The Girl on the Beach

Morton S. Gray

2016 Winner of Choc Lit's Search for a Star

Where heroes are like chocolate – irresistible!

Published 2018 by Choc Lit Limited
Penrose House, Crawley Drive, Camberley, Surrey GU15 2AB, UK
www.choc-lit.com

A CIP catalogue record for this book is available
from the British Library

ISBN 978-1-78189-419-4

Printed and bound by Clays Ltd

*Dedicated to Mom, Jeremy, James
and Daniel with love.*

Acknowledgements

Where to start? There are so many people
who have contributed to my writing journey
and my goal of achieving publication.

The Girl on the Beach was begun in 2014. A friend,
Kim Taylor from the lovely Bevere Gallery and Café
on the outskirts of Worcester runs art competitions
at the high school and this was the spark of the idea
from which this book developed. Thank you, Kim.

Thank you to all of those writers whose courses I've
attended, particularly Sue Johnson, Sue Moorcroft
and Alison May. I have also been to so many useful
sessions at writing festivals and the Romantic
Novelists' Association (RNA) conferences.

Margaret Ruess-Newland and Janice Preston read
early versions of the manuscript and made valuable
suggestions, as did my reader on the wonderful RNA New
Writers' Scheme. I would recommend this scheme to any
aspiring romance writer, as it offers priceless feedback.

Vital companionship and encouragement have come
from RNA members, especially those from the RNA
Birmingham Chapter and also from my little writers'
group the ADC's (you know who you are!).

My editor has been helpful and patient with this my
debut novel. Thank you so much for your help.

Susan Wood started the writing journey with me
and has been a constant support and inspiration.
My husband and sons have watched and wondered
as I scribbled in notebooks for years.

Thank you to my publisher Choc Lit, in association with
Lovereading, for running the Search for a Star competition,
which led to the publication of this novel when I won.
Thank you also to the Choc Lit tasting panel members
who voted for my story: Dimi E, Cordy S, Catherine L,
Alison B, Ester V, Kathleen H, Linda Sy, Jo O, Joy S,
Rosie F, Carol F, Cindy T, Alma H and Holly C.

Chapter One

How did she know him?

The headmaster, John Williams, began to introduce the man. 'Harry Dixon meet Ellie Golden, the inspiration behind our art competition. Harry will be taking over from me as headmaster in September and has agreed to help you decide who wins today.'

Rapidly searching her memory, Ellie shook Harry Dixon's hand. He had the physique of a rugby player, his dark hair cut short and straight. She didn't recognise the name, but the huge brown eyes and the cleft in his chin, almost hidden in short stubble, were somehow so familiar. She felt strangely uneasy.

He smiled, displaying even, white teeth. Did she imagine he was holding back, not smiling wholeheartedly? Did he recognise her too?

'Have we met before?' she asked, aware that her throat was suddenly dry.

'I don't think so. I would have remembered.'

The words brought heat to her face. His voice was warm and deep, clear in tone, but with a slight burr of an accent. She turned to examine the display to hide her blush. The exhibits were arranged on tall baize-covered panels at the back of the cavernous school hall. Each picture had a number with the Art Exposium competition logo, a stylised "A" and "E" with a swirl of paint joining the letters.

'We'd better get on with the judging, there's a lot to look at,' commented Ellie, trying to recover her composure.

The scoring sheet she'd typed up the previous evening seemed overcomplicated this morning, with its profusion of tick boxes. In her confused state, the columns merged and blurred. She knew she must sound prim and school-marmish, and look it too. What had possessed her to wear this suit? It was the one she'd once used for job interviews, grey and boring, even teamed with the scarlet silk shirt and pearl necklace. A clear case of dressing as she thought she should, rather than how she really wanted to. *Focus, Ellie.* She fought to bring her mind back to the competition, away from Harry Dixon and his identity. He was so good-looking and she still didn't know why she recognised him. *Those eyes! Stop it, Ellie.*

Examining the painting in front of her, she began to score it against her chosen categories. It was bright and used colour well, even though the brush strokes were a little primitive. The title didn't really fit the picture. Her mind drifted again to the cleft in Harry's chin. It was so distinctive that she couldn't have mistaken him for anyone else, could she? Recognition teased at the edge of her brain and she put her comments on the wrong line of the score sheet. *For goodness' sake, it's number three, not number four. Stay on track, what is the matter with you?*

She scrubbed at the score sheet with the rubber on the end of her pencil and re-marked the boxes correctly. Harry's voice cut into her inner turmoil.

'That's a pretty scientific rating system for a children's art competition.'

'I like to be thorough and fair.' She worried he'd noticed her confusion.

Harry's nearness as he looked over her shoulder made the hairs on the back of her neck stand to attention.

'I'd rather judge by eye. I can already see the winner.'

Ellie moved away a little, so she could turn to glare at him. 'Maybe, but every artist deserves a fair review. You haven't looked at all of the exhibits yet.'

'I must confess to having a sneaky look round earlier. You follow your system and when you've finished, I'll tell you which one I think is the winner. Bet I'm right in a fraction of the time.'

Her pencil pushed deeper into the paper, almost in danger of making a hole. Was he laughing at her? The arrogance of the man. She wondered if he had a degree in fine art too.

'I didn't realise there were two judges.'

'They probably didn't expect me to appear at the school before next term. As I take over as headmaster after the summer break, I suppose they felt obliged to include me as I'm here today.'

Ellie's son, Tom, attended the school, so she had a particular interest in the staff members. Tom, her darling. He'd coped very well with all the changes in his life, moving to a new area, new home, new school and occupying himself for all the time it had taken her to establish her gallery. It made it all the more important that she discovered how she knew this new headmaster. His aftershave was subtle, but spicy, reaching across the gap between them. Attraction and wariness began to fight within her.

'Are you from the Borteen area?'

'No, miles away.'

The way he averted his eyes and didn't elaborate raised her suspicions again. He definitely wasn't comfortable answering questions about himself, but then she didn't enjoy talking about herself either. Had she seen his face in the press or on television? Perhaps he'd been a competitor in one of those cooking competitions she loved watching so much. He didn't look like a cook, but appearances could be deceptive.

They moved around the display board and Ellie spotted tables laid out beyond.

'How lovely. They've entered ceramics and sculptures too.'

She went over to take a closer look.

Harry trailed after her.

Reaching out her hand to caress a large pot just at the

same time as he did, their fingers brushed against each other and she leapt back as if she'd been stung. He didn't show any sign of having noticed, but ran his palm disconcertingly over the glaze. She watched mesmerised. His fingers were strong, his nails short. Ellie wondered what it would feel like to have those fingers touching her hair.

What was happening here? She'd schooled herself not to react to men in this way. It was difficult to regain trust once it had been destroyed.

'How come you were chosen to judge this competition?' There was challenge in his voice now, but the hint of a smile in his expression.

She stopped ticking her score sheet. 'I've been working with the art groups at the school for the past year. I'm the sponsor of the Art Exposium competition.'

Passing Harry a leaflet from her clipboard, she wished the art competition had been a purely altruistic idea, but the truth was that it enabled her to put her name and work in the path of the parents, grandparents and all the staff of the school. She needed to raise the profile of her gallery as much as possible if the business was going to thrive.

Harry scanned the leaflet.

'You're Golden Design?'

'Yes, Ellie Golden, artist.' She chastised herself for doing a silly little curtsey to accompany the words.

'What's your style of art, Ellie Golden, artist?'

His head was on one side, his tone sarcastic again, but his smile suggested he was flirting with her. She was pleased and disconcerted all at the same time.

'Abstract acrylics and large ceramic pieces mainly. I'm inspired by the sea and the hills around here.'

He read aloud the address of her studio from the leaflet. 'That's off the High Street, isn't it?'

She nodded, trying to gauge his thoughts from the dark brown eyes. His eyelashes were impossibly long. She dragged her focus back to the score sheet and realised she'd marked her entry against the wrong number yet again. She was usually meticulous about detail. *What has got into you, Ellie Golden?*

'I'll have to come to your gallery and have a look at your work. The walls in my flat are looking a bit sad and bare at the moment.'

'You've moved to Borteen already?'

'Yes, I want to get familiar with the area before September. Are you a local?'

'No, I moved here after my divorce.' The words were out of her mouth before she'd censored them and she kicked herself for telling him that. It felt as if she'd told him she was single and open for offers. Harry Dixon was infuriatingly attractive, but she still couldn't shake off the sense that they'd met before.

Ellie Golden could be dangerous. Harry felt as if she was asking questions to whittle away at his painstakingly constructed story. Still, he'd have to convince a lot more people in September and he should be used to this by now. She'd recognised something in him, of that he had no doubt. He didn't remember meeting her before, but there was a niggling feeling that it could have been in that time he couldn't remember, his black hole ...

She didn't have the look of any other artist he'd seen. He knew he was stereotyping, but he always pictured them as flowing bohemian types, wearing smocks, with a dab of paint behind the ear. She appeared prim in her business suit and looked more like his idea of a librarian, if her blouse hadn't been scarlet. She'd no doubt dressed this way because she believed the judge of a competition should wear something formal. He imagined her carefully controlled tawny hair cascading around her face, daubed in the blues and greens she was using to paint. He had a thing about

5

wild hair. A quiver of interest sparked through him as he noticed the silver highlights in her blue eyes. *Steady, mate, don't get too interested. Remember you need to get on with your job and stay in the background the rest of the time. Safer.*

'Harry, have you had a chance to look at these sculptures? Some very talented work here – really impressive for eleven to sixteen year olds.' Her voice was full of genuine excitement.

He turned, after what he knew was a slight hesitation. Would he ever get used to that name, Harry? Why had he chosen that? It still gave him such a shock, when he pulled out his credit cards and his driving licence to see it. Even his degree certificate had been changed. They'd done a thorough job.

Ellie regarded him with that tight-lipped annoyed air he'd seen several times already. He'd drifted off into his thoughts and hadn't a clue what she'd said to him. He realised her hair had begun to escape its clip and had the promise of the wildness he'd imagined. A ripple of anticipation spiked through his body.

She abruptly put down her clipboard and rearranged it, as if she'd read his mind and sensed the effect the stray curls were having on him. *Phew, that was better, less tantalising.*

Touching a purple pot to distract himself and get back in control of his mind and body, he marvelled at the silkiness of the glaze.

'Is this the type of pottery you sell?'

'No, these are made from coiled clay. I throw pots on a wheel.'

Her long fingers were unadorned by rings, her nails clipped short. The image of those hands manipulating clay caused another shiver down his spine. It was only a short hop in his mind to her touching his own skin. *Whoa!*

She took ages over her scoring. Harry had given up

following her around the hall. He was impressed by the number of exhibits, but there were few that inspired him. Instead, he sat by the window, watching the dynamics of the schoolchildren at break time. The younger ones playing ball, the older ones hanging around in groups practising looking bored and disinterested. This world would soon be his responsibility. He relished the thought of belonging somewhere again.

'Finished!' Ellie announced. 'Come on then, I'm intrigued, which piece did you choose for first prize?'

Harry got up and went to the first display board they'd viewed. 'Number fifteen.'

'Oh, no! That one can't win.' He could swear that her face went white.

'Why not? It's by far the best.' He examined the canvas more closely. The title was "Fireworks" and it clearly depicted a sky full of colourful explosions above the buildings of a town, possibly Borteen. The perspective of the buildings and the reflections of the fireworks in some of the windows showed real skill. Harry could almost believe himself to be an observer of the scene.

'I agree, but it was painted by my son, Tom, so it can't win. It would look like favouritism.'

'Won't Tom be upset not to have his talent recognised?'

'He'll understand and I'll put it right with him later.'

She was messing with her hair again. Harry turned to stare at her son's picture as he fought down his interest. In his view, the canvas stood out like a beacon amongst the other work.

'He's obviously got your artistic genes. What about if I make a special award?' He grinned at Ellie.

'There's really no need.'

'Yes, there is. His picture is definitely the best here.'

She stared at him, curiosity written all over her features.

He reminded himself he needed to be wary and wandered

off to look out of the window again. Break time had finished and the school yard stood empty.

After a never-ending lunch with John Williams and the school governors, Ellie and Harry sat next to each other on the stage in front of all of the pupils of the school. Ellie tried to spot her son in the faces before her. Harry's leg brushed against her skirt. Her awareness of him was so heightened that she could feel the warmth of him, smell his subtle aftershave and settled her own breathing to the rhythm of his. She tried to look at him without turning her head and noticed he had a slightly deformed ear. It looked like a rugby injury.

He reached out to scratch his knee and she saw a strange mark above his wrist. It covered a section of his lower forearm.

Unbidden, a vision floated into her mind of a tattoo above a strong hand, a surf board, sandy legs …

She stiffened in shock and examined Harry more closely. No, it was impossible. It couldn't be him. He met her gaze and she was sure she could sense alarm in his expression. Her heart began to drum. She looked away, stared unseeing at her clipboard, tried to focus on her score sheet, but it was next to impossible given the turmoil inside her.

John Williams stood and welcomed Harry and Ellie as the art competition judges, talked about Ellie's gallery in the centre of town and her work with the school and introduced Harry as his successor from September. The young people sat silently in rows in front of her, oblivious to her confusion. In a few moments, she would be asked to announce the winners of the competition. A scream bubbled inside of her and she fought to control it.

Would she be able to speak, now that she knew for certain?

His name wasn't Harry Dixon.

It was Ben Rivers and Ben Rivers was dead.

Chapter Two

Ellie gathered all her reserves of strength to stand and smile at the expectant audience of young faces. She took the name Ben Rivers and by the time she'd reached the lectern, she had buried it in the deep recesses of her mind underneath a large pile of art canvases.

'Thank you, Headmaster. I would like to praise all of you who have entered the Art Exposium competition. The artwork is fantastic. This school is lucky to have so many talented students. It's been very hard to decide on a few winners given all of the brilliant pieces on display.'

Was that really her speaking? Her commanding voice belied the nervousness she'd felt earlier. Maybe Harry had been a useful distraction.

She waved her clipboard, knowing full well that the students would be unable to read it, but hoping to reassure them that the wad of scoring sheets meant that their own individual pieces had been taken seriously.

'I just want to take a moment to explain how we made our decision.' She included Harry, even though he hadn't really contributed to the scoring.

The audience were held in a kind of numb silence, hanging on her every word.

'The competition has been judged anonymously.' Ellie gestured towards the school secretary at the side of the stage. 'Each piece entered was given a unique number and that is all Mr Dixon and I have seen. Mrs Gibbons has the list of names. Everything entered was given marks for categories such as use of colour, portraying the title and finish. These scores have been totalled to arrive at a final ranking.'

She paused for effect. The tension was building in the hall. Inevitably, someone giggled at the back.

'I shall award three prizes. In third place, entry number fifty-two – "Autumn Sunrise".'

Ellie glanced over to where the school secretary rustled through the lists marrying the entry numbers and student names.

'Louise Stevens,' she announced in a squeaky voice.

'Would Louise Stevens please come to the stage?'

Ellie began applauding as a tall, spiky-haired girl with freckles stood up. The audience joined her clapping. Louise picked her way through the students on either side of her and came forward, her face as red as her school cardigan.

'Congratulations, Louise.' Ellie shook the girl's limp hand and presented her with an envelope. 'Third prize wins a fifteen pound voucher to buy art materials.'

The girl's beaming face reminded Ellie of one of the reasons why she'd wanted to run an art competition in the first place. She remembered winning prizes for her own artwork at school and the vital encouragement those awards had given to her. She waited until the clapping had subsided, before she spoke again.

'Second prize, of twenty-five pounds goes to entry number twenty-two – "Green Pot".' Ellie felt a shiver of the memory of Harry's hand meeting hers when she reached out to touch this exhibit. She wondered if he remembered too, but didn't dare to look at him for fear of destroying her focus and dissolving into stuttering confusion.

The secretary rustled through the entry sheets again. 'Zack Martin.'

The school hall erupted into cheers, as a cheeky-faced boy, his shirt untucked and his tie deliberately tied too short, bounded up the steps to the stage.

Zack pumped her hand enthusiastically, leaving Ellie's palm feeling uncomfortably moist. However, handing him his prize envelope, her heart contracted at his obvious joy. Zack paused at the edge of the stage to bow and pirouette to the wolf whistles of his friends.

Silence descended once more. Ellie wished that she could give everyone a prize.

'And the winner of the Art Exposium competition for this year is entry number ninety-nine – "Street Dancer".'

Ellie watched the secretary studying the name sheets carefully. Did she imagine the look of surprise that crossed the woman's face as she found the name listed for the entry? 'Nicholas Crossten.'

The students appeared to freeze. With shock? Amazement? The reaction puzzled Ellie. There was no movement from the hall and everyone remained completely silent.

'Would Nicholas Crossten please come to the stage?' Her voice had a slight wobble. 'For those of you who haven't seen it, his painting is a wonderful modern piece in black and white and depicts the title "Street Dancer" with few strokes, but maximum energy and passion.'

The headmaster rose from his seat, walked to the edge of the stage and beckoned to a boy on the front row. The youth got up slowly, almost reluctantly, and edged along the platform. His red jumper was washed out to pink and his trousers were dirty and too short.

'Nicholas, how wonderful. Well done, lad.' John Williams patted the boy enthusiastically on the back and raised his hands above his head to encourage the schoolchildren into clapping. They eventually put their hands together, but the noise level was nowhere near as loud as the previous applause.

Ellie wasn't quite sure what was going on, but the whole episode felt embarrassing. She gave Nicholas his envelope containing the voucher for fifty pounds' worth of art materials from the big art shop in the nearby town of

Sowden and told him about the gold rosette now gracing his painting. 'You have real talent, Nicholas. I'm very impressed with your picture.'

He half-smiled, pulled at the frayed edge of his jumper and wiped what Ellie suspected was a tear from the corner of his eye. As quickly as he could, he scuttled back to his seat on the front row. Ellie hoped that John Williams would explain the strange reaction of the students to his win.

The headmaster shook her hand and asked for a round of applause for Ellie and Harry's time and her donation of the prizes. The children began whispering and shuffling their feet, as they expected to be released soon and wanted to be ready to escape.

Harry Dixon stood up and stepped to the front of the stage. He lifted his arms to call for silence. 'If I may, Mr Williams, I'd like to speak to the students.'

John Williams nodded.

'Before you go, I want to make an award of my own. I can't claim to have any artistic training, but I know the sort of art I like to hang on my own walls. There is one painting I would happily buy from a gallery and I want to show my appreciation to the artist.'

Ellie held onto the edge of the lectern. Her legs had turned to jelly. Was that because she anticipated what Harry was about to say or because of her curiosity to see Tom and Harry together? Perhaps it just signified a release of tension now that her formal part in the proceedings was over, but she wasn't doing a good job of fooling herself.

'Entry number fifteen – "Fireworks".' Harry turned his head to the secretary in an echo of Ellie's announcements.

'Number fifteen was entered by Thomas Golden,' said the secretary after fumbling through the sheets of names.

Harry led another quiet round of applause. Ellie knew that Tom wasn't one of the more popular boys and the insipid clapping seemed to confirm it. Her son came forward, hands in pockets. Tom's large brown eyes were huge with surprise. She noted with pride that he was going to be tall.

He walked up the steps to the stage and grasped Harry's outstretched hand. It was a surreal moment. Ellie held her breath, but no one else appeared to be noticing what was so clear to her own eyes.

'I love your picture, Tom. Please accept my special award of ten pounds. If you name your price, I will happily buy your painting when the exhibition closes. That is, if you're willing to sell it.' Harry handed Tom a crisp banknote.

'Thank you, sir.' Tom beamed a smile at his mother, walked down the stage steps and then disappeared, blending into the throng of red cardigans and jumpers making their way out of the hall.

The tension drained from Ellie's body. She turned to the headmaster. 'What's the story of Nicholas Crossten? Did I make a huge mistake? The atmosphere in the hall turned very strange when I announced he'd won.'

'No, no. I believe you might have made a big difference to the lad. He has an unfortunate background, doesn't always come to school, a bit neglected. He was sitting on the front row so that the teachers could keep an eye on him. I think the students were just surprised, as he's more likely to be handed a detention than a prize.'

'Hidden talents then? There's such energy in his painting and it shows him to be a great observer of life.'

'Hopefully, your recognition of his artwork will help him. I must go and have another look at the winning entries. Would you come with me, Ellie and talk me through what you admired about the winners? I'd also like your opinion on something else ...'

Ellie walked down the stage steps. Her movements felt deliberate and stiff. She would have to go with John Williams, but her whole being wanted to ... wanted to what? Challenge Harry? Beat his chest and ask him why he had let her believe he was gone forever? Scream in his face, because he didn't recognise her, although she knew logically he was unlikely to given she'd changed so much? Ask why he had cut his hair and got rid of his tattoo? Cry? Or, deep down, did she long to be enfolded in those strong arms once more?

She shuddered, hoping John Williams hadn't said anything important or asked her a question, as he chatted away beside her on the way to the art exhibition. She looked behind her, but Harry Dixon had melted away … again.

Harry accepted a cup of tea from the school secretary. He juggled the cup and saucer, slopping some of the liquid into the saucer in the process, thinking it was rare these days not to be drinking from a mug.

What now?

Did he stay and see what Ellie Golden might say to him after that strange searching look on the stage, or did he leave?

He'd hoped this move to Borteen signalled a new phase, a new start. If Ellie had somehow recognised him from the past, he might have to move on again and that filled him with horror.

Decision made, he gulped his tea, which was tasteless and luke-warm, made an excuse about a meeting and strode out of the double doors at the front of the school. The school garden, car park, the drab housing estate, the Victorian shops and concrete wall that doubled as sea defence passed by in a blur. He didn't stop walking until his feet were on the sand.

Pausing to roll up his trouser hems, remove his shoes and socks, he headed for the water.

Cool sea, stony sand, the smell of seaweed in his nostrils. He laughed despite his tumultuous thoughts. His mother had often speculated that he was the son of a merman, as he loved the sea so much. Or was that just a story she'd concocted to cover the embarrassment of him being the product of a drunken one-night stand and the fact that she had no idea of the identity of his father? Much easier to plant a romantic notion in her beloved son's head of a merman coming out of the sea and seducing his mother on the sand.

He trailed along the water's edge trying to order his troubled mind. *Ellie Golden*. He said the name aloud slowly. *Ellie Golden*. As if voicing her name would help his recall. Why didn't he remember her? She seemed to remember him, but from where? For what? He couldn't recall an Ellie Golden in his past, but then that might not be her real name. Surely, he would have remembered her hair, if nothing else. She was an attractive woman; he wouldn't have forgotten her, would he? Unless of course, he'd met her in that period of his life of which he had no recollection at all ... that time he referred to as his black hole ...

He was tempted to return to his flat and pack up. It was probably an overreaction, but wouldn't it be simpler to disappear before he took up his post at the school? Sighing, he kicked the water, succeeding in soaking one leg of his best suit. Perhaps he could deflect Ellie, maybe convince her she didn't know him at all. Looking back along the beach, he resolved to brazen it out. He'd go and confront the woman at her gallery to see what she had to say. It would be easier if they were alone. He might be mistaken. She might be mistaken. He'd just have to find out.

It was silly to make assumptions that could affect his life in Borteen. He must find out the facts before deciding upon an appropriate reaction. Hadn't all his training for his former career been based upon that very principle?

A group of lads in the distinctive red jumpers of Borteen High School were coming towards him across the sand.

He'd been on the beach longer than he'd realised. School must have finished for the day. He turned around and passed close to the boys. Thomas Golden recognised him and raised his hand in acknowledgement. Harry waved back. As he was sure that Ellie's son was out of the way, it might be an idea to go to her gallery right now. He needed to know as a matter of urgency whether Ellie Golden was a threat to his future in Borteen.

Chapter Three

Ellie enjoyed talking to John Williams about the art competition. Amongst the one hundred and twenty entries there were a number of students who showed real artistic talent in Ellie's opinion. John, who had been the school's headmaster for ten years, had his students' best interests at heart and listened enthusiastically to her observations.

'I'm really sad that you're retiring,' she said with genuine feeling.

'I shall miss the school and the students, but it's time for a change.' A wistful look crept over his care-worn face.

'It must be difficult to leave a job you're so dedicated to.'

'Thank you for the compliment, Ellie.' He smiled at her. 'It is, but I have an idea that, hopefully, will help me to keep contact with the school. It's what I wanted to discuss with you. I'd like to set up a mentoring scheme to encourage students, especially those with particular talent and those who are disaffected, like Nicholas Crossten.'

'That sounds like a great scheme. Have you discussed it with the new headmaster?' The mention of Harry Dixon, even if not by name, started an uncomfortable churning in her stomach. She hoped that John Williams hadn't noticed the strained tone that had crept into her voice as she mentioned him.

'I've yet to discuss it with Harry. He might be totally against the idea, but I couldn't run the scheme single-handed, so I've been sounding out a few people to see if they'd be willing to help me by acting as mentors. I was wondering if you might be one of those people?'

'What exactly would this mentoring involve?'

'If I use Nicholas as an example. If you were his mentor, you'd meet regularly with him, probably once a week, to discuss his school work and any other concerns and, in his case, to encourage him with his art.'

Ellie reached out to smooth her hand over one of the pottery exhibits, as she took a moment to think. She realised right away that this was a bad idea as it reminded her of the brush of Harry's hand when they were judging the competition. She made an effort to bring her mind back to John's question.

'It sounds like a really good idea, but I'd have to be very strict on the time I could give to it. I'm a single parent, after all, trying to build up a business.' She hoped her reply didn't seem too sharp and negative, but she had to be realistic. She was the bread winner for her little family and she hadn't chosen the easiest of careers in which to make a living.

'Sorry, perhaps I'm asking too much. I'll find out Harry's thoughts first and, if he's in favour, I'll draw up clearer guidelines about levels of involvement. Then, maybe you'd give it some serious consideration?'

'I'd definitely think about it, particularly if I can help with budding artists like Nicholas. Although, I'll be running the after-school art class in September too, remember?'

'I do hope Nicholas will come to that.'

She smiled and decided to be brave. 'Can I ask how the school came to choose Harry Dixon?' Her heart began to thump. She glanced around to make sure Harry wasn't lurking behind one of the display boards.

'We advertised the post and interviewed the most suitable candidates. The school governors were keen to have a younger headmaster, had enough of old hands like me I suppose. Harry Dixon was ideal with his sports background and interest in using digital technology in schools. He's got impressive references and international experience.'

Ellie pushed her thumb against a rough edge of a piece of pottery, using the slight abrasion to steady her nerves. 'Sports background?'

'Yes, he was a games teacher at the start of his career. Borteen High doesn't have a strong sports tradition. Harry's determined to change that. He wants the school to compete in team sports and athletics. Not something we've done much of in the past.'

'Presumably anyone joining the school is thoroughly checked out?'

The headmaster's eyes widened. Maybe she'd gone too far.

'Yes, of course, vetted and references followed up. Why do you ask? Do you think there's a problem with Harry?'

'No, no. I suppose I'm just a bit sensitive as my son's at the school. I'm sure Tom will be more than happy to take part in more sport.'

Ellie took deep breaths. She couldn't continue her questioning without it appearing strange.

John put his hand on her arm for a second. 'Your son's okay, Ellie. Tom's starting to establish himself at the school.'

It took Ellie by surprise. Tears sprang to her eyes. 'Thanks for saying that. I worry he's still a bit withdrawn.'

John knew more about Ellie's life story than most people in Borteen. She'd shared most of her past with him at the point Tom joined the high school. Right now, that fact made her uncomfortable, as she knew his mind would be replaying the details and looking at her face more closely.

She went to stand in front of the competition winner's canvas, to give her time to compose herself. The depiction of a young man dancing in the street, his cap on backwards and a beat box at his feet was almost alive.

'Nicholas has a lot of talent. To be able to show a scene in so few brush strokes is masterful. I can teach him to add just a touch of colour to his pictures to make them even more striking. If he can paint to this standard already, he could be famous one day.'

John came to stand next to her. 'Yet, he's the sort of lad

who could be totally overlooked. He could quite easily leave school with no qualifications or prospects. He's come close to being excluded because of his behaviour many times. The fine line between famous artist and school drop-out, eh?'

'I can see why you would prefer him to have a mentor, but he would need to be willing to accept help for it to work.'

John sighed. 'The biggest challenge of a teacher is to help students fulfil their potential and, sadly, it isn't always possible. You can't do it for them. You have to sow seeds in their minds and just hope that one day they germinate.'

'The challenge of being a parent too.'

Her eye was caught by a crude picture of a camper van; she'd seen it when she was judging the competition, of course, but since her insight into Harry's identity, it had taken on a different significance. It was enough to transport her back to the day after Ben died, the day when his camper van was towed away from the beach road and Ellie had wanted to grab onto the drying rack at the back where Ben's wetsuit always hung. It felt as if they were taking Ben himself away and she had no memento to remind her of the love of her life, the man she'd given her virginity to …

John Williams was looking at her with a strange expression on his face. It was time to go. She forced herself to smile, made her goodbyes and walked out of the school towards her gallery with a lot of things on her mind, not least Harry Dixon.

After putting his socks and shoes on over sandy feet, Harry brushed sand from his tie and jacket. The day had become hot and airless, the sky deep blue. He hoped that it would be a warm summer, although a glance at the waterfront confirmed his suspicion that the sea here wouldn't be suitable for surfing. It was more a beach for sunbathing, sandcastles and paddling. Never mind, it was close to his beloved ocean. He took a deep breath of salty air. A wistful yearning for his long lost campervan and surfboard rose up in his heart. Life used to be much less complicated.

Borteen was typical of many small seaside towns. It had a promenade along the seafront, butting up to a high street, where shops sold wetsuits, kites and beach gear, in amongst the butcher, bakery, newsagent and the, seemingly these days, obligatory charity shops and cut-price chemist.

Gaps in the buildings revealed small alleyways, the homes of craft shops, galleries and cafés. Harry knew from Ellie's leaflet that Golden Design, her gallery, lay in one of these streets. When he found it, he was impressed by the crisp white paint and the large window displaying colourful artwork and pottery. The shop sign was a mosaic of brightly coloured pieces of glass with "Golden Designs" outlined in gold paint on top.

He squinted through the window, trying to see if the paintings were Ellie's. The ones on display all had the same stylised signature and, although he couldn't tell what it said, he imagined it must be her work.

They were large canvases with bold blocks of colour, somehow not the sort of artwork he would have imagined being produced by the woman in the drab grey suit he had met today. She must have hidden depths, using her painting to express a part of herself she didn't reveal in real life. His reflections added to the intrigue surrounding Ellie Golden, but, he reminded himself, she could pose a threat to his new life and even his safety.

There was a big "Closed" sign on the gallery door. Harry tried the shiny brass handle, just in case, but the door was locked. He would have preferred to tackle this risk to his future straight away, but it was clear that wasn't going to happen. He needed to plan the most effective way to deal with Ellie Golden and her knowing stare, or else decide to abandon his life in Borteen before it had even begun.

Ellie had finally begun to relax on the walk to the gallery. The knots in her shoulders unwound one by one in response to the sight and sound of the sea and the warmth of the sun.

The tension flooded back all at once, as she reached the entrance to the alley and spotted Harry Dixon outside of her shop. She moved behind the nearest wall and watched him peering through the window at her artwork. He took his time, examining the display closely. She wondered what he thought about her paintings. When he tried to open the door, she thought for a moment he was going to break in. Amazing how when your suspicions are raised, you can imagine people capable of anything.

She debated whether to stroll casually up the alleyway and confront him, but she knew that he would then have the upper hand, standing between her and the gallery door. Cornered men could be unpredictable, as she knew to her cost. Her hand unconsciously traced her nose and cheekbones. She needed to find a place and time where she felt safe and in control to have a conversation with Harry, to get the answers to the questions buzzing around her brain, but right now was not that time. She could afford to be patient.

As Head of Borteen High, Harry was going to be around for a while, but did her suspicions about his past make his position at the school impossible? How did someone die and then reappear with another name? Why did she think it necessary to consider his feelings and career? If he was who she believed him to be, he was deceiving everyone.

Harry turned. There was no other way out of the alley, so he would walk straight past her if she stayed where she was. She scurried round the corner into the bakery, hoping he hadn't seen her. Her heart thumped in her chest. He couldn't find her spying on him, that would be just too embarrassing.

She studied the display of pies at the back of the bakery for a long time, hoping Harry had left the street. As soon as her heart rate and breathing had calmed down, she bought a chicken and mushroom pie for herself and a steak and onion one for Tom's evening meal.

Emerging cautiously into the late afternoon sunshine, she scanned the seafront. There was no sign of Harry, but she didn't want to risk him still being near the gallery. Annoyance at her reaction to the man caused her steps to speed up as she made her way up the hill towards home. How dare Harry Dixon or Ben Rivers, or whoever on earth he was, invade her space and make her uneasy in her own town, her own skin. The situation would need to be sorted out as quickly as possible. She refused to live with insecurity again.

Chapter Four

Ellie was puzzled when she reached home as Tom wasn't in the house. She could tell because the post was still on the doormat and there was a package for him. Normally, he rushed back up the road from school and sat ensconced in front of a computer game until teatime. Nonetheless, Ellie went upstairs, calling his name. His pristine bedroom lay empty. She worried that he still felt the need to keep everything neat and tidy, a hang-over from living with his step-father's temper.

She tried not to worry that he wasn't back and, of course, trying made the worry even worse. She made a cup of tea in the tiny kitchen. Peeled potatoes to boil for mash to go with the pies. Checked she had frozen vegetables in the freezer. Tidied a couple of shelves. Still, no Tom. It had gone five o'clock; he should have been home ages ago.

Exasperated with both herself and Tom, she dialled his mobile number. He didn't answer; the call went to voicemail. A rush of fear passed through her, but she argued against going out to search for him. Not just yet, he was fourteen, after all, she needed to get used to giving him more freedom.

Anxious to occupy her troubled mind, she took a large sheet of paper and pencils to the table. On her walk home, she'd begun to doubt her suspicions about Harry Dixon. Was her mind playing tricks on her?

She drew two columns. One she headed Harry Dixon, the other Ben Rivers. Writing Ben's name stirred up a turmoil of emotions. Had she made him into a sort of god-like hero with the passage of time? She gritted her teeth and began a clinical comparison of the two men.

Harry Dixon, about five inches taller than herself, so

just over six feet tall. Brown eyes, *big* brown eyes. Dark short hair, stubble, unmistakeable cleft in chin. Even, white teeth. Muscular rugby player's build. Damaged ear, left side. Possible tattoo removed from forearm. Well-spoken, slight accent, but she couldn't decide where from. Alive.

Ben Rivers. Oh, Ben Rivers. Ellie traced the letters of his name, overcome with unexpressed emotions. She forced herself to continue with the analysis, gripping her pen like a lifeline. Five inches taller than herself, about six feet tall. Huge brown eyes. Long blond hair that flopped over his face. Cleft in chin. Even teeth. Muscular rugby player build. Tattoo on forearm. Voice accented with soft West Country tones. Dead.

Could she be mistaken? After all, it didn't make sense. She'd seen Ben Rivers buried in a Cornish graveyard. She'd visited the spot numerous times, especially when she needed to escape from the house and her now ex-husband, Rushton's temper. She'd taken shells from the beach to decorate the earth. She'd planted primroses in the spring and watered them with her tears.

The memory of the raw sensations in her body when she'd discovered that Ben had died in a surfing accident could even now reduce her to sobs, despite the passage of nearly fifteen years. How could she even imagine that he still lived? Was she deluded? Had her mind played tricks on her and made her believe that Harry and Ben were one and the same man?

For a moment she was back on the beach in Cornwall, watching Ben surfing a wave. All the girls loved him, which is why Ellie never stood a chance of getting close to him. It was a warm summer, her skin was tanned, her bikinis bright and tiny.

'Mum, I'm home,' yelled a voice, making her jump and draw a line across her notes.

She wiped a hand across her face, as if to close down the

past, and quickly folded the paper several times so that it could be shoved into her pocket. She didn't want Tom to question what she'd been doing.

'Where've you been? I've been worried.'

He stood in the doorway, school jumper tied around his slim hips, tie hanging loose round his neck.

'Mum, it's you who's always saying I should be making friends. I went to the beach with some mates. Bought them ice creams with my winnings.'

Ellie immediately wondered if the crisp ten pound note that Harry Dixon had given to Tom was the source of the sudden friendliness of the other boys. Still, Tom seemed happy and that should be all that mattered.

'We've got pie and mash for tea.'

'Sounds great.'

Harry, about a mile away in his rented flat, paced the lounge. It was easy to pace, it was small and he hadn't got much furniture yet.

Had he become too big for his boots? If he had stayed a games teacher, moving school and occasionally country every few years, it might have been safer. He'd worried that the deputy head-ship at his last inner-city school had been too prominent, but he was competent at his job; he was bound to get promotions.

Was a headmaster's post a step too far? Had he raised his head too high above the parapet of anonymity?

He wanted to be the head of Borteen High, dammit. Why should his early career choices and actions in his twenties colour his whole life? He felt sure that he could do a valuable job at the small senior school, but was it inevitable that, sooner or later, the past would catch up with him? He'd had one or two near misses before when someone thought they recognised him, but Ellie appeared much more certain.

The expression on her face at the prize-giving haunted him. She looked as if a light bulb had suddenly ignited in her brain. He'd seen her eyes widen with an emotion or memory – recognition, a remembered scene?

He might have made nothing of it, but hadn't she already asked if they'd met before and had he heard a soft Cornish accent appearing sometimes when she spoke? How likely was it that she'd known him in his past life? He certainly didn't recognise her, but then there was that period in his history which refused to be anything other than a complete blank.

He wished he'd been able to keep photographs of surf gatherings, he might have identified Ellie from the pictures, but, on the other hand, if he had met her, he didn't really want any proof of the fact. At the moment, she believed she knew him, but he didn't think she felt totally certain. What could she accuse him of anyway, even if she did recognise him? Did it matter?

If he made one phone call, he could be whisked away and his existence in Borteen erased. But, could he face reinventing himself yet again?

He looked at his suitcase and rucksack in the corner of the lounge. They contained all of his belongings. He'd learned to travel light in his nomadic existence and not to get attached to things, or people for that matter. His was a solitary existence.

He wished she'd been at her gallery this afternoon. Then, he could have tackled things head on and be feeling more settled tonight, or at least have a sense of which way the wind was blowing.

The art exhibited in Ellie's window was pleasing to the eye. There had been several pieces that he would have happily bought, although she had cleverly hidden the price tags. Any prospective buyer had to actually go into the shop to ask for the prices and he suspected the pictures he liked might be beyond his budget.

Harry's stomach started to rumble, reminding him that he hadn't eaten. He decided that a walk on the beach, followed by a take-away meal might clear his head and help calm his troubled thoughts.

'Della's coming to sit with you tonight.' As she said the words, Ellie felt her stomach muscles clench and brace for Tom's reaction.

'Mum, I'm too old for a babysitter.'

'True, but I can't enjoy myself thinking of you at home on your own, while I'm out till late.'

'Della smells.' Tom crashed the plate he'd just wiped up onto the pile in the cupboard.

'Thomas Golden, that's a horrible thing to say.' As he hadn't broken it, Ellie didn't mention the plate.

'Maybe, but it's true.' He stared at her defiantly and, after a few moments of staring at each other, they both dissolved into laughter.

Ellie hugged her son close, noting that he'd grown again and they were almost the same height. It wouldn't be long before he'd be towering over her. She ruffled his hair. 'You know I worry. If Della's here, at least I can relax. I don't go out very often, do I?'

He pulled away from her. His brown eyes were liquid pools. 'Okay, Mum, but I'm going to be upstairs doing homework anyway. Della won't see me. It's a waste of money.'

'I'm sure that will suit Della. She can watch her favourite TV programmes. I'll be back after eleven. Make sure you don't stay up too late.'

'Yes, Mum.' He saluted her, a cheeky grin on his face and disappeared out of the room.

Once every couple of months, Ellie allowed her friend, Mandy, to drag her to the local wine bar for an evening out. They'd met when Ellie had first come to Borteen four years ago and set up a temporary art exhibition in the local craft centre, which Mandy Vanes owned.

The rapport had been instant, as if they'd always been friends. A past life connection, Mandy called it. Ellie trusted Mandy above all others, but did she trust her enough to tell her about Harry Dixon and Ben Rivers, even though she badly needed to discuss the situation with someone?

She pondered her dilemma, as she applied a swish of eye shadow and a flick of mascara. She didn't normally bother with make-up, but, as Mandy used it heavily, Ellie couldn't face feeling pale and pasty sitting next to her friend. She'd given up trying to tame her hair. It bubbled around her head, the mass of curls more exuberant than ever after her shower. She peered into the mirror and sighed. She'd have to do.

The doorbell sounded and Tom pounded down the stairs to open the door.

'Mandy!' The delight was obvious in his voice. Ellie wondered what sugary treat Mandy had bought for him this evening. She'd become the auntie that Tom had never had, to the benefit of both her son and her friend. Ellie couldn't decide if it was a blessing or a curse to have no brothers and sisters. Her parents had both died while she was married to Rushton. With hindsight, it felt as if they'd both stayed alive just long enough to support her through Art College, looking after Tom whilst she studied.

As she came down the stairs, Ellie could hear Tom telling her friend all about the art competition and his special prize from Harry Dixon. The joy was evident in his tone.

'I hear Tom's inherited your artistic talents,' Mandy said, as Ellie came into the room. 'Special new headmaster's prize, eh?'

'Tom has an artistic style all of his own. His paintings are very different to mine. He'll be exhibiting in the gallery before I know it.'

Mandy looked sleek and glowing in a bright strappy top and leggings, her straight blonde hair falling over her bare shoulders. Ellie lamented her own uninspiring wardrobe, her white shirt and wide-legged trousers worn to help her fade into the background.

The doorbell sounded again, but this time Tom didn't rush to answer it. Ellie shot him a glowering look, as she went to let Della in. She reflected that Tom might be right, as a faint smell of body odour followed the older woman into the house. Della was their neighbour and she happily sat with Tom when Ellie wanted to go out. Della relished the pocket money, free range over the treats in Ellie's kitchen and the chance to watch what she wanted on television without her husband's grumbles.

Ellie grabbed her jacket and bag, nodding at Della.

'Thanks for sitting with Tom, Della. We'll be home by half eleven.'

They left the house, already giggling. It was nice to have the freedom to chat with a like-minded soul. The responsibilities of being a single parent often weighed heavily on Ellie's shoulders, especially since Tom had become a teenager.

'Come on then, what's been happening with you? I want to hear all about the school art competition and, most of all, about the new headmaster. Rumour has it that he's rather dishy?'

It seemed Ellie was to be confronted by her demons straight away. She didn't answer immediately and realised, belatedly, that it was a mistake, because it aroused Mandy's interest even more.

'Hey, hey, come on, spill the beans. You fancy the new headmaster, don't you?'

Ellie was horrified, particularly as heat bathed her face. 'No, Mandy. You've got completely the wrong idea. I do *not* fancy Harry Dixon.'

Did she? Was that the problem? Did she fancy Harry

Dixon, despite her suspicions that he used to have a different name, be a different person?

She'd never really had a proper relationship with Ben Rivers. It had been more like a fantasy, then a tantalising glimpse of possibility, followed by dashed hopes. She'd been much younger and more naïve then. Time had given Ben immortality and a god-like status in her memories. Harry, on the other hand, was real and alive.

They walked to the wine bar on the seafront. It was the busiest evening for a long while, now that the hotels, guest houses and self-catering properties were filling up with those who wanted and could take a break before the school holidays. Settled in the comfortable leather seats by the window, Ellie began to feel more relaxed as she sipped a glass of white wine. The wine bar was newly refurbished with tall chrome lamps and glass tables. The wooden floor still smelled new and mingled with the scent of the curry listed on the specials board.

'Sorry if I upset you earlier about the new headmaster thing. It seemed a pretty extreme denial though.' Mandy smiled, a question in her eyes.

'Ghosts from the past, Mandy. Ghosts from the past.'

'Do you want to talk about them?'

Ellie pushed her hands through her curls and pulled her locks behind her head. 'To be honest, I'd love to tell you all about it and ask your opinion on a few things, but tonight, I'd just prefer a girly chat, relaxation and a few glasses of wine.'

'Okay by me,' Mandy said, with a laugh. 'Just say the word when you are ready to talk and I'll be all ears.'

Ellie nodded, sipped more wine and then choked on her mouthful.

A man was looking at them from outside the window.

It seemed just as if their conversation and her thoughts had called him to be right here, right now. It was Harry Dixon.

Chapter Five

'Oh, who's the dish? He's having a good look at us. Wonder which one of us he likes the best? Please let it be me,' said Mandy, running her hands over her already smooth hair.

Ellie wiped spilled wine off her lap and the front of her shirt, thankful that it was white wine, not red and peered through the window again, wondering if she'd been mistaken.

Had the wine genie conjured up an image of Harry Dixon? She'd hardly drunk anything, so couldn't be hallucinating yet.

But, it wasn't a mirage.

It was the man himself.

He appeared as surprised as she did to be face to face through the glass.

Raising his hand in a half wave, he walked away.

Ellie leaped to her feet. 'I won't be long, promise. I need to talk to that man.'

She moved before reason told her not to, before Mandy could speak.

The pavement outside the wine bar was busy with people, mainly tourists, out for the evening. She dodged an elderly couple and set off up the high street in search of Harry.

She soon caught up with him.

'Mr Dixon, Harry, could I have a word with you please?'

'Good evening, Ms Golden. I tried to find you earlier, but your gallery was closed.'

Ellie swept her mane of curls behind her shoulders. Chasing him down the road didn't seem such a good idea any more. She felt hot and out of breath. 'Oh, yes, you wanted to buy a picture?'

'I'd like to have a better look at your artwork, whether

I can afford anything is a different matter, but, also, you seemed to think that you knew me earlier. I wanted to talk to you to see if we could work out when and where we could have met before.'

The initial enthusiasm for following Harry and challenging him began to flood away, leaving behind just embarrassment about her behaviour.

'That's why I came after you, so that I could get the questions out of my mind.'

This evening he looked somehow different and her earlier certainty that he was Ben began to wane.

'And ...'

'Why don't you come and have a drink with my friend, Mandy, and I. Then we can discuss it?'

Mandy had a twinkle in her eyes, as Ellie, followed by Harry, returned to the wine bar. Ellie shot her a 'don't you dare' look, as she introduced Harry and they sat down. Harry perched on the bench seat at the other side of the table, his back against the window. Ellie noted his faded denims and dark blue shirt. She told him about Mandy's craft centre and couldn't believe that her friend blatantly fluttered her eyelashes at him as she spoke. Why did that make her feel so uncomfortable? What was wrong with Mandy flirting with Harry? He didn't belong to Ellie after all.

'Can I get you ladies another drink?'

They sent him off to get glasses of white wine and Mandy huddled closer. 'What's going on?'

Ellie schooled her features and her breathing. Harry glanced across at them a couple of times as he stood at the bar waiting to be served.

'When I met Harry, I had the impression that I already knew him. It's been eating at me all day, which is why I asked him to have a drink with us. Hopefully, I can find out if we have met each other before ... to put my mind at rest.'

Mandy twisted on her seat to look blatantly over at Harry at the bar. 'Whoa. Have you told him that you think you know him from somewhere?'

Know didn't quite cover it, but Ellie didn't say that. 'He doesn't seem to remember me.'

Mandy looked at her quizzically. 'Not usual for you to make a mistake though. You'll have to tell me more, but not now – he's coming back.'

Harry was aware that the next few minutes could make or break his future in Borteen. He stood well and truly in the lion's den, with Ellie throwing daggers of suspicion at him and Mandy firing arrows of apparent lust.

As he moved away from the bar, carrying a tray with two wine glasses and an orange juice, he took a huge breath to steady himself. It was all he could do to keep the drinks upright on the tray, with the women studying him as he crossed the wooden floor. He placed the glasses in front of the two very different females. Ellie nodded. Mandy thanked him with a wink.

He didn't react, merely sipped his orange juice. Ellie was by far the most attractive woman, with her wild hair and petite figure. Mandy seemed friendly, but was too loud and brash for Harry's taste. He found it disconcerting that she appeared so openly to be trying to attract a man, or rather … him.

'The art competition was a success, Ellie. Do you organise it every year?'

'I've been considering it for a while, but it was actually the first one.'

'Well, I hope you'll do it again next year.'

She looked at him with a strange expression on her face. She was studying his features, of that he had no doubt.

'I'd love to. Thank you, by the way, for giving that special award to Tom. It's really boosted his confidence.'

'I stand by my opinion. Tom's was by far the best picture in the exhibition.'

'Which picture did Tom enter, Ellie? Was it the fireworks one?' asked Mandy.

Ellie nodded.

'Oooh, that's a super picture, my favourite too.'

Harry grew fed up of skirting the real issue and when Mandy left them to visit the toilet, he decided to dive straight in. 'Now, tell me, where do you think you've met me before? It's been intriguing me ever since I met you this morning.'

Her cheeks grew pink. He couldn't tell if this was with embarrassment or the effects of the alcohol; he suspected the former.

'I knew a guy in Cornwall, years ago. I thought you were the same person, although he wasn't called Harry Dixon and he had long blond hair, a surf board and a tattoo.' Her face held a challenge. She locked eyes with him and when she couldn't hold his gaze any longer, she looked at his left arm, which was covered by his shirt sleeve. It took all of Harry's concentration not to flex the muscles of his forearm.

He forced himself to scratch his head, using the techniques he had mastered over the years not to show a flicker of reaction on his face to her words. 'Cornwall? No, sorry, not guilty. I've only been to Cornwall once, as far as I am aware, on a family holiday. I must have been about ten.'

She looked up and he fixed his eyes on hers again. She broke eye contact first.

Certain aspects of his past training were useful. He could tell by her expression that she hadn't been convinced by his answer, so he decided to go for reinforcement. 'Are you sure it was Cornwall? Could we have met at college?'

He felt pleased to see confusion pass through her eyes. 'I went to college in Cornwall. Have you got a brother?'

'I had a step-brother, but he looked nothing like me.'

Harry felt hot. Ellie had stared at the exact place where his tattoo used to be. This was more than a coincidence. He needed to keep calm. He found Ellie very attractive, but there was no flicker of recognition. If he'd known her before, it had to be around the time of his memory-destroying head injury. The thought was disconcerting, their connection could have been close or distant and he wouldn't know.

She put her head on one side, as she thought. 'You don't cook, do you?'

He laughed. 'Beans and cheese on toast is my speciality. Why do you ask that?'

'I love cookery competitions on television. If you'd been a competitor in one of those, I might have recognised you from that. Oh well, I must be mistaken, or else you have a double.'

That was a much better response. If Ellie remained uncertain, she wouldn't make trouble for him and perhaps he could continue with his original plans.

When Mandy returned to the table, he diverted from the subject of his identity by asking her a few questions about the local area and places to visit nearby. He showed an interest in the goods she stocked in the craft centre and asked for the address so that he could go and have a look for himself. He worried that he was encouraging her attentions, but he'd have to deal with that danger another time.

Satisfied he'd averted disaster with Ellie and got Mandy on his side, he finished his drink and made his excuses. He was pleased with the encounter. Hopefully, he'd cleared the air and secured his future in the town.

But, could it really be that easy?

'What was that all about?' Mandy's eyes sparkled in the wine bar's lighting.

'What do you mean?' Ellie had developed a fascination for the hem of her trousers.

'Come on, Ellie. In all the time I've been friends with

you, I've never seen you run down the street after a man. In fact, I've never seen you talk to a person of the male gender, unless it was to do with business or your son.'

'That's a slight exaggeration. I just needed to clear up if I'd met Harry before. It's been bugging me.'

'You mean, before … before?'

'Yes, before!'

Mandy was acquainted with certain parts of Ellie's history. She had told her friend about the night Rushton Jacob, her ex-husband, had let his temper get the better of him and beaten her badly enough for her to need surgery, because it explained why Tom, who had witnessed the attack, was sometimes withdrawn.

Mandy always managed to get through to her son with her bright breezy approach to life. She often did jigsaws, or played board games with him, to encourage him to talk and interact. Things had got better the older he'd become, but he still had his moments. Ellie was grateful to Mandy for the part she'd played in helping Tom to adjust to life in Borteen.

Her face, which she ran her hands over in response to Mandy's reference to her past, little resembled the girl who'd been infatuated with Ben Rivers all those years ago. Her reconstructed nose was smaller than the original. Her new cheekbones were higher. There were occasions when she didn't even recognise her own reflection in the mirror.

'So, you now know it was a case of mistaken identity and Harry isn't who you thought he was?'

'Maybe …'

Mandy's eyes widened. 'Are you suggesting that he lied?'

'Who knows? I just have a gut feeling that he wasn't telling the complete truth.'

'I don't get why he'd deny living in Cornwall.'

'I'm probably deluded. Please forget I ever said anything.'

Ellie definitely wasn't ready to tell Mandy the full extent of her suspicions about Harry Dixon.

Chapter Six

The next day, Ellie was pleased not to have a headache. She'd drunk more wine than she would normally have done on a night out, but, thankfully, there were no ill effects.

Tom went off to school in a happy mood. He'd given her a rare kiss, before hoisting his school bag onto his shoulder.

She dusted the arms of the battered rocking chair, which had been one of the first items of furniture she'd bought after arriving in Borteen. She'd always wanted a rocking chair and this one had seemed to be waiting for her in the window of the charity shop. Rocking soothed her nerves in a way nothing else did and she couldn't imagine being without the chair.

Ellie and Tom had moved a lot in the early years after Rushton had been sent to prison. It had been hard to settle and to trust that they were safe, given the type of friends Rushton mixed with and the threats he'd made.

The times she awoke in the middle of the night with his voice yelling at her, "I'm going to kill you, if it's the last thing I do," had lessened, but the memory was never far from the surface of her mind, as if he sat on her shoulder repeating his maxim if she dared to get too comfortable. The dreaded man might be in prison, but she was still haunted by him.

Thankfully, she'd had money to finance the moves. Before they'd discovered Borteen, she'd even been considering Australia. Her concerns about Harry Dixon had reawakened her urge to move on. These thoughts were demons, nagging at the edges of her mind. How on earth would Tom react if she told him they were moving again, particularly just as her gallery was beginning to take off?

He'd probably refuse and ask Mandy if he could move in with her.

At nine-fifteen, she began to walk down the road to the seafront and her gallery. She found it hard to believe that she'd been brave enough to rent her own shop, rather than exhibiting in other people's galleries and craft shops as she had done for many years. It made the urges to move on again more difficult to act upon.

Borteen was the first place she'd tried to put down permanent roots and leave the past behind. Harry Dixon turning up here had unsettled her. Even if he wasn't who she believed him to be, and she was pretty certain he was, the rush of memories from the past had invaded her peace and caused her to re-examine her past and her future.

She walked at a steady pace down the hill, past the white-washed cottages, reminiscent of those in her native Cornwall. The air was warm already and it promised to be a blisteringly hot day. The blue sky merged with the sea in exactly the same shade at the horizon, making it difficult to distinguish one from the other. Seagulls circled, calling and squawking. She breathed in the unmistakable scent of the sea, the smell that felt vital to her very existence.

Whenever she intended to spend time painting in her studio at the gallery, she loved to find inspiration on her short journey to work. Today, the overwhelming colour was blue, the dominant sensation heat and her emotions were in turmoil. She'd see what she could make of it all on canvas. Art and her own imagination never ceased to amaze her.

She stopped by the sea wall to enjoy the sight of the early morning beach, cleansed and levelled by the tide. A man jogged across the sand. Ellie watched, fascinated by the sand wisps thrown up by his trainers and the trail of footprints, tracing across the seashore, showing the route he had run. Her fascination changed to discomfort as she realised the identity of the runner – Harry Dixon. Her first instinct was to walk off in the opposite direction, but she forced herself to stay still.

Blue running shorts displayed muscled, tanned legs and his orange vest top revealed well-toned arms. To her horror, he noticed her watching him and raised his water bottle in a wave, as he sprinted past at the water's edge. Thankfully, he ran past fast enough that Ellie didn't need to respond, but, nevertheless, she walked away from the seafront with a blush on her cheeks.

She knew from experience that creative activity would calm her mind. First, however, she needed to make sure that the gallery was ready for any visitors. She cleaned the large window and door of the shop before she did anything else, standing on a beer crate to reach the high bits. She exchanged pleasantries about the weather with Maeve, who owned the gift shop in the corner of the alleyway. Maeve arranged brightly coloured windmills in a basket as she spoke.

The front room of the gallery housed Ellie's exhibits. Paintings hung on the wall, or were propped on easels. The walls were painted white and she had sprayed the easels with gold paint to fit in with the Golden Designs theme. The wide window sill and a central table contained carefully arranged ceramic pots. Ellie tried to keep the ceramics she displayed to a theme of colour or subject. At the moment, the pots were all glazed in blue and white with wave patterns on them.

The lighting was strategically placed to illuminate the canvases and reflective surfaces, mirrors and a large glass vase full of marbles were positioned to reflect the light around the shop.

She'd noticed that displaying less led to more sales. People preferred to be able to see exactly what they were buying and to be sure that they were purchasing unique pieces.

Ellie whizzed a duster over the pots and frames. It wasn't wise to let dust build up and give the impression that products weren't selling. She wondered for a moment whether the perfume diffuser's scent of vanilla was too strong.

The gallery had been open nearly a year and she was breaking even, just about holding her own. She had great hopes for the summer holidays and had been building a stock of artwork to replace any that, fingers crossed, sold. Ellie kept her stock of pictures and pots in a big cupboard off the kitchenette.

The studio room of the building was where she felt most at home. A square room, it housed her pottery wheel in one corner and easel and paints in another. Sometimes customers would wander through from the gallery to watch her working. She wasn't terribly comfortable with people spectating, but, on the other hand, it reassured customers that the designs were original and made them more inclined to buy from her after they had watched her with a brush or wet clay in her hand.

Beyond the workroom lay the kitchenette and toilet. In the yard outside the back door was a stone outhouse into which her kiln just fitted with necessary ventilation around it. This outhouse would once have contained an outside toilet and a coal shed.

Ellie moved to the easel and placed a blank canvas on the stand. She needed to work out her pent-up emotions and she was determined to use these unsettled feelings to fuel her creativity.

Pausing to put on her paint-daubed overall, which she didn't always remember in her enthusiasm to get going, she picked up a large brush and covered the canvas with water. Working quickly, she added different shades of blue paint. The brush strokes merged, carried by the water on the surface, blurring the hues together in a pleasing chaotic mix. At the bottom of the canvas, she painted sandy shades and as the canvas began to dry, she detailed footprints along the sand, emanating from a small running figure in an orange T-shirt.

She stood back, astounded at what she had just painted, as her canvases were usually more abstract, but pleased nonetheless with the resulting image. Oh that every canvas filled as quickly. She chuckled, wondering if Harry Dixon would recognise himself in the window of the gallery when she displayed the painting. If he was going to unsettle her mind, she may as well earn some money by translating her churning emotions about him into artwork.

She finished several canvases, each very different, working swiftly and decisively as her mood began to calm and lighten. When they'd dried she'd see if she needed to add more detail with paint or ink.

By the time she turned the gallery sign to open, she was feeling much more serene and ready to talk to prospective customers.

When Ellie returned home from the gallery later that afternoon, Tom was in a foul mood. He banged around the house and refused to speak to her. She had learned over the years to let him burn out his anger and only to try to talk to him when he was ready to communicate. Stamping up and down the stairs was his usual method of tension release.

As she prepared their evening meal, mushroom risotto, she noticed a change in his behaviour. He came to sit at the dining room table, resting his chin on his hands. He looked exhausted, dark rings circling his eyes. Ellie stopped what she was doing and came to sit opposite to him. She mirrored his posture, resting her chin on her hands.

'Are you going to tell me what's eating you?'

He met her gaze with those huge brown eyes.

'You know me too well, Mum. I'm just angry with myself for being played like a fool.'

'In what way, love?' Ellie believed she could already guess, but wanted Tom to tell her the story himself.

He banged his fists on the table, making her jump. 'The lads I thought had made friends with me yesterday. They ... they didn't want to speak to me today. It was just the fact I had money to buy them ice creams. Tossers, the lot of them.'

'Oh, Tom, I'm sorry. That's so unfair.' She clenched her fists in a frustration magnified because someone had picked on her beloved son.

'Bollocks to the lot of them, I don't need them.'

Tom stretched out his long legs and arms in a huge yawn. She could almost see the tension flowing out of him. The crisis was over.

Ellie's heart felt as if it had been wrung out. Tom had been so happy the previous evening when he'd believed he'd made friends. Children and young people could be so cruel to each other. The times she'd wished she could wade in and sort out injustice metered out to her son. She hated him to be hurt, hated him not to be loved and accepted as the wonderful creative being that he was. Just when she was feeling so upset, Tom flashed her a huge smile and changed the subject.

'The new headmaster, Mr Dixon, is cool though. He came into school this afternoon to meet us properly. He's running sports events in the summer holidays. Can I go, Mum?' Tom virtually bounced up and down with excitement flowing out of every pore.

'What kind of sports events?' She hoped her overwhelming suspicion for the man didn't show in her voice as much as she was feeling it in her body.

'Taster sessions of rugby, football, cricket, hockey, athletics and cross-country running. Oh and netball, but that's for the girls. They're sampler classes to help Mr Dixon spot talent for the teams he's going to set up. We're going to be competing with other schools. There will be league tables.'

'It sounds fantastic. Of course you can join in.'

'Awesome! I've got a form in my bag.'

He ran up the stairs to get it, his mood transformed in an instant.

She filled in the details on the form, as Tom stood over her watching.

'Won't you need extra kit for these sports?'

'Mr Dixon says we can just wear a T-shirt and shorts for the taster days. If we're chosen for the teams we might need proper kit, but he said he's hoping to raise sponsorship for that from local businesses.'

Tom's growing admiration for Harry Dixon shone in his voice. Ellie was pleased by his enthusiasm and wary all at the same time.

'The summer season is my best chance for making sales, so I'm going to have to open the gallery every day anyway. I'd be happier if you were doing something interesting.' Before she could stop them, words came out of her mouth. 'Your dad was always very sporty.'

'Really? I'd like to hear more about him, Mum.' The expression on his face, full of expectation, tugged at her heart strings.

Ellie always tried to avoid the subject of Tom's father if she could. Tom knew that her ex-husband, Rushton, was his step-dad and not his biological dad. A good job, given what had happened. Ellie thanked her lucky stars every day that she hadn't had a child with Rushton.

'Your dad loved surfing and running. I don't know anything about his childhood though or if he played team sports at school.'

'He died in a surfing accident in Cornwall, didn't he?'

'Yes, he did.' Her heart began to thud.

She could see Tom's mind working on the information.

She turned away, a lump in her throat even after the passage of years. She could remember the day of Ben's death as if it were yesterday; that's why Harry's appearance was so confusing. Who had been buried in Ben's grave if Harry was actually Ben?

Tom's voice brought her back from her reflections.

'He never actually met me, did he?' Tom's brown eyes, fixed on her, were heartbreakingly similar to her memories of Ben's eyes.

'He died before you were born, love. I'd just fallen pregnant when it happened. Very sad.'

Tom sat down at the table again, deep in thought, folding and refolding the consent form for Harry's sporting events. Ellie planted a kiss on his head and with a quick hug, went to finish preparing the meal. She was thankful that he hadn't pushed her to answer any more searching questions. One day, she would tell him the whole story, but he seemed too young to understand the raw realities of life and the choices she'd made when she herself was only a few years older than Tom was now. She couldn't bear the idea that her son might judge her and think badly of her.

How would she feel about Tom spending the summer in Harry Dixon's sports classes? She was so distracted that she burned her finger on the hot pan. It was a small burn, but it sent her scurrying to the sink to run cold water over the reddened skin, batting away tears at the sharpness of the pain.

Ellie Golden you have to stop this. Forget that man and get on with your life.

Of course, keeping that resolution was easier said than done.

Chapter Seven

The end of term came and went, along with celebrations for the retirement of John Williams at Borteen High. As Ellie had hoped, sales at the gallery began to pick up with more tourists arriving in the area for their holidays. The downside was she had to be more vigilant for unsupervised children near her paintings and pots. Thankfully, they were always fascinated by the jar of marbles she had near the door and these proved a useful distraction for keeping sticky fingers away from her art.

Tom relished the sports training sessions. He declared he loved every sport.

'Even netball?' Ellie asked, with a wink.

'Mum, you know what I mean.'

Ellie laughed, pleased that Tom was happy.

A side effect of the sports training was that Tom had met genuine friends and spent more time out with them than at home. His skin bronzed in the sun, despite Ellie's liberal application of sun cream every morning with her ears ringing with Tom's protests.

Ellie tried very hard to let any references he made to Harry wash over her. At least he was having a positive effect on her son.

For the first time, Tom showed an interest in the gallery and took to coming down to the shop if he wasn't training or socialising, wearing an open-necked shirt, his school trousers and shoes, to help with the customers. Ellie had never mentioned a dress code and found it touching he had thought about looking smart for the job, even polishing his shoes, which he never did for school.

Tom asked if he could have commission for any artwork he sold and Ellie readily agreed. She listened with pride to his sales patter, as she painted in the studio room. He was able to sell her work without the self-consciousness she herself displayed. It was a win-win situation and she loved spending time with him in this new business arrangement.

'Mr Dixon's coming into the gallery today,' Tom said, arriving at the shop one afternoon. His hair was still wet from his shower after the morning's sports sessions.

Ellie forced herself not to overreact.

'Really? You haven't been doing a hard sell on him too have you?'

'No, Mum. He said he promised to come and look at your pictures ages ago. He needs a few to brighten up his flat.'

Ellie wondered if she could make an excuse to be away from the gallery when Harry arrived, but she decided she would have to brazen it out. She couldn't avoid him forever. Borteen wasn't that big.

A short while later, she returned from checking the kiln to hear Tom talking in animated tones. She knew exactly who she would see when she walked into the gallery, but still she almost dropped the large almond-coloured pot she was carrying. Harry Dixon was sitting on one of the leather seats in the gallery talking to Tom.

His hair slick from the shower, sunglasses perched on his head, wearing an orange T-shirt and blue shorts, he looked as if he'd come straight out of a magazine advertisement. Ellie couldn't help following his long, muscular, tanned legs down to blue flip-flops.

'Good afternoon, Ms Golden.'

Had he noticed her looking at his muscles? Embarrassing!

'Ellie, please.'

He nodded his head in acknowledgement.

'Ellie, your son is making an excellent job of selling me one of your paintings for the bare walls in my lounge.'

She turned to see the picture Tom was holding up and

nearly dropped the big pot she was carrying once again. She put it gently on the floor, to keep it safe and to hide her reaction at the same time. Tom was displaying the picture of the runner on the beach. The runner she had modelled on Harry Dixon.

'Tom, have you shown Mr Dixon a range of my pictures?'

'Sure, Mum, but this one reminds me of Mr Dixon. He goes for a run on the beach every morning.'

Ellie willed her face not to colour. 'I've seen him running a couple of times on my way to work.'

'I've even waved to your mum,' said Harry, winking at Ellie. The blush was now inevitable.

'Can I ask about the colour scheme of the room you want the picture for?' asked Ellie, in an attempt to divert her embarrassment.

Harry laughed. 'I don't believe there is one. The landlord must have shares in magnolia paint.'

Ellie was determined not to be unnerved. 'So, you can choose whatever you want to display against the neutral background. What are your favourite colours?' She'd gone into her familiar sales questions without thinking.

Harry looked thoughtful for a moment, but Ellie couldn't shake the feeling that he was observing her closely from under his lowered eyelashes. 'Blue and orange, I suppose, and this picture has both of those.'

'As long as you're sure you like looking at it and haven't let Tom talk you into buying one of his own favourites. You've got to live with it remember, not him.'

'He's got pretty good taste if this is his choice. By the way, your son is showing real sporting talent. If he carries on learning so fast and trying so hard, he'll be in the school teams for several sports.'

Ellie saw Tom grow visibly taller in front of her as Harry spoke. This is what he needs, she thought, encouragement and praise from a male role model. Why couldn't Harry Dixon be just any man?

At that moment, Mandy came flying through the door.

'Hello ... whoops, sorry, you have a customer. Oh, *hello, Harry*.' The way she stressed the words hello and Harry made the sentence sound like a chat up line.

Harry nodded at Mandy and sat up straighter in the chair. He crossed his legs, as if he was afraid she might sit on his lap. To be fair, Ellie would not have been surprised if her friend had done just that.

'You're not buying my favourite picture, are you?' exclaimed Mandy, looking at the painting Tom was holding.

Tom took a step backwards, clutching the canvas and moving it away from Mandy.

'Yes, I'm afraid it's sold.' Harry took his wallet out of his pocket. 'You'll have to ask Ellie to paint another one.'

'Aww, Ellie would you?'

'Bear in mind each picture is unique, another one wouldn't be exactly the same.'

'I'll have a look when you've painted the new one to see if I like it. Anyway, I must dash. I popped in to invite everyone to a barbecue on the beach on Saturday night.'

'I'm not sure I can get a sitter for Saturday.'

'Nonsense, Tom can come too. He's fourteen and he's finished school. There'll be people of all ages there. Harry, are you up for it too?'

'Sounds great, I'd love to come. I'm trying to meet as many of the locals as I can before I take up my new post.'

'That's settled then. See you all on Saturday. Byeeee.' Mandy winked at Harry and breezed out as quickly as she had arrived.

'She's rather a whirlwind, your friend Mandy.' Harry uncrossed his legs and relaxed back in the chair.

'Sure is,' said Ellie, through gritted teeth. Why did it upset her so much when Mandy flirted with Harry? She should be used to her friend's behaviour by now, but somehow this was different and personal.

Tom held up the picture of the beach runner once more. 'Are you sure you want to buy this one, Mr Dixon?' he asked.

'Yes, please.'

Tom wrapped the canvas thoroughly in bubble wrap and Ellie dealt with the payment.

'I'm really looking forward to putting your painting on my wall, some colour at last. See you on Saturday night, Ellie?'

She nodded and thanked him for his purchase, trying to keep her doubts about the beach barbecue under control.

As soon as Harry had left with the painting tucked under his arm, Tom studied her with an odd expression on his face. 'Mum, why do you act so strangely around Mr Dixon?'

'I *do* not!' she exclaimed, horrified.

'I think you fancy him.' Tom dived out of the way in case she whacked him.

'I do not, Thomas Golden!' She crossed her arms tightly across her body, as if trying to hold in something she might reveal.

'Okay, I'll believe you, thousands wouldn't.'

If Tom was aware she acted and spoke differently with Harry around, would Harry himself have noticed too? Disturbed by the idea, she tried to distract herself in the studio.

Harry walked deep in thought towards his flat. The picture got heavier and more uncomfortable to carry the further he went. Ellie Golden was lovely. Surely, he would remember if he had met her in the past. It was Tom who looked familiar, but how could that be? Perhaps he'd met Tom's dad before.

The thoughts kept circulating around his head. It was a mystery and no doubt the answer lay in that period of time he couldn't recall. His own personal black hole. The medical professionals had told him he was unlikely to ever retrieve those lost memories, so he would have to get by without the knowledge of that time. It hadn't seemed to matter much before, but somehow now it seemed vital to be able to remember what had happened back then. How did Ellie and possibly Tom's dad fit into his personal history?

Chapter Eight

As Ellie pondered what to wear on Saturday night, she worried again about Tom's comments regarding the way she acted around Harry Dixon. Others might notice too, if she wasn't careful.

What if someone said something to Harry?

She'd have to be alert this evening.

Harry was the first man she had been remotely aware of for ages. Was it wrong to fancy him despite her confusion? She'd fancied Ben, so why shouldn't she fancy the man she believed he was now? Maybe the whole thing was an illusion stemming from the fact she was attracted to him. After all, he reminded her strongly of the man she had believed at one time was the love of her life.

Could she finally let go of the memory of her infatuation with Ben Rivers and the trauma of her rebound marriage and allow herself to find love?

Was it possible that Harry might feel the same about her? She'd noticed, or rather thought she'd seen, his eyes lingering on her face on several occasions. Was it just curiosity triggered by her questioning, or the spark of an interest?

On the other hand, might it be better, if she truly was ready for a new relationship, to pick a man with no associations to the past, no demons lurking in the background to rise up and scupper her happiness? Her thinking went round and round in circles as she tried on and discarded items from her wardrobe.

One thing was for sure, she'd felt her hackles rise when Mandy was flirting openly with Harry. She would bet her life savings that her friend would be prowling around him this evening and Mandy would no doubt be dressed to kill too.

Abruptly, she changed her mind about what to wear and pulled the tie out of her hair, allowing her newly washed curls to bounce uncontrolled around her face.

Tom gawped open-mouthed, as she came down the stairs. 'Whoa, Mum. You look hot.'

'Thomas Golden, I'm not sure it's entirely appropriate to say such things to your mother.' Secretly, however, she was pleased at his spontaneous comment. She was even more delighted when she answered the door to Mandy's ring and got a similar reaction.

'Goodness me, where has *this* Ellie Golden been hiding? I've got competition tonight, girlfriend!'

Ellie didn't dare say a word. She smoothed her pink mini-dress over her hips, hoped her perfume wasn't too strong and her silver heels weren't too high.

Harry sat on his newly acquired second-hand leather sofa and examined the picture yet again. The splash of colour was very welcome in the bland room. He had a strange suspicion it was a painting of himself. Ellie must have painted it after she had seen him running on the beach one morning, or was it arrogant to think that? He would never dare to ask her.

Whatever the inspiration, the picture looked perfect on the wall and it suited him to have a reminder of his morning runs, the only time he could truly be himself. It was also nice to have a bit of Ellie here. He wished circumstances were different and that she didn't keep giving him those searching, suspicious looks. It was unnerving that she had questioned him about Cornwall.

The picture aroused strange feelings in him. In it, he was immortalised and somehow linked forever with Ellie, as she'd painted it. The thought of her choosing paints and moving her paintbrush to create an image of him was incredibly arousing. One, because she'd been inspired to paint him and two, because of how she'd depicted him: athletic, tall, muscled, at home on a run.

Part of him longed to hold her, to be part of a couple, to not feel so utterly, heart-wrenchingly alone in the world. It had been too long since he'd allowed himself to be attracted to a woman.

Stop it! You don't need the complication. It would only end in tears.

He had a horrible feeling that if he went to the barbecue, Ellie's friend Mandy would make a play for him. She seemed a nice person, rather too exuberant for his taste, but he didn't relish the idea of having to fight off her advances, perhaps alienating her in the process. Perhaps he should give the event a miss completely. He could tell them he'd fallen ill, food poisoning seemed a realistic excuse.

After half an hour of trying to concentrate on the thriller he was reading, the idea of another night in front of mindless television held no appeal. Better to flirt with danger, perhaps ...

Ellie, Mandy and Tom arrived at the beach to a party warming up nicely.

Two huge barbecues were set up on the paving at the edge of the sea wall and a steel drum band was in full swing below on the beach. Ellie and Mandy immediately kicked off their shoes and began dancing on the sand. Tom raised his eyes heavenward when Ellie asked him to join them and slumped against the sea wall looking sulky to be left in charge of handbags and shoes.

Ellie beckoned him over again, but he just crossed his arms and looked the other way. His hair was getting longer and his blond fringe blew across his eyes. It struck her again, how quickly he was growing up and how closely he resembled his father.

She looked up into the darkening sky to let the tears

resulting from this thought settle in her eyes rather than roll down her face.

The two friends danced with abandon, until Ellie suddenly realised Harry had joined her son, sitting next to him with his back against the sea wall. Her heart lurched and she became self-conscious and uncoordinated. She could no longer pick out the beat in the music, was hardly aware of the music at all, despite how loud it was.

'Let's go get a drink, Mandy.'

Mandy stopped flailing her arms and noticed Harry too. 'Oh yes, let's get one for Tom and Harry too. They both look as if they need cheering up. It's a party for goodness' sake.' She rearranged her dress to display more of her ample cleavage.

After her earlier resolution to flirt with Harry, Ellie had completely lost her bottle. She was nervous about going over to speak to him, especially as he was playing with her discarded shoes.

There was something far too intimate about the way he was tracing along the silver straps of her sandals with his fingers. She felt a corresponding tingle on her feet as Harry played, experiencing the sensations as if he were touching her bare skin. An ache took up residence in her body.

He looked up, saw her watching him and smiled. It was a warm, genuine smile.

Mandy had no such inhibitions about her advances to Harry. She marched straight over to him and held out a bottle of beer.

'Good evening, Harry. Drink?'

'Thank you for the thought, Mandy, but I don't actually drink alcohol. I'll go and get myself a lemonade.'

He got to his feet and, with another smile for Ellie, headed for the bar.

Mandy was left with the unwanted bottle held in mid-air, her expression initially surprised and then tight-lipped.

'You can't have beer yet, Tom. I'd better find someone else to give this to.'

Ellie could almost see Mandy's man-tracking antennae extend from the top of her head as her friend walked into the crowd intent on finding someone who would like the beer and give her some attention.

Ellie was transported back to a similar scenario in her own history.

In the mists of time, it had seemed like a dream, although all too soon it had turned into a nightmare. The conversation leading up to the event that changed her life was so clear even after the passage of years.

'You've been lusting after Ben Rivers for ages.'

Ellie had been surprised that her inner thoughts had been read so easily.

'You imagine yourself in his arms?'

She'd nodded.

Norrie had turned his back on her and she heard him take a bottle of beer from the cool box at his feet. He messed around taking off the cap. It seemed to take forever, but then he turned back to her, holding out the bottle.

'There you go, lovely Ellie, give this to Ben and stay close to him. If you kiss him, he won't be able to resist you. Trust me and my magic potion beer.'

Norrie had winked and pinched her bottom as she turned to walk away, thinking he was teasing her.

'You can give him a message for me too.'

She'd walked down onto the beach to find Ben, repeating the message to herself so she didn't forget the exact words.

Harry was glad to be able to step away from Mandy. As he had suspected, she had that predatory look in her eye and had singled him out for attention, beginning with the present of the bottle of beer and a flash of her cleavage.

He hoped he'd foiled her approaches for the time being by admitting he was teetotal.

Ellie looked amazing. Her long, slim legs were tanned and toned. The mini-dress showed her figure to its best advantage and her hair was something else. Brushed out, its curls allowed to bush out naturally, the effect was stunning. Unlike Mandy though, Ellie had yet to properly meet his eye, despite the fact he'd smiled at her several times. Was she playing hard to get or just not interested in him?

It would help if he could remember any connection with her in Cornwall. Another trawl of his memory banks couldn't find a trace of her.

He debated whether to go home. The thing with Mandy would undoubtedly come to a head at some point, but, if he was honest with himself, there was only one woman here tonight who could ignite his interest and she was wearing a pink mini-dress.

He bought two bottles of lemonade and took one to Tom. The lad had been joined by a girl he recognised from the art competition, Louise Stevens. The pair were talking animatedly in the late sunshine about art, of all things. Tom had acquired a drink from somewhere, so Harry gave the bottle of lemonade to Louise. She looked awe-struck that the new headmaster would speak to her, let alone give her a drink. He had the impression she might take the empty lemonade bottle home as a souvenir.

Leaning against the wall, he watched the dancers. Music for the middle part of the evening was being provided by a DJ, with sound blasting out of huge speakers. Harry was surprised at how many people he already recognised on the beach. His deliberate networking was beginning to pay off. He began a game, seeing how many names he could remember. He'd got to seven acquaintances, when he felt a warm arm slip through his own. His breath stilled, as for one moment he let himself imagine it was

Ellie, but a waft of sharp perfume confirmed that Mandy had returned.

Having slotted her arm through his, she squeezed.

'Aren't you going to ask me to dance, Mr Dixon?' Her eyelashes flicked her face; they were longer than eyelashes were supposed to be, he guessed they were false and being deployed in a seduction routine that left him cold.

'Like most men, I don't really do dancing.'

'That's why you should drink alcohol to remove your inhibitions.'

The mention of alcohol had the same effect as tipping a bucket of cold water over him. He would have to be cruel to be kind. Pulling his arm from her vice-like grip, he put a foot of space between them.

'Look, Mandy, we're both adults. You're a lovely girl, but if I tell you I'm not interested, will you take the hint?'

Mandy looked as if she too had been doused in cold water. Her face assumed a scowl.

'Are you gay as well as anti-alcohol?'

He paused before answering, trying to assess how much Mandy had drunk.

'I think my sexuality and my drinking habits are my business. I was only trying to save you from wasting your time. I'm sorry. I don't want to upset you, Mandy. I like you very much, but, please, please, just be a friend.'

She stared at him for a moment. The way she swayed made him think that maybe she had been drinking quite heavily. She shot him a disgusted look, twisted round on her heel and stalked away. He hoped she'd had enough to drink not to remember their encounter.

It was then Harry realised that Ellie was standing close by and had probably overheard everything. He shrugged his shoulders and Ellie smiled, meeting his eyes at last. Great, now the woman he found most interesting and attractive in Borteen believed he was more focused on the men at the party.

Harry was aware of how small towns and rejected women worked too. Before the start of the new school term, if he was unlucky, this juicy bit of gossip about the new headmaster's personal life could be all around town.

Ellie moved closer. In contrast to Mandy's perfume, Ellie's flowery, powdery scent bridged the gap between them and made Harry inhale more deeply. He wanted to get closer to her.

'Is there a particular reason why you don't drink?' she asked. He had the distinct impression they weren't talking about his alcohol consumption. He was trapped in a halo of her enticing scent. The pink of her dress shaded more peach in the fading light and he had a great desire to reach out and put his hands on her slender waist.

'No medical reason, if that's what you mean. I had a bad experience in the past that I don't want to repeat.'

'Hmm, we all have those ...'

'I think mine might be a bit more extreme than most people's ... unfortunately.'

She looked curious and he was grateful she didn't press him for any more detail.

They stood side by side in silence and watched Mandy honing in on an unsuspecting tourist who was dancing with his mates.

Ellie shrugged in her friend's direction. 'That's Mandy for you, fickle I'm afraid, a bit like a cat where men are concerned. I love her though. She's been a loyal friend to me. I don't think she really knows what she's looking for in a man and, unfortunately, she seems to put most of them off.'

She didn't need to elaborate and he wasn't surprised or upset that he could be replaced in Mandy's affections so easily, more relieved.

Ellie was the picture of loveliness. Her hair brushed out was doing strange things to his senses. He wanted to bury his fingers in her curls. Shaking himself, he wondered where his preference for wild hair like Ellie's had come from. Could that be the link to Ellie? Was it her hair that had excited his interest before? It was a memory buried on the edge of his consciousness and, similar to many recollections from the early part of his life, it refused to become clear.

The music changed. An old track, one he could hum along to and his mood transformed with it.

How did a situation between two people change so quickly?

One minute she was standing next to Harry feeling rather disappointed that he preferred male company to female, the next they were slow dancing on the sand and her senses were on fire.

A glance at Tom confirmed he was far too busy talking to Louise to notice what his mother was doing. Mandy, however, was another matter. She'd seen what was going on and, after standing staring at the couple for a moment, she flounced off in the direction of the bar.

Harry's breath was warm on her neck, his hands held her waist gently but firmly. It felt normal, natural and so lovely that her bare toes curled in bliss. She tightened her arms around his neck and he inched closer. Her legs brushed up against the warmth of his and now their bodies were resting against each other. They seemed to fit together like the pieces of a jigsaw. His hand moved to cup the back of her head, drawing her closer. She couldn't remember the last time she had been handled so tenderly, had been so close to a man with her animal instincts kicking in.

Would he kiss her? Her lips burned in anticipation and her heart skipped a beat. How had this happened? There had been no words, simply a mutual closing of the gap between them and a united humming of a well-known song. Right now, she wanted the track to go on forever.

She fervently hoped Harry hadn't danced with her just to

quell Mandy's inevitable rumour-mongering, but surely, the dance only replaced one rumour with another. She nuzzled her chin a little closer into the warmth of his shoulder. Did she imagine his sigh? The heat from his body was chasing away the slight chill that had enveloped her since the sun had gone down.

The only lights were from the disco equipment and the street lamps above the sea wall. The tide was edging in slowly. It would eventually bring a natural end to the party and right now that thought sparked panic as she didn't want Harry to let go of her. She could hear the swish of the waves on the sand. This clinch had to stop sooner or later, but then what?

Stop it, Ellie. Enjoy the moment.

The track finished and Harry pulled gently away. Ellie couldn't breathe. She needed to see the expression on his face.

He smiled sheepishly as they pulled apart.

'Thank you for the dance,' he whispered.

Right, so it was just a dance.

Ellie's spirits sank as the warmth of his body faded.

'I'm going to call it a night. Goodnight, Ellie.'

He turned abruptly away and began to walk off across the sand into the growing gloom.

As her disappointment grew, Ellie's hackles rose and before she could stop herself, she had followed him across the sand and opened her mouth.

Chapter Nine

'Ben!'

Her voice rang out clear into the night air. She was shocked that she had spoken aloud the name that had become sacred to her over the years. The name that had been on her mind again most of the time, ever since she had met Harry.

He froze, a silhouette framed against the sky and then he spun round to face her.

'Are you talking to me, Ellie? Have you forgotten? My name's Harry.' There was grit in his tone.

She stopped about a yard from him, stood her ground and stared.

He locked his gaze with hers and stared back, but he was the first to look away.

Had that moment of intimacy during the dance really happened or had she dreamt it? Her stomach churned. She was surely destroying the beginnings of something that could be special.

Harry appeared to be about to walk off again and his movement inflamed her anger even more.

'Ben!'

He visibly jumped.

Ellie was certain she hadn't imagined it.

'What do you want me to say? You're mistaking me for someone else.' His voice was full of exasperation.

'No. I don't think I am. Now I've danced with you, I'm even more sure.' It wasn't actually true, but she felt the need to try and goad him into an admission. This ghost needed to be laid to rest once and for all.

'Look, Ellie. I've no idea who you believe me to be or how you feel you've known me before, but you have to stop this fantasy. I'd hoped we could be friends.'

The way he emphasised the word friends suggested he meant much more.

She'd started, so she might as well continue. It was like being on a slide with no way of stopping on the slippery surface. She glanced around to make sure no one was within earshot.

'You have a mole two inches below your belly button.' Her voice was quiet, but determined.

His hand moved to protect the area she'd mentioned and his shocked eyes widened. To Ellie, it was as if she had shot a gun at him, with the mole as her target.

'Now you're freaking me out. This is getting far too personal.'

'Well, you have, haven't you? You've a mole exactly where I said.'

'That's not really any of your business.'

She acted as if he hadn't spoken.

'Like the tattoo you've had removed from your wrist. It was a snake with a green and purple pattern.'

Whereas he had seemed curious, even amused before, his eyes now glowed with anger.

'I don't know what you think you're doing, Ellie, but I've had enough. Stop this please.'

There was a shout. A fight had broken out further down the beach. Ellie glanced behind her and saw that Tom and Louise had got up to go and see what was going on. At least no one was focusing on them.

'Maybe the school governors will be interested to know your real name.'

She might be going too far, but couldn't stop herself. The frustration of his refusal to admit what she believed to be true built to a crescendo.

Did you ever forget the feel of a lover, the scent of their skin?

Harry took a step towards her. Fear flared through her

mind and she stepped backwards, poised to run. No man was going to hurt her physically ever again.

'Look, Ellie, I don't know what you think you know, or what bearing it has on my job as headmaster. Why would you want to cause trouble for me? This is a new start, a promotion. I'm having difficulty understanding what you want from me.'

'Borteen is a fresh start for me too. I've just begun to make it work and then you turn up with a new look and a new name. You're supposed to be dead. I cried at your funeral for heaven's sake.'

'Hey, hey. Stop it, Ellie. I'm confused about who you think I am or what I'm meant to have done, but surely there's room for both of us here?' A pleading tone had crept into his voice, but his features were calm.

'I'm not sure about that. You're about to pull the wool over the eyes of this community, a community I've come to care about. My son goes to Borteen High for goodness' sake. Don't you think I should be concerned if a person I believe has a false identity is taking up the post of headmaster at my son's school? A son I've had to protect and keep safe from harm, a son who's been damaged enough by things that have happened in his past.'

Her words sounded, in some ways, hypocritical. After all, she'd reinvented herself too, but that was different, wasn't it?

'I still don't understand what you're talking about, but I tell you now, I'll fight for my job and for my reputation. For the record, I like your son very much and would never do anything to harm him. I like you too. I thought we could be friends, maybe even more, but it seems I was mistaken.'

This time, he did walk off and rapidly disappeared into the growing darkness.

Heart thudding, Harry lurched across the sand. It felt as if

Ellie had blasted a hole in his stomach. He fingered the mole two inches below his belly button through the fabric of his shirt. How did Ellie know such an intimate thing? Surely, he would remember a woman who had been that close to him?

He searched his memory banks again, but could find no trace of Ellie from the past, but then he did have that big black hole. What a nightmare. For the umpteenth time, he wondered if he should back out of the new job and move on. Was all the meticulous preparation for nothing? Could Ellie Golden, artist, pose a real threat to him?

It was years since he'd had his tattoo removed. He still missed it. The days of being a long-haired, blond, care-free guy with a snake tattooed on his wrist and a surfboard on top of his campervan seemed a long way off, but of course all of that had been an illusion too. In reality, it had just been a job, but it was so easy to remember only the good bits with hindsight.

Those were the days, before the nightmare began. Before he had to be aware of his every word and action, always watching his back for lurking potential danger. With the passage of years, he'd maybe relaxed too much. Forgotten … lost his edge.

He walked to the end of the beach, where the rocks reared up to form a cliff. Pent-up anger and swirling emotions made him want to thump something, but he knew that violence rarely achieved anything. He settled for kicking over an abandoned sandcastle. The action didn't make him feel any better. He was angry with himself mostly. Angry that he had allowed himself to be lulled by the moment, danced with Ellie and imagined it could be all right between them, despite her suspicions.

He'd enjoyed their dance. He couldn't remember the last time he'd swayed to music with a lovely woman in his arms, bathed in the shadow of the warmth of her, the scent of her skin, not just the scent she had applied to her skin. She was the right height to dance with and her closeness had aroused his senses and his body. He could easily have taken it further. Wanted to take it further.

He liked Ellie Golden.

Liked her very much.

Harry tried to imagine himself in her position. If roles were reversed and he suspected she was someone other than she portrayed, wouldn't he be like a dog with a bone until he discovered the truth? Wouldn't he want to solve the mystery? Of course he would.

Where did that thought process leave him? Did he make that phone call and find himself displaced and homeless once more, or did he stick this out and try to make the best of things?

As far as he knew, Ellie couldn't prove anything, not beyond reasonable doubt, not without discrediting herself in the process. If only he could remember her, place her in time; be aware of what their relationship might or might not have been in the past.

When he reached his flat, it appeared emptier than ever. The fragile shell of relaxation he'd begun to build was gone and his mind was unsettled, even here. He needed to buy more furniture, but what was the point, if he was in danger of having to move on again?

How could a woman he liked, who he had imagined he could spend time with as a friend, maybe even a lover, be such a threat?

He stood in front of Ellie's painting. If the figure running near the sea had been modelled on him, what was she thinking as she painted? He was the running man, forever running, belonging nowhere.

He asked himself a question and realised that if he didn't know the answer, there was little hope of happiness here or anywhere else.

Who is Harry Dixon?

Chapter Ten

Ellie couldn't believe what had just happened. She smoothed her dress and made her way back along the beach, being careful not to fall into any holes dug in the sand during the day.

What was she thinking? What happened to keeping things low key until she was sure? Or even forgetting her suspicions altogether? She glanced warily about her. People were beginning to gather their belongings to go home. Had anyone overheard the heated conversation between herself and Harry? She hoped that the fight further down the beach had distracted people, but she couldn't be sure.

She'd enjoyed dancing with Harry. Her skin tingled with the feel and warmth of him and her hope that he might kiss her had somehow made her outburst seem even worse. Why couldn't she just accept that Ben was gone and move on? Harry must think her touched by madness. Yet in the midst of all of this, she still had an inner belief that she was right and, when she thought about it, Harry hadn't denied anything.

Where did their argument leave them? She'd threatened to contact the school governors, but what could she say to them that she could actually prove? Wouldn't she create trouble and uncertainty for herself and Tom if she made unsubstantiated accusations about the new headmaster? Harry must have the right credentials and references or he would never have been appointed.

If Harry was Ben reincarnated, renamed or whatever, why? She tried to imagine what could have happened to him. Of all people, surely she should understand the need to get away from a situation, to leave the past behind.

What if she was wrong? Harry had appeared genuinely

perplexed and hadn't admitted or denied anything. What was she hoping to achieve by badgering him?

Right now, she wished the sand would open up and swallow her whole.

She scanned the people on the beach, hazily outlined by the promenade street lamps. Mandy was draped over one of the tourists she had been chatting to earlier. Tom wasn't sitting by the sea wall. A familiar anxiety rose in her chest. Where was he?

Just when she had, in her mind anyway, alerted the emergency services and begun to head up a huge manhunt, her son appeared at her side. His grin was unstoppable and, uncharacteristically in public, he hugged her.

'Mum, you'll never guess. I've got a girlfriend.'

Ellie managed to smile and say appropriate things on the way home. She showed an interest in Tom's news, exclaiming when he told her about Louise, as if she hadn't seen them sitting against the sea wall talking all evening.

Tom was happier than she'd known him in a long time and seemed oblivious to the fact that Ellie was faking a brightness she didn't feel.

As soon as her son had gone up to bed, she went down to the shed at the bottom of the garden, which doubled as her home art studio.

Her mood always fed her artwork.

Still clad in the pink mini-dress, only pausing to wrap a scarf around her hair and remove her sandals, she shivered in the post-midnight air, as she daubed canvas after canvas with bright confused colours and shapes.

She would later recognise these paintings as some of her more inspired work, even if in the depths of the night, she acted totally unconsciously. Wave after wave of bewilderment and despair surfaced to be translated into desperate painting.

Replaying her encounters with Ben in Cornwall and the intricate details of that fateful night, she tried to put herself in Harry's shoes. She knew the feeling of wanting to disappear and start again. What was she trying to achieve by challenging this man, whoever he was? She recalled the nightmares when she'd felt responsible for Ben's death, for leaving him on the beach. Was that what this was all about, her own guilt?

By dawn, she had filled five large canvases and was exhausted. Her mini-dress was pink no longer; instead, it echoed the confusion of the canvases and would never be worn again.

The waves crashed against him again and again. He'd always taken pride in his mastery of the surf. The bruising, uncontrolled tumble was hurting more than his ego.

He knew his life was in danger, as the breath in his lungs was replaced with salty water. His surf board trailed behind him on its retaining cord, flailing ineffectually and occasionally bashing painfully against his legs and feet. What surprised him most was the name his mind was silently calling over and over again, as he tumbled on and on to oblivion – *Ellie*.

Ellie's mane of curly hair and her blue eyes seemed to be with him on this journey, as if he held her in a tight embrace in the sea. Then, the surfboard connected in a bone-shattering thump with his head and darkness took over accompanied by searing pain.

He came to awareness with a jerk of his limbs and choked. Green bile covered the patch of sand beneath his face. He rolled away from the mess and lay stunned, looking up into the azure blue sky. Seagulls circled overhead, reminiscent of vultures. How was he still alive?

His body was bruised and bleeding. In a rush, the water left his ears and his hearing returned. Somehow amplified, the sounds of the ocean and the birds stunned him, replacing the name he had been silently screaming. How could he have survived such an ordeal? How different to his usual landing on the beach, the jubilant whoop, after he had ridden a wave, balancing on his board, straining his muscles and enjoying the thrill. His proficiency in the water was why he had been chosen for the job.

The sea had thrown him up, like a piece of drift wood and he knew he ought to move, before the ocean claimed him again. The men in the darkness kept punching him, bruising his body beyond tolerance, kicking him, biting him. One had a knife.

He could hear someone shouting his name above the sound of the wind and sea.

'Harry, Harry ... Ben?'

Ellie's face came into view. She gently tested his limbs for fractures, mopped at his face with a towel. Her tears flowed down her face, were caught by the wind and shone like jewels in her curls.

He felt himself lift from the ground, looked down to see a slender girl leaning over a man on the beach, before he zoomed towards the sun, screaming 'No' to the sky as the light went out yet again.

Harry woke bathed in sweat. He gulped lungfuls of air to fight off the panic. The nightmare had been so real. Similar haunted dreams had recurred many times since that night in Cornwall. However, this particular one had been different. Was the addition of Ellie a reaction to their argument? She'd said last night that she'd cried at his funeral.

He was shaken by the dream and didn't go for his habitual early morning run. He needed to make that phone call and he was putting it off. He snuggled underneath the duvet. He was too hot, but the thought of relinquishing his sanctuary was not appealing.

Even before the nightmare, he had argued with himself that Ellie could have found out about his mole through one of his sporting activities, but knowledge of his tattoo, since it hadn't been on his wrist for many, many years, was a different matter. Ellie had described it as if she was remembering the colours of it, as if she had traced her fingers around the curl of the snake on his skin.

He emerged from his hibernation to sit cross-legged on the floor in front of Ellie's painting. If he closed his eyes, he could feel her hair tickling his cheek and remember the desire to run his hands through her curls and onwards down her body. How would she have responded if he had? Would she have reacted in the same way if he'd taken things further? Was she just annoyed that he'd walked away?

If his call resulted in him being told to pack and leave, he'd have to abandon the painting; it was too big to take with him and that knowledge made him doubly reluctant to pick up the phone.

Chapter Eleven

Ellie craved activity to take her mind off her confrontation with Harry; it had been whirring round and round in her head for a week now. She always needed new ideas for painting and pottery and, as there were several fruit farms in the countryside around Borteen, she decided to visit a couple to get inspiration for a series of orchard-themed paintings.

By the time she had driven to two farms, coaxing her ancient Mini that didn't get much use along the narrow lanes, buying juicy plums, raspberries and strawberries, her fingers were eager to get working with both cookery and art. The only shadow over a happy morning had been an irrational feeling that she was being followed. She reasoned with herself that the occupants of the blue van she had seen behind her several times were probably visiting fruit farms too. After all, who could resist fresh local fruit?

Her reaction to the lines of fruit trees and bushes surprised her, with the sight taking her artistic spark in a totally different direction to that which she had imagined that morning when she'd been planning her trip.

As soon as she'd stowed away her purchases at home, she headed down the hill to the gallery. Leaving the closed sign in place, she set the pottery wheel in motion. Fashioning a tall wide pot, she attached tree shapes cut from slabs of clay to the outside using liquid clay as glue. She set several of the trunks higher than the others to give the impression of an orchard of trees. Details of foliage, branches and trunk were added with a modelling tool, not too many as they would shrink during the firing process.

In her mind, she could already see the glazes she would apply to the pots to ensure the trees stood out in relief. Looking at the first pot, she was so pleased with the result that she made another and another. She loaded the resulting orchard of pots – that thought made her giggle – onto her drying shelves, where they would dry a little before being loaded into the kiln for their first firing. She could already visualise the finished results displayed in the gallery.

The attempt to distract herself from the turmoil of her thoughts about Harry was sort of working, wasn't it? But then, if she was thinking his name right now, he was still on her mind.

She replayed the night of the barbecue on a never-ending loop, particularly dancing with Harry and the delicious feelings it had evoked in her body, but then she would remember the things she'd said to him afterwards. She almost wished he was a drinker, because, by that time in the evening, he might have been drunk enough to forget some of their conversation. However, stone-cold sober, he would recall every word, including the bit about her crying at Ben Rivers' funeral.

She had to convince herself that Ben had been just an infatuation, a flirtation and one-night stand that she had not been able to leave behind, an event that had been amplified because the man she'd admired from afar for so long had died and by the circumstances she shortly found herself in; married to a man who was not her son's father and someone who wasn't always kind.

She was annoyed that she was thinking about her marriage as if it was something that had happened to her, rather than something she had agreed to and co-created. Okay, she'd felt desperate and was pregnant, but she'd said yes. It had been in many ways a marriage of convenience, but convenient for her as well as Rushton at the time. She just hadn't imagined it would become such a huge, painful compromise over the years.

Her fantasies about Ben and might-have-beens about their relationship had become a sanctuary from the nightmare her life back then had become. Now, she recognised that for her sanity and so she could continue to live in Borteen, she had to consign Ben to the past. He had to stay in his grave. Harry was real, rather than a fantasy embroidered over time. She had to accept him as Harry Dixon, headmaster, draw a line under the past and move on. She could do that, couldn't she? It was a pity she hadn't been able to do it before she opened her mouth after the beach barbecue. Would Harry ever be able to forgive her for hounding him? Would he even speak to her again?

Although she felt she had got things straighter in her head, Ellie realised that she hadn't seen anything of Harry since that night. Subtle questioning, when Tom was eating his tea, confirmed that Harry wasn't around. The summer sports sessions were being run by another teacher from the school. Her son complained that it wasn't as much fun when Mr Dixon wasn't involved.

Ellie wondered if she had scared Harry away from Borteen and the headmaster's job. Part of her felt sad, but the other part relieved. Uncomfortable truths from the past could remain dormant and not touch the world she had built up around herself and her son.

She didn't dare ask anyone if they knew where Harry had gone, but she so wanted to know what had happened to him. She'd been keeping her ears open for any mention of his name, but so far, she'd been disappointed.

It was good to observe Tom's summer playing sport and his constant contact with Louise. He lived on cloud nine. If he wasn't on his mobile talking to the love of his life, they were stuck together on her settee, or else, she presumed, at Louise's house in a similar position. Tom in love was a new person: mellow, funny, friendly and happy.

Louise was an easy person to have in the house. She was quiet and always made sure she helped with meal preparation and washing up.

The gallery attracted noticeably more visitors as the

tourist season ramped up. Ellie was excited that there were more actual sales, rather than people who spent ages looking, admiring her work, promising to come back and buy, but then never returned.

She was on a particular high one lunchtime, having sold three canvases to a couple who were renovating a barn. They had wanted splashes of colour in their vaulted lounge and bought some of the pictures she had painted after her confrontation with Harry on the night of the barbecue. Ellie was elated about the sale and secretly relieved that the canvases, which constantly reminded her of that evening, would soon be gone. A familiar face popped his head around the door – John Williams.

'Ellie. How are you? You're certainly looking well,' said the retired headmaster.

'Mr Williams, I haven't seen you around for a while.'

'John, please. You won't have done, my wife and I took a long cruise as a treat when I retired from Borteen High. We returned at the weekend.'

He walked further into the gallery, looking at the canvases and cautiously picking up one of the finished orchard pots. He moved it around in his hands. 'I love this. It might be just the thing for my wife's birthday present.'

'Inspired by my visit to some of the local fruit farms, along with several million pies and jars of jam. When's your wife's birthday?'

'On Friday. I'll take it. Now, before I get too distracted, I'd also like to talk with you sometime about my mentoring scheme idea. I've got more concrete guidelines, now that I've spoken to Harry Dixon.'

Before she had thought it through, Ellie blurted out, 'Is Harry Dixon back in Borteen?' She watched a puzzled look pass over John's features.

'Yes, of course. I spoke to him yesterday about my proposals. I do hope you'll consider taking part as a mentor.'

Ellie felt cautious about committing to anything, but then the gallery became much quieter once the summer holidays were over and the tourists returned to their home towns. It might be healthier to have other things going on in her life too. She had also found marketing for her business worked in subtle ways. Often, it was activities she was involved in totally unrelated to the gallery that brought people, especially locals, through the shop door. Even so, she was reluctant to sign up to something that might bring her into even closer contact with Harry. At least, not until she had gauged the nature of their ongoing relationship, given what had happened between them at that party.

On impulse, she decided to humour John. 'Have you time for a coffee right now? I've had a brilliant morning sales-wise, so I can indulge myself with a break.'

A smile lit up his face. He put the wrapped orchard pot on the table. 'Can I collect this afterwards?'

Ellie locked the till, put the closed sign on the door and they walked round to the seafront chatting about the school, Tom and a new shop in the High Street. She marvelled at how her steps felt lighter and the colours of the town brighter, because she was encouraged by her morning's success.

They sat on one of the beachside tables of the seafront café and sipped coffee. John Williams stretched his long legs out towards the sea wall. Ellie sniffed the sea air appreciatively.

'I loved being on the cruise ship, but it is nice to be home. We're so lucky to live here next to the beach.'

'I agree. I never get tired of the seafront. Where did you travel to on your cruise?'

'We cruised the Spanish and Portuguese coast, nice and slowly. Called into Gibraltar and then toured the Canary Islands.'

Ellie thought it remarkable how relaxed John seemed,

compared to when he was the high school headmaster. Had she imagined the furrows that used to line his forehead? His brow was now smooth and tanned, as he described the highlights of the cruise. In fact, she decided that he looked at least ten years younger.

'Thank you for letting me talk to you about my retirement project, Ellie. Can I say right at the beginning that I've never run a mentoring scheme before, but I've been doing lots of research into how other schools manage them. I visited a few schools running similar schemes last year and I gave an outline of how one at Borteen High might work to Harry Dixon. His approval was, of course, crucial.'

'I haven't seen anything of Harry for weeks, I wondered if he was still in town.'

'He's been away on holiday, but I managed to catch up with him yesterday morning.'

As if on cue, a familiar figure came into view, running across the sand at the waterline, in a replay of Ellie's painting. It was high tide, so Harry wasn't running far from where they were sitting. To her horror, John saw him too, stood up and yelled, 'Harry!'

The running man turned, recognition slid over his features and he jogged over the sand towards them.

'John.' Harry shook the older man's hand. He nodded to her. 'Ellie.'

Nothing in the way he greeted her gave any suggestion of what had occurred between them the last time they'd met.

'I'll get you a coffee, Harry. That's, if you can spare a moment? I'm trying to persuade Ellie to be one of our school mentors.' John's voice had acquired a more cautious tone.

'A black coffee, please. Just a small one.' Harry wasn't even out of breath after his run, but Ellie watched fascinated as a bead of sweat traced down the side of his face.

John Williams disappeared inside the café and Harry did a couple of leg stretches before sitting on the bench seat opposite her. They avoided eye contact and the silence stretched on.

Ellie could see that John was waiting in a queue to be served and, eventually, she couldn't stand the silence any longer.

'Harry, I'm sorry if I upset you.'

He surprised her by smiling. 'At least you're speaking to me. Let's forget that evening ever happened, shall we? I think we need to start again. Hello, I'm Harry Dixon.' He emphasised his name and held out his hand.

Ellie sighed and raised her own hand to meet his. 'Ellie Golden.' The sparks flying between their palms were difficult to ignore.

'What's this? Have you two agreed to something without me?' John Williams returned to the table with three mugs. 'I got you another too, Ellie.' He unloaded the tray.

'No, John, nothing about the mentoring scheme, but Ellie has agreed to continue her work with the art groups at school and to run another art competition next summer.' Harry winked at her.

She glowered back. He'd cornered her nicely, but she was going to do those things anyway, so it wasn't much of a victory. She was glad John was too caught up in his ideas for mentoring the talented and disaffected youth of the seaside town to pick up on the energy swirling between the two of them.

'Tell me more about the mentoring scheme, John.' She needed to focus on something other than Harry and the sensations his nearness was causing in her body. Even if she avoided looking at him, his subtle aftershave distracted her and she was ultra-aware of his presence.

John described passionately how he felt mentoring would benefit the school and a provisional outline for how the scheme would work. Ellie found it fascinating that he could talk so seriously without being aware of her inner turmoil.

'So, what makes you think that I'd make a good mentor?' she asked, after listening quietly to his suggestions and plans.

To her surprise, it was Harry and not John who answered her question.

'One, you have a teenage son yourself, so you understand the trials of puberty. Two, you can use the processes of art to reach and relax your mentees. Three, you're quietly spoken, calm and approachable. Four, you're known by the pupils and parents at the school and, as a bonus, you already have the necessary clearances and checks to work with young people.'

She was impressed with Harry's quick, spontaneous response and stunned that he appeared to be able to see her in such a positive light. 'Oh,' was all she could think to say in response.

John nodded his agreement. 'That about sums it up. I agree with Harry's points, but I do also understand that you have a business to run. We can't assume that you are willing to take part and we definitely can't overload you.'

'It sounds a very worthwhile scheme. As long as my time commitment can be kept to a manageable level, I'd be happy to be involved.'

John jumped up and hugged her. It took her by surprise, so the embrace was rather awkward. Harry was laughing when she was finally released from the older man's arms.

'If that's settled, I'll get back to my run. We can arrange a meeting for the mentors at the beginning of term, John. I look forward to seeing you there, Ellie.'

With those words, he was gone, back down to the water's edge.

Ellie watched him go and had to tear her eyes away from him so she could concentrate on John's continued conversation. Regardless of Harry Dixon's actual identity, she was attracted to him in a way she had never known since her infatuation with Ben Rivers and it both excited and unsettled her. She wasn't quite sure how she felt about this morning's encounter, but at least they were speaking again, if only in a professional capacity and very much on Harry's terms. She got the impression he had forbidden her to mention Ben Rivers ever again. Wouldn't life be so much simpler if she didn't?

Harry ran down the beach in a lighter hearted mood than he'd felt for a long time. It had seemed ironic to go on a holiday when he'd just moved to a seaside resort, but he'd recognised the need to clear his head and think things through without the distractions of the new life he was building and the close proximity of Ellie.

He'd booked the tiniest holiday cottage he could find on the west coast of Scotland. There was a white sandy beach, rugged rocks and he rarely saw anyone, just the occasional dog walker. The weather hadn't been brilliant, so he hadn't done much running and there wasn't even internet or mobile coverage, but it didn't matter as this was a time to regroup and think.

He couldn't decide if Ellie's confrontation or his nightmare had unnerved him most. Another thought was worrying him: if Ellie had been in Cornwall at the same time as he was working there had she been embroiled in the drugs racket he'd been working to expose?

Who was Tom's father? This seemed important, especially as the boy looked so familiar. She'd mentioned a divorce. Had he known her ex-husband?

He lay on the bed in the tiny bedroom, watching the rain pour down the window and tried to piece together what he actually remembered about Cornwall, rather than what he'd been told after the event.

When he'd been asked if he was interested in an undercover role, it had been because he was good on a surfboard. The reason he'd signed up and trained for the job, leaving his regular police role in Devon, was personal. His younger step-brother, Simon, had died after taking dodgy pills he'd bought from a guy in a nightclub. Simon had been experimenting with drugs ever since the sudden death of his father, Harry's step-dad. As a result of the loss of her youngest son, Harry had watched his widowed mother sink into depression, neglecting herself and her declining health. She'd died barely a year after Simon, leaving Harry all alone in the world. There had been no one to miss him when he disappeared from Devon to take up his undercover role.

There were strict rules and regulations around an undercover job that were often difficult to maintain: no sexual relationships, no drugs. The latter was nigh on impossible when you were working alongside those peddling drugs, especially when you needed to infiltrate a group and seem legitimate. He'd tried as much as possible to limit his drug use to smoking an occasional cannabis joint.

It had all seemed surprisingly easy to begin with, almost like a long holiday, surfing by day and drinking in the main suspect's bar by night. Norrie came to trust him after he'd helped on many occasions to throw out rowdy drink and drug-fuelled customers when the bar closed. Before he knew it, he was being paid in beer to act as a bouncer and was allowed to park his camper van at the back of the pub overnight.

The undercover role didn't sit easily with his conscience. He'd loved his previous work at a small local police station. His main focus there had been to help people. The role in Cornwall involved living a lie, being deceitful every day and helping, at least for a time, to perpetuate the sales of his hated drugs. He knew it was a means to an end, but still it made him uncomfortable.

He'd witnessed numerous drug deals without batting an eyelid and Norrie had eventually asked if he'd act as an occasional driver to fetch supplies for him. He'd been given the destination of a crossroads on the moors. That first time it had just been a case of slowing down and accepting a package thrust out of the window of a car coming in the other direction.

The main target wasn't this small drug-selling band, but a drug factory and supply team for the whole South-West. After a couple of drive-by collections, he'd been asked to accompany Norrie and his mate Rushton, he guessed as extra back-up, when they went to negotiate a deal with their suppliers.

The remote moorland farm was conveniently located near to an old wartime airstrip. A small plane had been leaving as they pulled up. Harry had to try and memorise the letters and numbers on the fuselage to report to his contact later, along with the vehicle number plates at the farm.

It was a major feat to act relaxed and nonchalant, when he was trying to memorise details, conversations and faces. As far as he'd been aware, this was the closest any of the undercover officers had got to the supply chain. It was vital that he related the information to his contact as quickly as possible, in case the suppliers got spooked and moved on before they could be arrested, or indeed, in case his own identity was discovered.

He remembered calling in the information and being advised to pack up and leave right away, as the police would be closing in on the moorland farm immediately. His surfboard was on the rack at the beach and he had walked down to fetch it. Try as he might, he couldn't remember anything after that.

Stretching, Harry went to make a cup of tea. A memory played at the edge of his brain, but he couldn't bring it forward. It was like having an itch he couldn't scratch.

He guessed he must have stayed just that little bit too long and information about the raid and his part in it had got back to Norrie and Rushton, but he didn't actually know that. He turned his mind to what he'd been told when he was recovering in hospital.

They'd found him on the beach with his surfboard. Someone had tried to make it look as if he'd had an accident in the sea and been washed up with the board still attached to him by its tether. He guessed this information was the seed for his recurrent nightmare. He'd been treated for injuries that suggested he'd had a prolonged beating: broken ribs, internal bleeding, cuts and bruises all over him and a nasty bash on the head. An analysis of his blood had shown signs of a cocktail of drugs, including one often used in date rape cases. He'd been told the drug was usually administered in a drink and that eventually when the stimulants he tested for had worn off, he would have been rendered immobile, almost paralysed and at this stage he must have been beaten senseless. He had no memory of having a drink, but they'd found he'd drunk beer. He would have been focused on just getting away from the area so it made no sense at all. Why would he have stopped to drink a beer in those circumstances? He'd never touched alcohol since that time.

The plane had been traced, the drug warehouse and cannabis growing farm on the moors raided and shut down. There had been many arrests. Norrie and several other dealers had been charged and sent to prison. He'd been praised for his role in the operation, but all he'd felt was ill, bewildered and, for a few months, incapable of much at all. His body had healed, but his mind was a different matter. One thing he'd been very clear about was that he no longer wanted a career with the police, undercover or otherwise. He'd left to train as a teacher with a brand new identity.

After a week of mulling over the details of the things he remembered and the aftermath of his attack, the weather cleared and he began to run again. He had to move on. He refused to let that small period of his life dictate the rest of his existence. The second week of his holiday was relaxing and if his thoughts strayed back to Cornwall, he reminded himself of his resolution. Life was for living and not for dwelling on a past he couldn't change.

When he arrived back in Borteen, Harry had made his dreaded phone call to his contact about Ellie and related the strength of her conviction that she had known him before. He'd been told to brazen things out for now. Ellie Golden couldn't prove anything. She was more likely to damage her own reputation and business by making outlandish accusations about Harry. His contact, Sam, promised to look into Ellie's past in Cornwall and let him know if she had any known link to the drug ring. Harry sincerely hoped that she wasn't involved.

As he ran across the beach with renewed energy after the meeting with John and Ellie, he chuckled to himself as he remembered the expression on her face when he had ensured her continued art connection to the school. His contact had told him to be nice to Ellie and to get her back on his side. His mission was to smooth over any possible past link and to get her to trust him as Harry Dixon. He wasn't sure how it was going to work, but, on reflection, it might be fun trying. After all, he didn't have to pretend to like Ellie, he did like her. He was fascinated by the suspicious artist and mesmerised by her hair.

He still wondered if he should tell her the full story. She might empathise and be completely on his side, but could he take such a risk, particularly if she might have been involved with the drug ring? It sounded very much as if she too had needed to disappear and reinvent herself, but without the slick mechanisms that had helped him. Unfortunately, his training forbade any admissions about the past. Ben Rivers was dead and buried and would have to stay that way. He had to be wholeheartedly Harry Dixon, even when he was at home alone, for his life to work.

He returned to his flat following his run and looked around with pleasure at the improvements he had made to the place. Immediate concerns that he was getting too comfortable rose into his mind. He'd never been able to put down roots. Contentment was alien. Would he ever be able to settle down fully and maybe buy his own property? Would he always have that feeling that he might have to move on at a moment's notice, that he might be discovered and in danger?

The relief at having broken the ice with Ellie after that terrible evening at the barbecue was physical. He hadn't realised how much tension he'd been carrying in his shoulders. Despite this, he kicked himself yet again for the way he'd handled her accusations. He knew his shock and inappropriate words would have added to Ellie's suspicions that she was right about his former identity. He'd become lazy, or rather he hadn't ever had a direct challenge like this to test him. He'd found that most people were trusting and accepting of someone new to an area and, so far, he'd been taken pretty much at face value wherever he had been.

His mother had always said that everything happened for a reason, particularly co-incidences. Why had Ellie come into his life at this point with knowledge of his past identity? Why here? And why a woman he found so intriguing and lovely, but might never be able to trust?

Sinking down onto his new-to-him, battered leather sofa, he stared at the picture she had painted, as if he could trace the brush strokes and conjure the hand, arm and body that had made them. Ellie Golden in his flat, now there was a thought. Her essence seemed to invade his space and fill him with longing. Then, with a bump, he'd come back to earth as his questions about her resurfaced.

Chapter Twelve

After the coffee and unexpected encounter with Harry, Ellie returned to the gallery with John. When he'd gone, proudly clutching his wife's birthday present, she set about rearranging the display room. It was exciting to rediscover work in her stock pile. Sometimes, she didn't even remember painting the canvases, as if she had pixies living at the gallery who came out at night to paint for her.

The bell sounded on the gallery door. Ellie put down the canvas she was examining and went to find out who was there. Mandy and a dishevelled youth came into the display room. Mandy was holding the lad firmly by the shoulder and he was squirming in her grasp. 'Caught this thing perving at you through the window.'

'I was only looking at the art,' he protested.

'Yeah, right,' said Mandy, causing the lad to squeal again as she pushed him further into the room.

'Hey, Mandy, let go of Nicholas.'

'You know him?' Mandy let go and Nicholas Crossten leapt away from her. He stood out of reach of her grasp.

'Nick, call me Nick. I hate Nicholas. It's what teachers call me, and mum, when I've done things wrong, which according to them is nearly all the time.'

Ellie laughed. 'Mandy, meet Nick. He won the Art Exposium competition I ran at the high school.'

'Really?' said Mandy, looking at Nick as if he was an alien being.

'I haven't seen you around this summer, Nick.' Ellie carefully repositioned the pottery she had been moving earlier.

'No. I've just come back. Mum packed me off to stay with grandma for the holidays.'

'Did you have a nice time?'

'No. I hate gran. Doesn't let me watch television or anything. Expects me to read books and play in the garden.'

'Sounds a lovely summer to me,' said Ellie.

'I agree with Nick. It sounds like hell. Sorry about the pushing thing, by the way.' Mandy was busy wiping her hand on the back of her jeans, as if she feared she might have caught something by touching Nick, who was scruffy and dirty as always.

'I get worse at home.'

Ellie exchanged a meaningful look with Mandy.

'What did your parents say about you winning the art competition?'

'I didn't tell mum.'

'Why ever not?' exclaimed Mandy. 'Surely she'd be pleased and proud.'

Nick had a shifty expression. 'Not sure she would.'

'Have you painted any more of those wonderful monochrome paintings?' asked Ellie, hoping to lighten the mood.

'Can only paint at school. I'll have to wait till the new term starts.'

Ellie began to wonder about Nick's home life. John Williams had hinted things might not be ideal for him.

'Great news then. I'll be running an after school art club from September. So if you join, you'll be able to paint more, not just in lessons.'

'Whee!' Nick punched the air, making Ellie worry about the safety of her nearby pots. 'That's made my day, Miss. See ya.' With that, he ran out of the door and was gone.

'Sorry about that, Ellie. The way he was dressed and was behaving, I thought he was a yob planning on stealing something from the shop.'

'Hmm, I don't know his full story yet. The picture he put into the competition was brilliant. One of those minimal strokes, but maximum impact canvases. It would be a crime if such talent went to waste and his parents, or rather, his mum, because he only mentioned her, doesn't sound very supportive.'

'I wonder how many undiscovered artists there are out there. People whose talents were never recognised or nurtured?' Mandy dipped her hand in the big vase of marbles by the gallery door and let them trickle through her fingers.

'Far too many, I suspect. Even if you do get support, it isn't an easy way to make a living. I should know.'

'Well, at least you are doing your bit for the students at Borteen High.'

'Yes, but is it enough, Mandy?'

'Come on, you know succeeding in the art world has always been a mixture of talent and luck.'

Ellie fell silent, wiping dust from the edge of a picture frame.

'Are you up for a night out on Friday? That's what I came to ask.'

Ellie sighed and brought her attention back to her friend. 'What did you have in mind?'

'Not a lot of choice round here as you know. We could go to the wine bar or the pub. Or really push the boat out and get a taxi to the bright lights of a Sowden night club.'

Sowden was the biggest nearby town, where Borteen residents had to go for bigger supermarkets and shops.

'Prefer Borteen, if I'm honest. It's a pain getting a taxi home.'

'So be it. We'll have fun anyway, no matter where we are.'

Mandy had quickly thawed after being annoyed with Ellie for dancing with Harry, or rather, being peeved because Harry preferred her friend.

Ellie knew that Mandy had never viewed her as competition before. Her reaction to Harry was the first time in a long while she'd been aware of her long dormant attraction antennae picking up and buzzing.

Mandy had not asked any direct questions about why Ellie wasn't dating the new headmaster, but she occasionally threw hints into the conversation that Ellie refused to comment on. She knew her lack of response must be driving her friend crazy.

Mandy was fickle where men were concerned, but Ellie had quickly come to realise that her flirtatious nature hid a deep-seated terror of commitment. What a pair they made. One scared to give her heart, the other scared to put herself in a position where a man might have control over her life.

Ellie considered her friend's invitation to go out and laughed. 'Why not, let's go and have some fun. It's about time I let my hair down and relaxed. This summer's been a bit intense.'

The name Harry Dixon hung unspoken in the air.

Chapter Thirteen

Seemingly, in next to no time, the summer holidays had slipped by and the school term had begun. Tom had grown so much in size and maturity. He had needed a completely new school uniform and larger shoes. Ellie realised that when he grew out of the new ones, purchased on their school uniform shopping trip to Sowden, they would fit her, as they now had the same sized feet.

Tom had also grown in confidence as a result of his relationship with Louise and his new-found sporting prowess. Ellie offered up a prayer that he would be able to maintain his blossoming self-assurance when faced with his classmates at the start of the new term.

The date of the initial meeting of the mentoring steering group arrived. A gathering of teachers, ex-teachers and other people from the community sat around a table in the school library. The heavy oak furniture smelled of beeswax polish, taking Ellie right back to her grandmother's house, where she used to polish the intricately carved oak sideboard on her Sunday visits.

John Williams chaired the meeting with the directness and clarity that Ellie had come to expect from him. She respected the fact that Harry allowed John to take control. She'd made up her mind not to look at Harry at all, but couldn't help sideways glances. The sight of him in a crisp white shirt, navy polka-dotted tie and a dark suit turned her insides liquid. There was something so alluring about a man in a smart suit and tie, well, this man anyway. It was difficult to concentrate on the content of the meeting when she kept remembering the warmth of his body against hers when they'd danced on the beach.

Ellie would need to go on a mentors' training course,

but essentially mentors were to meet with the students they were assigned at least once a fortnight to give them the opportunity to discuss any problems and/or aspirations. The whole thrust of the scheme was to try to ensure that young adults facing life's inevitable challenges had somewhere to go to discuss any issues that might be affecting them and their performance. The mentors were asked to be independent sounding boards and to encourage excellence in all aspects of school life.

Harry sat near to John and took his turn to speak in support of the scheme.

'I've asked the teachers to draw up a list of pupils who they think would benefit from mentoring.' He waved a piece of paper. 'I already have an initial file with cases that came straight to mind.' He turned to John Williams. 'How many mentees do you envisage us having each, John?'

'I would think a maximum of two. We all have lives and businesses outside of this initiative and I wouldn't want anyone to get overloaded.' He looked pointedly at Ellie in acknowledgement of their previous conversations. 'Of course, that means we're likely to end up with a waiting list pretty quickly.'

'Shall I read the first list of names?' Harry put the sheet of paper on the table in front of him.

Ellie glanced quickly away as their eyes met across the table. Would he be able to see the effort she was making to move on from her initial thoughts about him?

'Good idea, if we can assign pupils to mentors, we can get going quickly and, hopefully, start to make a difference right away.' John Williams looked pleased.

'Okay, first on the list is Nicholas Crossten.'

Ellie put her hand up and put it down again, aware she'd, unconsciously, fallen into schoolgirl mode. 'Nick, he prefers to be called Nick. He told me only teachers and his mother, when they're angry with him, call him Nicholas.

I'd like to put myself forward as his mentor, as I know him quite well.'

'I don't think that's wise,' said Harry, straight away.

'Why ever not? We've a link through art and he's started to open up to me about his home life.' Ellie felt almost as if Harry had slapped her. It seemed doubly sharp given her thoughts a few moments previously.

'That's precisely why not. You're already too close to him to be detached. You'll be more valuable to him as an art teacher.'

'I'm not too close to him.' Ellie's hackles were rising. How dare Harry Dixon make judgments about her relationships?

John held his hand up. 'Okay, boys and girls. If we argue over every case, we'll never get anywhere. I'm afraid I agree with Harry, Ellie. You can be of more use to Nick by nurturing his artistic talents and knowing too much about him, which inevitably happens with a mentoring relationship, might create a barrier to that.'

Ellie didn't agree, but recognised they would be getting nowhere fast if she continued to argue her case for mentoring Nick. She bit her lip to stop herself from continuing the argument.

'I think I should mentor the boy,' said Harry. 'He's the one every single teacher flagged up when I asked who to put on the list. There may be some serious interventions needed, particularly at the family end.'

Ellie sank back into her chair feeling sulky. The list of children was read out and people were assigned as their mentors; Ellie was given Zack Martin, the cheeky-faced lad who had won a prize in the art competition too. She was ambivalent about this.

She could see one name left on Harry's paper. Before reading it, he glanced across at her and then away. Her suspicions were aroused and she sat up straighter in her chair.

'And last, but not least, Thomas Golden.'

Ellie didn't know why she felt so stunned that her son was on this list. She knew he was troubled at times, but it was as if the air had been squeezed out of her lungs. She felt concerned for Tom and embarrassed for herself all at the same time. Colour rushed to her face and she couldn't raise her eyes from the table for a few moments.

'Tom shows some sporting prowess, so I'd propose to take him as my second mentee.'

'No!' The word was out of her mouth before she'd censored it.

'Is there a problem, Ellie?' said John, a concerned tone in his voice.

She had to ignore her red face and marshal her thoughts quickly. 'For the same reason as Mr Dixon stopped me being Nick Crossten's mentor, actually. Mr Dixon would be better helping Tom with his sporting aspirations and, as they're already close, it would be difficult for him to be impartial, in my opinion.' Ellie uncrossed her arms as soon as she realised they were clasped defensively across her chest.

'Touché,' said Harry, with a shake of his head and a mock salute.

It was a difficult moment. The other members of the mentoring team remained silent watching the drama unfold. Ellie had the feeling a spotlight was shining on her and it was not comfortable.

John Williams broke the silence. 'What about if I were to mentor your son, Ellie?'

She smiled at the older man, grateful to have him on her side. 'That would be lovely. I can't think of anyone better for the job.' She glanced at Harry, but couldn't read the expression on his face.

She had intended to sneak out of the meeting as quickly as possible, but when the formalities had been completed and she'd gathered her things, Harry stood in the way of her escape route.

'Excuse me.'

'Ellie, can I have a word before you go?'

She hated being cornered. Every nerve in her body was telling her to push past him and run, but of course, you didn't do such things in polite society, especially when your son's headmaster wanted to speak to you. Instead, she squared her shoulders and stared up at him, trying not to notice the intensity of his eyes. 'Mr Dixon?'

He waited until the room had emptied and pulled out a chair for her. There appeared little choice but to sit on it.

'I wanted to check that you are still going to be running the after-school art club.'

'Yes, Tuesday afternoons at three forty-five, if that works.'

His expression was guarded. 'How soon do we need to advertise the next art competition? I mean, do you allow pupils to prepare work throughout the year, or is the point that they paint for the competition nearer the time?'

'Last year, we announced we were running the competition at about this point in the year and put up a few posters. The art teachers in school kept an eye out for outstanding pieces amongst coursework throughout the three terms, so we ended up with a healthy number of entries in July.'

'Great, thanks. That's all I wanted to discuss.'

All he wanted to discuss! *All he wanted to discuss?*

Why then the rigmarole of getting her to sit down?

Was he goading her?

Had he let her believe he was going to confront her about her objection to him mentoring her son and then avoided the big issue? Or, had he accepted her arguments and moved on?

Confused, and she realised, a little disappointed they weren't going to discuss their differences, Ellie fought not to notice Harry's aftershave. It was a delicious scent, which, combined with his big brown eyes, made it somehow hard to be angry with him.

She picked up her bag and papers yet again and stood up. As she reached the door, he spoke again.

'So, when and why did I become Mr Dixon and not Harry? I thought we'd agreed on a truce.'

She turned to face him, fixing a smile on her face.

'You're the headmaster now, so Mr Dixon is the most appropriate title, especially in front of other teachers and at mentoring meetings.'

'I'll let you get away with that, if and only if you'll call me Harry outside of those situations.'

'Yes, Sir,' said Ellie, knowing she was pushing her luck.

'Ellie, I'm truly disappointed not to be mentoring Tom. I'm sorry if it was a shock finding him on the list.'

'Not a shock exactly, more an unwelcome confirmation.'

'You're aware he's seen as withdrawn at school, not fulfilling his potential?'

'Yes. It comes up on his reports time after time. I wish I could change things, but then you can't change the past, can you?'

'I can reassure you that the teaching staff and I will do everything we can to help him. Hopefully, with John Williams as his mentor, we can make real progress.'

'Thank you.' Ellie studied the tiles on the floor.

'Did something in particular happen to make him like this? You don't have to tell me if you don't want to, but it might help.'

Ellie closed the door again. Her heart began to drum, as she thought what to say. She was alone in the room with Harry, but the huge boardroom-style table was between them and she had her hand on the door handle.

'Most of the problems stem from him witnessing an attack. Rather a violent attack. He was six. He must have been so scared and there was nothing he could do to help against a big, angry man. I also believe that at the time, he must have thought he was next for the same treatment.'

Harry dropped down into one of the chairs. 'My God, Ellie. I ... I had no idea. Has he had counselling?'

'Yes, he saw a psychotherapist for four years. The counselling stopped when we moved here. Maybe I should consider more intervention, although I have to say that having a girlfriend over the summer has done more for his attitude and state of mind than anything or anyone else ever has.'

'He's dating Louise Stevens isn't he? Was the attack he witnessed on someone ... close to him?'

She paused. 'Yes, it was ... me.'

Harry visibly blanched.

She couldn't continue the conversation. Her chest tightened with panic. 'I'm sorry, Harry. I still find this a difficult topic of conversation, it's painful in many, many ways, but at the same time, it might tell you something about my own trust issues. I'll say goodbye for now.'

She wrenched open the door, hurting her fingers on the handle and fled down the corridor with tears in her eyes. Maybe she was the one who needed more therapy.

Harry sat in the meeting room for a long time after she'd gone.

Who had attacked Ellie? Her ex-husband seemed the most likely culprit. As she had suggested, it explained some of the behaviour he had observed in her, but not this deep distrust of himself.

Harry wasn't a violent man, not unless his life depended upon it or that of someone he cared about. He couldn't ever imagine beating a woman. The way she touched her face as she was speaking suggested that she'd taken blows there. Could this be why he didn't recognise her?

He had been genuinely disappointed not to be assigned Tom Golden as a mentee. He asked himself the reasons for this. Was it because he wanted to know more about Ellie? No, he concluded that he had formed a bond and rapport with the lad, mainly though sport. If he'd had a son of his own, Harry would have wanted him to be like Tom.

Chapter Fourteen

If Ellie was totally honest, she wasn't looking forward to being Zack Martin's mentor. If only they'd let her look after Nick Crossten. She could relate to Nick.

Harry had probably been right though, even if she hated to admit it; she would have been in danger of getting too close to Nick. Something about him ignited her maternal instincts.

Her charge, Zack, looked just as she remembered him, when he slunk into the office Ellie had been allocated for the meeting. Cheeky round face, overweight, shirt untucked even though school rules were strict on neatness, and his tie deliberately tied to be jauntily too short. On first appearance, he was brash and cocky, but as the boy sat down in the chair opposite to her, Ellie could see fear in his eyes. He seemed to shrink as he settled on the edge of the seat.

'Miss, what's this about? Have I done something wrong?'

'What makes you think that, Zack?' Ellie smiled as broadly as she could, hoping to reassure him.

'No one said why I've got to come and see you.'

'Really, oh dear. What exactly was said to you?'

'Mr Dixon shouted across to me in the playground and told me to go to room G45 right away.'

Ellie made a mental note to raise this issue at the next mentoring meeting. Pupils must be aware of why they had been singled out for mentoring, as it was supposed to be a two-way process. She smiled again in what she hoped was a reassuring manner.

'You've been asked to see me because you are special, Zack.'

His expression changed to puzzled and then his face split in an answering grin. 'You mean, because of my pottery?'

'Partly, Zack. The idea is that you and I meet every

week and at those meetings you can tell me about anything bothering you, or anything that is stopping you being the best you can be at school. We'll work together to change anything you're unhappy about. We can talk about your pottery too.'

'You mean you're like an American shrink?'

She was taken aback by his terminology, but could see what he meant. 'More a friendly auntie I suppose.'

'My aunties aren't friendly. They hate dad's guts.'

Ellie chuckled and retreated to familiar territory. 'Are you enjoying your art classes? Is it just pottery you like, or painting as well?'

'Art's my favourite lesson, Miss. I love working with clay, but I already have three pictures to choose from to enter in the next competition and it's only September. I want to win the next one. I can hear everyone in the school clapping and cheering.'

Ellie was touched that her competition was so important to him. Despite her initial wariness, she began to warm to the boy. 'That's great, Zack. We could see if we can find other art competitions for you to enter, if you like.'

'Seriously, Miss? There are other competitions around here?'

'Let me have a look and I can tell you at our next meeting.'

She made a note on her pad.

His eyes assumed a dreamy look and she wondered if he was seeing his artwork illuminated in a spot light, or on a news report on television. Nothing like having ambition.

'Is there anything you're worried about at the moment, Zack, anything you want to talk about?'

'Don't think so, Miss. I enjoy school most of the time. It's better than home anyway.'

'And you've got some good friends at school?'

'Ish, Miss. Not sure you can really trust anyone.'

She explored his comment a little, wishing that she'd had

her second training session before the meeting. She was making it all up as she went along.

When their time was up, Ellie emerged from the room a little breathless. It was the result of the unpredictability of the subject matter and the way your brain had to move from subject to subject so quickly. Still, the first meeting had gone far better than she'd imagined. She laughed that Zack would have been surprised if he'd been aware how nervous she was.

After her initial explanation, he seemed to have taken it in his stride that he'd been chosen for the mentoring scheme because he was special.

Unlike Tom, who was not best pleased to have been put on the list at all. He'd stood in the kitchen doorway when he returned from school with a look like thunder on his face.

'Did you put me forward for it?'

'No! The teachers made the nominations.'

'So, the teachers think I'm a repro.'

'Repro?' Ellie was mentally trying to keep up with Tom's explosion, but didn't recognise this expression.

'A lost cause, a good for nothing, mental problems ...'

'Tom Golden! It's not about that at all.'

But then, he had been put on the list because he was withdrawn at times. Even Ellie had difficulty getting a response from him if he was in one of his moods.

'Why then?' He pulled his school jumper over his head, then yanked off his tie.

'As far as I understand it you were nominated for extra support because of your sports ability.'

'Yeah, right.'

He stormed off upstairs and didn't speak for the rest of the evening. Ellie sketched on page after page of art paper, trying to distract herself from her feelings of helplessness and frustration. The path of a single parent was far from easy.

Chapter Fifteen

Ellie's after school art class was very popular. She felt flattered to have a waiting list for the club. At these sessions, she felt truly alive, wondering, not for the first time, if she should have become a full time teacher. She'd finished a teaching qualification in the month before Rushton's attack and after her recovery, they'd moved several times, so she'd never applied for a teaching role.

Nick Crossten was blooming. Ellie had encouraged him to stick with the theme of the street dancer in his art, but to include splashes of colour to accent his work. His canvases were truly amazing and each one seemed better than the last. Ellie decided to discuss options for funding his work with the mentoring group. He was skilled enough to gain a scholarship or grant to continue learning and developing his artistic skills.

There could be other possibilities to provide funds for Nick. Up until now, she'd kept the gallery exclusively to promote her own work, but she was tempted to try selling a couple of his pictures to give him money for things he needed and possibly, more importantly, to give him encouragement to continue. She wished Harry Dixon wasn't Nick's mentor, because it meant she would have to discuss her ideas with him.

As if her thoughts had conjured him yet again, Harry walked into the classroom at that very moment. The noise level in the room diminished immediately. Harry nodded to Ellie, smiled at Nick, admired his work, and did a tour of the other desks to see what the students were working on. Ellie noticed that he focused exclusively on each child, one at a time, giving the individual his full attention. He managed to skirt around Ellie and only came to where she was working when he had done a complete circuit of the room.

'Everyone's having such fun. Can I have a go?' he asked. The expression on his face was like that of a cheeky schoolboy.

Ellie was surprised. It was the last thing she'd expected him to say. She wasn't sure if he was joking, but wordlessly, she spread a large sheet of paper on a spare desk, put a water pot and paints next to it and held out a brush. He took the brush and his eyes seemed to hold a challenge. He was wearing the aftershave she had come to delight in. One day she must ask him for the name of it, so she could get a bottle just to sniff.

Harry exchanged a grin and a wink with Nick, who was working on the opposite table. 'I've not done painting for years. Can you give me some tips please, Miss?'

Nick laughed aloud. Ellie couldn't help but smile too. 'Do you want to paint people, buildings, landscapes or abstracts?'

'Too many questions. Can't I just pick up the brush and see what happens?'

'Of course, but painting is usually better with a theme or shape in mind. The mistake most people make is to think art is about daubing paint. Do you agree, Nick?' She turned to her protégé.

'Yes, Miss. I need to have in mind what mood or emotion I'm trying to show with the paint before I start.'

Ellie stopped in her tracks. It seemed such a mature statement from a young lad. She exchanged a meaningful look with Harry.

'So, Nick, what mood or emotion are you working with today?'

'Joy!'

Tears sprang to her eyes and she tidied the desk in front of her to regain control over her emotions. 'How wonderful.'

'Yes, I'm happy. I'm allowed to paint, what more could I want?'

A mischievous thought went through Ellie's head.

'Mr Dixon, what mood or emotion are you going to be working with today?' She winked at Nick.

Harry's face was a picture as he contemplated the question, she could almost see cogs whirring in his head. Ellie and Nick exchanged several glances before he replied and she wondered if she had been wise to ask the question.

'I'd have to say surprise and hope.'

The way Harry looked at her made a blush tinge her cheeks.

Harry brandished the paintbrush, dripping with blue paint, at the paper in front of him. He wasn't sure what he was playing at. The art class was Ellie's domain. They hadn't spoken much since the mentoring meeting, just polite salutations in the corridor or town.

He would prefer it if they were on better terms. It might be difficult for them to be friends, or anything more with Ellie's suspicions about his past, but they, at least, needed to have a working relationship. He might have to talk to her about Tom, her art support or anything else for that matter.

Since she'd told him about the attack she'd suffered, he couldn't get imagined images and rising anger out of his head every time he looked at her or even thought about her, which was more often than he would allow himself to admit.

He sat with the blue paint dripping onto his paper and froze. What now? All of the students were watching him and he was no artist.

Ellie seemed to sense his confusion.

'Do you need help, Mr Dixon?'

'I'm afraid so, my mind has gone completely blank.' He flashed her a 'help me' look.

Taking him completely by surprise, she grasped his hand,

complete with paintbrush and pulled it over the paper in a wide arc. Harry's senses went into overdrive. Ellie's skin was warm against his own, her perfume was floral and her body pressed against him felt heavenly. He had to remind himself that he had ten teenage pupils staring at him. Otherwise, he might have floated up to the ceiling in bliss.

'Does that help at all?'

She released his hand and moved away a little. The paper was three quarters covered in blue.

Was she serious? His mind was further away from the painting than it had been when she'd asked if she could help him. He washed the blue from his brush and dipped it into the white paint, trying to cover up his state of confusion.

'I need more help than I thought.' He wondered if he had gone too far, whether she would walk away in disgust, but she was probably as aware of the students watching them as he was.

She lifted her eyes heavenward and grasped his hand again. This time edging the blue sweep with a zigzag in white.

Realisation dawned. She'd painted a wave. Not just a breaker, but a rolling wave fit to be surfed.

'Now all you need to do is add a surfer to the picture.'

The reference to her version of his past brought him back to the present with a bump. Her suspicions were still there, not far below the surface, and she was making that perfectly clear. He'd thought they'd made progress towards an understanding, but he'd obviously imagined it.

'Wow, Sir, that's really good,' said Nick, wandering over to peer over his shoulder.

'I haven't exactly done any painting yet, Nick. The teacher's done it for me. Isn't that cheating?'

Ellie had moved across the room and was busy discussing shades of yellow with another student. Harry could still feel the imprint of her body warmth beside him.

At the end of the club time, he waited until all of the students had gone. Nick was the last out and almost had to be evicted.

'That boy adores you.'

'He relates to me, because I listen and encourage him. From what he's said, I don't think he gets either of those things at home, but I shouldn't judge as I don't know the full circumstances.'

Ellie picked up Harry's artwork. Instead of a surfer, he'd rebelled and painted the shape of a badly formed, but recognisable dolphin. Her eyes flared for a moment and then she laughed.

'Touché.'

'Ellie, I know you still don't trust me, but please believe I have the best interests of the students of this school at the forefront of my mind.'

She sighed and sat down opposite to him. 'I don't doubt it. I've watched you with them, watched you with Tom on the sports field. I have no issue with ... who you are now.'

He held his breath to stop from speaking until she'd had her say.

'I've a few issues with your previous incarnation, but you obviously had your reasons for making the change.'

He was wary. Was she trying to trick him into an admission or was she offering an olive branch? What had appeared conciliatory suddenly felt hostile. He looked at her almond-shaped eyes and her curls, barely contained by a band. She had red paint on a strand near her ear.

It would be so easy to reach out ... and ...

Trust was most definitely the issue here. He didn't trust her motivations and she didn't trust him at all. Any friendship or working relationship was difficult without at least an element of trust. They had little, if any, between them. There was, however, obvious animal attraction, he believed on both sides. Where did they go from here?

'Ellie, would you have dinner with me?'

The response was instant and negative. 'No, thank you.'

'I don't mean a date dinner. I meant some time out to allow us to clear the air between us.'

She was gathering her things to leave. Had he managed to destroy the fragile working relationship that had been emerging between them? He kicked himself, wondering what on earth he could say to bring her back on side. 'You can bring Mandy with you too if it would help.'

She stopped what she was doing. 'There are things in my past that not even Mandy knows. I love her dearly, but she's the biggest gossip in the area. Do you really believe we should discuss the subjects we need to talk about in front of her?'

'Maybe not then. It was a long shot to try to get you to reconsider.'

'I'm not in the mood for reconsidering anything today. Goodnight, Mr Dixon. Please feel free to take your painting home.'

She was gone, leaving him with the memory of a fleeting touch and a picture only fit for the rubbish bin, except he might keep it for a while, to remind him of the feeling of Ellie's hand on his skin.

Chapter Sixteen

Ellie and Mandy sat in their usual seats in the wine bar fronting the promenade. The nights had begun to draw in and it was already difficult to see the sea in the gloom of the evening. It had drizzled for days and the girls both had umbrellas propped against the bench seat opposite. Ellie's hair was uncontrollable in damp weather. It stood out at strange angles from her head and refused to be tamed.

She'd been telling Mandy about Nick Crossten's latest painting. She had decided against displaying his work in her gallery, as it was so different in style from her own work, but she'd asked if Mandy might take a few of his pictures for the craft centre to see if they would sell.

'I'll have to ask Harry Dixon first, of course, after all the pictures were painted using school materials and Nick is under age.'

'What about his mum? Won't she need to give permission?'

'I was hoping Harry would deal with that side of things.'

Mandy twisted round in her seat and fixed her with the type of stare Ellie had come to recognise as the expression her friend wore when she had something niggling away at her.

'Why do you always say Harry's name in that tone?'

'What tone?' She shifted uncomfortably in her chair.

'That strange, wary tone.'

'I do not.' She crossed her legs.

'You do so. What's it all about, Ellie?'

'I don't know what on earth you mean.' She crossed her arms, annoyed she was being typically defensive.

'From where I'm sitting, you two would be perfect for each other.'

Ellie's nerve endings jangled.

'What!'

'In my opinion, you're very well suited,' Mandy persisted.

'But, I'm not looking for a man.' Ellie started to pull her fingers through her hair.

'No, but if you were, Harry Dixon would be an ideal candidate.'

'In your eyes, maybe, but not in mine. Anyway I thought you were convinced he was gay.'

'That was before I saw the way he looks at you and how he held you when you danced at the beach.'

'He does not, did not.' She crossed her arms and legs even tighter.

'Why won't you even consider it? I know you were suspicious of him when he first arrived, but he denies ever being in Cornwall. He's good-looking, the right sort of age, intelligent and to top it all, he gets on well with Tom.'

Ellie laughed. 'And these are the main ingredients for romance are they?'

'It's bugging me. He's made it clear he doesn't want me, but I reckon you'd be in with a good chance. Think how thrilled Tom would be if you were dating his hero.'

'He's not Tom's hero.'

'Really? Wake up. Haven't you heard the way Tom talks about Harry?' Mandy changed her voice to imitate Tom's way of speaking. 'Harry said I was good at this. Harry said I should try that.'

'What if it went wrong?'

'Oh, Ellie, I despair. He even looks enough like Tom for people to think he's his father.'

Ellie spluttered and spat wine all down her top. It left a dark stain that she mopped at with a tissue as she tried to marshal her thoughts. She was anxious to move away from this topic of conversation.

'I worry, Mandy. I worry that I'm not a good enough mother for Tom. That I'm not … enough.'

'Rubbish! You're a brilliant mother. Tom's just going through those difficult teenage years. Don't you remember what it was like yourself?'

'I worry what happened with my ex has damaged him for life.'

'I'm sure whatever happened in the past makes Tom value you more, even if he doesn't show it most of the time. That's lads for you. We can't change the past though, can we? We just have to cope with the here and now and move on into the future.'

'If only it was that simple.'

'Look, I have your best interests at heart, all I ask is that you think about it. Harry has been good to Tom, good for Tom too, so why don't you cut him some slack, even if you won't consider dating him?'

Mandy's words stuck in Ellie's mind. *We just have to cope with the here and now and move on into the future.*

It was true, she had seen no sign that Harry was up to anything sinister. His heart and soul appeared to be engaged in the interests of Borteen High and its pupils. She'd been suspicious of his motives in the beginning, but now that seemed unfair. She couldn't change the past. Anyway, would she want to? It would mean a life in which Tom had never been conceived and that was unthinkable. Her son had been the source of almost all joy in her life for the last fourteen years.

She felt jumpy today. Tension lodged between her shoulder blades. A letter addressed to Ellie Jacob had somehow been forwarded to her through a roundabout route. The letter was from the solicitor she'd used in Cornwall and detailed the date when Rushton Jacob, her ex-husband and attacker, would be released from jail. Ellie had felt sick as she read the words. She was even more on edge, because it had taken a while for the letter to reach her. Rushton had been out of jail for over a month already.

If the letter had found her in Borteen, there was a chance that her ex-husband could too. Would Rushton still want to find her? They were divorced, she'd served the papers on him whilst he was inside. She'd changed not just her name, but thanks to his attack, her appearance too. There was, however, the small matter of his threat to kill her and also, his stash of cash. She'd found the money after he had been taken away by the police. She knew that she should probably have handed it in, but she also knew that they needed it to survive.

Her weekly mentoring meeting with Zack seemed to come around with great regularity. Ellie had become used to the boy's blustering swagger, with which she realised he actually tried to mask a deep-seated insecurity. The way he dressed and behaved were just for show. Underneath it all, he was an uncertain adolescent trying to find his way in the world.

She didn't think Zack was opening up to her entirely. Of course, she worried it was her fault, due to her way of talking to him or lack of training. She'd begun to browse websites about mentoring in the hope of finding the key to unlocking Zack's potential.

They had arranged to meet first thing in the morning before the start of the school day. This meant Ellie could get away to open her gallery by nine-thirty. She'd rehearsed various ways to open the session today, right down to how to arrange the seating, but it was all unnecessary, when Zack bounded in with his eyes shining with excitement.

'Miss, Miss, can you guess what happened to me this morning?'

'You'll have to tell me, Zack, I've no idea.'

'A man stopped me round the corner from school and asked if I wanted to buy drugs. He had all these tablets, all different colours ...' He beamed as if it was some sort of badge of honour to be asked such a thing.

The hairs at the back of Ellie's neck stood to attention. 'What! Just now?'

'Yes.' Having looked thrilled, as if he was telling her something exciting, Zack subsided into the chair, as he became aware of her reaction to his news. He looked as if he'd been caught smoking behind the bike sheds.

'You didn't buy any drugs did you, Zack?'

'I hadn't got any money.' His tone suggested he was disappointed.

Ellie thought quickly. 'Stay right here. I'm going to fetch Mr Dixon so you can tell him exactly what you just told me.'

'Have I got to, Miss?'

'Most definitely.' She suddenly worried that Zack might run off. 'Actually, Zack, come on, we'll go and find him together. Hurry up. I think it's important we move quickly.'

Harry was in his office when the two of them burst in unannounced. He glanced from one to the other. 'By the looks on your faces, you'd better sit down.'

Ellie quickly told Harry what Zack had told her. He jumped to his feet.

'Zack, tell me what the man looked like.'

Poor Zack had lost his earlier bluster. 'Sir, he was as tall as you, but with darker skin.'

'Black skin?'

'No, sir, just darker.'

'What was he wearing?'

'Smart trousers and a shirt, but no tie. He'd got a blue jumper tied round his waist and it hid a bag where the drugs were.'

Harry ruffled Zack's hair. 'Well done for the description, Zack.'

He turned to Ellie. 'Ms Golden, I'm going to go out and see if I can find this man.'

'Do you want me to call the police?'

'Leave it till I get back, we don't want police cars scaring him off. I won't be long.'

He rushed out of the office. The door banged against the wall.

Ellie wanted to shout, "be careful", but somehow it didn't seem appropriate.

'Zack, you'd better go to your form room. School is about to start.'

As if in answer, the bell to signal the start of the school day rang out.

Ellie jumped despite knowing it was going to happen. 'Probably better if you keep this to yourself until Mr Dixon has spoken to you again. I know it will be hard, but please try.'

Zack's eyes were full of unshed tears. 'Did I do anything wrong, Miss?'

'No, Zack, on the contrary. You did the right thing to tell me. I'm very proud of you.'

He grinned uncertainly and went off to class looking much less cocky than usual. Ellie knew it was a vain hope he would be silent about the drug dealer.

She sat in Harry's office feeling as if she had no right to be in his personal space. It was a very functional room, with a desk and chair for the headmaster and two visitors' chairs opposite. On the side wall was a huge mahogany bookcase full of books and papers and a sad looking plant that needed water. Harry didn't appear to have personalised the room at all, but the air held traces of his aftershave. In the end, Ellie stood by the window, looking out over the school grounds.

Harry returned fifteen minutes later, his face flushed.

'Any sign?'

'No. I ran all around the surrounding roads. Good job I've been training every morning. I guess whoever it is disappears when school starts and the potential customers dry up. I'd better question Zack again, find out if any other students were approached and contact the police. I really hope no Borteen High students have bought drugs or taken any on the premises.'

'That's a scary thought. Although, surely the teachers would have noticed changes in behaviour?'

His face became serious. 'Drugs are dangerous things and can change lives. I can testify to that. They fill me with horror.'

She squirmed. 'You've taken drugs?'

'My step-brother died after taking Ecstasy and someone once laced my drink and it led to me losing my job, losing everything I had, actually.'

The image of Norrie's back as he fumbled to open a bottle of beer rose up in her mind. Was Harry referring to that beer? *My God. Did I give him that laced drink?*

Had Harry lost everything because of her? She wanted the floor to open up and swallow her. She became hot and sweaty. Thankfully, Harry was busy talking to the local police station on the telephone and didn't notice her discomfort.

Chapter Seventeen

Ellie couldn't sleep. She tossed and turned until her bed clothes were tied in knots around her body. She wanted to ask Harry what had happened back then, when he said he'd lost his job, but to do so she had to ask about Cornwall again, re-voice her suspicions about his identity and jeopardise the fragile truce that had been building between them.

Her mind replayed that night in the past on constant memory loop. The guilty feelings from back then, about leaving Ben on the beach after they'd had sex and the new growing questions about whether she'd given him the laced beer without realising it, threatened to overwhelm her.

How would Harry react if she asked him more questions and, more to the point, if he realised she had maybe unwittingly led to his downfall? She hadn't actually seen Norrie put anything into the beer she had offered to Ben, but she seemed to remember it had taken him a while to remove the lid.

Her eighteen-year-old self had longed for Ben to notice her, but he was unattainable and aloof. He'd always been on the edge of the group. After sipping that beer, he suddenly couldn't take his hands or his lips off her. It had felt wonderful to be the focus of his universe, so she hadn't questioned his change of heart.

They'd walked along the beach together into the shadows. Ben took off his jacket, laid it down, pushed her gently onto the sand. She could remember the silky texture of the jacket lining against her spine. His eyes had sparkled, lit by moonlight in the darkness. She hadn't cared about anything, because his body was pressed against her own, one hand in her hair, one exploring her neck, then cupping her breast, circling and playing with her nipple through her thin T-shirt and then pushing back the fabric to kiss and nip her skin. She'd arched her back, pushing herself closer against him. The sound of the zip of her shorts. His fingers exploring under the band of her bikini bottoms. His inquisitive tongue.

If she closed her eyes, Ellie could still imagine the sensations. Hear his and her moans, framed by the sound of the ocean close to them and see the moon in the darkness above. He'd tasted of beer and her lips tingled.

She'd always thought of this part of that night as a time of magic and pleasure, but with hindsight, she realised that even if Ben had still been alive the next day, there was no guarantee he would have wanted anything further to do with Ellie or her baby.

If that beer she gave to him had been drug-laced, their encounter that evening made more sense. He hadn't wanted her at all. It had just been drug-fuelled lust on his part and stupidity on her own. The endearments and caresses she'd let herself believe were the beginnings of a relationship had meant nothing. Ben hadn't really known what he was doing, which was probably why he didn't remember her. She must have appeared like a dream, an hallucination, a figment of his imagination, to be forgotten when the drug wore off.

Ellie tortured herself with her thoughts. Repressed tears began to pour onto her crumpled pillows.

She was a fool.

Deluded fool.

Idiot.

She had meant nothing.

He didn't even recognise her.

Her rational mind added that her face was different after her surgery.

It didn't help.

She tried to think exactly what had happened after they'd

made love, had sex, she wasn't sure how to describe it any more.

Ben had gone to wash in the sea and the other men from their group had joined him. She remembered them laughing and splashing about in the surf.

She had grabbed her clothes, scrabbled up the sand dunes and disappeared into the night, not wanting to be embarrassed in her state of undress, not wanting Norrie and the others to be certain of what had happened, however much they might speculate.

What had happened to Ben afterwards?

It had always been a mystery.

She wouldn't know unless she could get Harry to talk about it, but to do so would risk exposing what she now suspected was her part in what he had described as his downfall.

Ellie disentangled the sheets and, although it was only five in the morning, went to shower. She was unlikely to get back to sleep and perhaps she could use this torrent of emotion to fuel her painting.

Harry stared out of his office window. He didn't see the students milling around the playground. The phone call he'd received earlier had stolen all of his thoughts.

'Harry, I'm afraid I'm ringing to give you a warning.' His contact's voice always cut through whatever had been happening before his call. Sam only rang if there was information important to keep Harry safe and for regular calls to check on him. It was one link with the past he couldn't afford to sever.

'Warning? What do you mean?'

'We have reason to believe that the drug selling incident outside Borteen High might be more serious than you imagined.'

'How did you find out about that already?'

'The man we believe to be involved is on our watch list.'

'Please explain.' The neckband of his shirt suddenly felt too tight.

'It's more than likely linked to the prison release of one of your old associates.'

Harry had loosened his tie and undone the top button of his shirt. He wasn't nervous exactly, more unsettled. What if he'd found the drug seller that morning and been recognised?

'How could he have found me?'

'We've thought about that. We came to the conclusion that it wasn't you he'd traced, but the lovely Ellie Golden.'

'Ellie! Why would they be after her? And how do you know she's lovely?' He regretted the last question, he'd given his feelings away. 'Who is this man?'

'It's her ex-husband. Nasty piece of work. Don't think a spell in prison has improved him at all from the reports we've had. Rushton Jacob.'

Harry felt a whooshing sound in his head as the words filled him with shock. Here was Ellie's link with the drugs world. The link he'd hoped he wouldn't find. Rushton Jacob, the man who more than likely had been involved in his beating on the beach and might even have thrown some of the punches. He rubbed his damaged ear, as if the connection would conjure up the face of his attacker, but as usual there was nothing but emptiness where memories should be.

'Just be wary, Harry. If he realises who you are, he might want another shot at revenge.'

'I don't like the sound of this. I can't endanger the children of this school.' He fought a sudden panicky feeling in his stomach.

'At the moment, nothing suggests he's even aware of your presence in Borteen.'

'What about Ellie? Should I warn her?'

'How do you propose to do that without admitting your past identity? You haven't admitted it already, have you?'

'No, of course I haven't, although she does suspect I was once Ben Rivers, as I told you.'

'Best keep it at speculation, not certainty.'

Harry fell silent, mulling over the options.

'But, she could be in real danger if he's gone to the trouble of tracking her down.'

'Maybe wise to keep away from her, Harry.'

Keep away from her. How could he when every cell in his body wanted to protect her from this dangerous man?

Chapter Eighteen

Despite a number of students making statements about being approached by someone peddling drugs, the local police were unable to find the man. They staked out the area around the school for several days, but either it had been a one-off attempt at sales, or the man had been tipped off that he'd been spotted.

Regardless of the risks, Harry made a point of walking the school perimeter several times before school and made stern assembly speeches on the subject of drugs and their dangers. At the next mentoring meeting, he made a request that the mentors broach the subject of drugs with the students they were coaching. It was difficult to relax, given the information his contact had shared. He tried to keep an eye on Ellie when it was possible, but it was difficult to do much without worrying she would think he was stalking her.

Ellie didn't do birthdays, hers anyway, if she could help it. She hated being in the limelight and having to open presents and cards in front of other people. She believed her almost-phobia dated from when she was five or six and had reacted badly to an elderly aunt buying her a present exactly the same as someone else. Her mother had been mortified by her behaviour and most of that fateful birthday had been spent in her room in disgrace. Far from being a pleasant experience, being given a present made her heart speed up and put her nerves on edge.

This year her birthday fell on a Saturday. Mandy and Tom arranged lunch for her at the restaurant at the end of the high street. They all ordered seafood and sparkling water. The food was delicious. Ellie would never tire of eating fresh fish almost straight from the sea.

She braced herself for the inevitable appearance of a birthday cake. It came, complete with one flaming candle. Mandy and Tom sang "Happy Birthday", joined by most of the other diners in the restaurant. Ellie was bright red by the time the singing had finished.

Feeling incredibly uncomfortable, Ellie opened the cards they gave her, knowing it would be presents next. Mandy had bought her predictable gifts, perfume, make-up and a sparkly top for one of their evenings out.

Tom's present was a large heavy parcel.

'What's this? It's an intriguing shape.'

For once, her curiosity was aroused and she felt an unfamiliar spark of excitement. Inside the wrapping was an intricately formed piece of driftwood, which had been sanded and varnished to make its surface smooth and shiny. It was a natural sculpture.

'Oh, Tom, it's beautiful. Did you find it, or buy it?'

'Mr Dixon came across it on the beach when we were out running one day and I asked if I could have it for your birthday. He suggested that I sand and varnish it. He spent ages helping me. Do you like it, Mum?'

'I love it.' She kissed him and then twirled the piece around to find the best angle to display the wood. There was something so unique about artwork provided by nature and it made it even more special that Harry had found it and helped Tom to finish it for her. She ran her hands over the smooth shape and couldn't help imagining Harry handling the wood, as if his energetic presence had been sealed in by the varnish. She stowed it carefully back into its wrappings and carrier bag, looking forward to displaying it at home. It would almost be like having a piece of Harry in the dining room.

Mandy clapped quietly. 'You did do well, Ellie. Please tell me your present opening wasn't scary this time.'

'Surprisingly, I quite enjoyed it, but thank you for being conscious of my fears.'

She had promised not to work on her birthday, but wanted to pop into the gallery to check for post. Tom had a date with Louise later that afternoon, but agreed to carry her birthday presents home safely first. Mandy and Ellie had planned a birthday trip to the cinema in Sowden for the evening.

As she turned into the alleyway, Ellie jumped out of her skin when Nick lurched out of the shadows.

'Nick Crossten you scared me half to death.'

'Sorry, Miss Golden.' He looked even scruffier than normal, probably because he was wearing home clothes and not school uniform.

'Were you looking at my pictures?'

'Not exactly. Could I come inside?' He kept looking around him, as if he expected someone else to jump out of the shadows too.

'Of course. You can help me unload the kiln. I put a batch of new pots in to fire three nights ago. The kiln should be cool by now. They're some of the pots I want to decorate and sell for Christmas and you can be the first to have a look at them.'

She was puzzled that Nick didn't show any of his usual enthusiasm. He came through into the gallery after her, pausing to let her pick up the post and shut the door. She stuffed the three envelopes into her bag and went to walk through into the studio room.

'Miss, can you lock the door behind us please?'

Ellie was surprised and wary, but did as he asked. 'Are you okay, Nick? Is something wrong? Is someone following you?'

He seemed happier when they were out of sight of the windows at the front of the shop.

'No, no one is following me, but I came to tell you that I think someone is following you.'

Ellie felt a cold shiver snake up her spine.

'Following me? Who?'

'A man. I've seen him outside the gallery and outside school after art class. He's been following you.'

'Are you sure, Nick?'

He nodded his head, with a look more serious than any expression she had ever seen on his thin face.

Touched by Nick's concern, rattled by what he had said, but sure there must be some rational explanation, Ellie fought down a sudden vision of the letter about Rushton's release from prison.

Surely not.

To cover her alarm, she led Nick into the back yard and opened the door to the kiln room. Out of habit, she put a hand on the side of the kiln to make sure it had cooled.

'Did you see what I did first?' She said, with a tone that sounded falsely bright even to her own ears. 'If you work with a kiln, you must always make sure it's stone-cold before you open it. If it isn't, the sudden change of temperature can ruin your work, besides burning you badly if it's still hot. These babies should be cooked. Oh, I do hope they're nice. You never truly know until they come out of the kiln safely.'

Nick was not a young man to be fobbed off. 'Aren't you worried about this man following you?'

'I'm determined not to be unnerved. I'm sure there must be a simple explanation. Thank you, by the way, for warning me. It is very good of you to look out for me.'

'You've been very kind to me and I wouldn't want anyone to hurt you.'

'Why do you think anyone would want to hurt me?'

The boy shrugged.

Ellie felt shaken by his interpretation of why a man would be following her, but tried not to worry Nick further by any reaction to his words. She refused to act in haste. If this man was following her, she could easily make a mistake and fall into his hands by panicking.

His hands.

She'd already given this unknown stalker Rushton's face.

She forced herself to continue unloading her work. It was not a process that could be hurried. As she focused on removing the supports and packing, she was alarmed to see her fingers shaking.

They spent a companionable half an hour gently taking the fired pots out of the cooled kiln and placing them on the table in the studio. It was always exciting to see how pottery turned out. Somehow, it was always a surprise. You could never totally predict the finished result in terms of shape or glaze colour and often Ellie found things were even better than she had imagined, or alternatively a complete disaster.

Nick admired the pots, turning one carefully in his hands. The green and red of the glaze looked very festive. They would look fantastic as part of the gallery's Christmas window display and it felt good to get them finished in plenty of time. Christmas displays in the big stores in Sowden seemed to start impossibly early from the end of August.

'We have some lessons at school with pottery clay, but not using a wheel. You are just supposed to roll it into snakes and then coil them up into a pot. Can I have a go on the potter's wheel sometime, Miss? These look really cool.'

'I tell you what, Nick. We'll see if anyone else in the after school club would like to have a go and then maybe we could hold one week's class here. I could bring the pots to school once they'd been fired in the kiln.'

'Sounds great, Miss. Yes, please.'

Her mind kept being drawn back to the seriousness of their earlier conversation.

'Nick, the man you believe you saw following me, was it anyone you know, anyone you've seen before?'

He shook his head. 'No one I've seen in Borteen before.'

'Can you describe the man?'

'He was tall, sort of looked like one of those rugby players. Had black hair.'

Ellie didn't want to hear this description. There was a distinct possibility that Rushton had found her after all.

When they had finished unloading all of the pots and they were safely stored away, Nick went out of the gallery door first and had a look to see if the man he had seen was around. He came back and reported that there was no sign. Ellie locked up and began to walk home. She walked quickly, uncertainty fuelling her steps, glancing behind her every few yards along the route, despite her escort.

Nick insisted on accompanying her as far as her front door. She was both pleased and alarmed at his protectiveness. She made him promise not to hang around outside her house to watch for the man, assuring him she would lock all of her doors and windows. She was worried that if it was Rushton, he could take exception to Nick trailing after him and it could be dangerous if the lad challenged him.

When the front door was firmly closed and she had satisfied herself that no one lurked in any of the rooms or the garden, she finally looked at the gallery post. There was an advertising letter for insurance, a bill and an obvious birthday card. She opened it in trepidation. She had an irrational thought that Rushton might have remembered her birthday.

To her surprise, the card was from Harry.

The front of the card was a lovely photograph of the bay at Borteen and inside, he had written: "Happy Birthday, Ellie. Regards Harry". There was one kiss.

Even though it was a simple message, the one kiss made Ellie wonder if was trying to tell her that he was beginning to think of her fondly. If she was going to risk her heart a little, she needed a sign from Harry that her feelings would be reciprocated. Could they possibly consider a romance after such a terrible start?

The doorbell rang. Ellie had been shaken by Nick's warning, so her heart began to beat faster. Rather than fling the door wide, she put the security chain across before she opened it and peered out through the gap.

The man standing on her path was a stranger, although she knew that she'd seen him somewhere before.

'Ellie Golden? I'm sorry, I've been trying to catch you for a while. I'm Louise's father.'

'Hang on.'

Ellie shut the door to remove the security chain and as she did so, she took a huge sigh of relief. This must be the man who Nick had seen hanging around the gallery. He was tall, dark and broad-shouldered. Phew!

'Come in, Mr Stevens. Tom and Louise aren't here at the moment.'

'Good. No, they're in town. I was actually hoping for a word with you on your own.'

Ellie made tea and they sat in her tiny lounge with the view of the street and beyond it the sea. Today, the sea and the horizon merged in greyness. Mr Stevens looked huge in her small chair.

'My wife and I thought it was time we made contact with you, being as Tom and Louise have become a regular boyfriend and girlfriend.'

'Yes, they do seem to be besotted with each other. I can hardly get a word out of either of them when they're here.'

'It's the same at our house. We're a bit concerned that they might get ... erm ... physically close. They are a little young, so we felt we should talk to you about it.'

Ellie was aware a blush was starting on her cheeks. It was weird discussing her son's potential sex life with someone she'd just met. Meanwhile, Mr Stevens had gone white with his own embarrassment.

She'd thought about the question of underage sex too.

She'd tried to speak to Tom about the issue, but he'd brushed her off, saying that he wasn't a complete idiot.

'I've spoken to my son about it and I expect you've had discussions with your daughter too, but you're right, it's time to have a more in-depth serious chat. Hormones are strange things and it's easy to get carried away.'

'I'm glad we're thinking along the same lines. I guess as the parents of a girl, we're always going to worry about boyfriends.'

For a moment, Ellie could see a vision of her own parents with disapproving faces.

He was slurping his tea as fast as he could. He'd delivered his embarrassing message and seemed keen to make his escape.

'I promise to have another discussion with my son.'

'And we'll be doing exactly the same with Louise.' He sat on the edge of his seat and looked ready to make a run for the door. 'Happy birthday, by the way. Louise said that Tom was at your birthday lunch.'

'Thank you. Birthdays seem to come round very quickly these days.'

'Yes, I can agree with that. Right, I'd better be off. Enjoy the rest of your day.'

He handed her his empty mug and stood up. Ellie was pleased to have solved the mystery of the stalker and couldn't wait to tell Nick the good news so he could stop worrying about her. Her relief was short-lived, however.

'Mr Stevens, you say you've been trying to speak to me for a while. Can I ask if you've tried to see me at the gallery?'

'Graham, please. No, just at this address.'

Her heart sank. She hadn't solved the mystery after all.

Chapter Nineteen

The days flew by. It was hard for Ellie to believe it had been a week since her birthday. She hadn't seen anyone following her, no matter how often she had looked behind her as she went about her daily life. She'd experienced several confused dreams containing scenes from the past, with Rushton angry and dominant. Also, she couldn't help an obsession for checking locks on her house and car and scanning the people on the beach and in town. After no further alarms or sightings, she'd almost allowed herself to relax.

As she walked down the hill on the following Saturday morning, she noticed that the leaves on the trees were beginning to turn to reds and browns. She loved autumn and the inspirational hues in the landscape. She was planning a huge canvas of stylised trees in autumn colours. In her mind, she had painted it already and had to caution herself that the paint rarely worked in the way she imagined in her head.

Today, she felt joyful. Life had real purpose again, with Tom happy, her business taking off and her involvement in the mentoring scheme making her feel useful and valued. If she could whistle, she would be whistling a tune as she walked.

With her usual scan of the beach and the sea, she walked down between the buildings and came to an abrupt halt. Her heart began to hammer. The gallery window was shattered, jagged pieces of glass stuck out at all angles and inside on the broad window sill, her carefully arranged display of orchard pots was no more.

On closer inspection, she could see that pottery and glass shards combined in a chaotic heap of destruction inside the gallery. She stared in disbelief, shock blocking her throat. She let out a silent scream. *No!*

The glass door was untouched, its closed sign hanging forlornly on its chain. There was no one around. It was early, so there weren't even any other shop owners around to talk to about the damage. The wool shop and the gift shop occupying the same alley were closed. Their windows were intact. The gallery alone had been targeted, so Ellie couldn't believe it was a case of random vandalism. Sickness flooded her body, but then outrage took over.

She took out her mobile phone and reported the incident. A policeman arrived within ten minutes. Ellie had waited, leaning against the wall of the alleyway shaking, she wasn't sure whether with shock or anger, until he arrived. He introduced himself as PC Giles.

Nothing appeared to have been stolen, even though many items had been smashed or damaged, so he gave her an incident number, made a few notes and left her to the clearing up. The missile used to break the window was a half house brick, but had nothing to distinguish it or to identify the culprit. Ellie asked if there had been any more windows smashed nearby, but a call to the police control room confirmed the gallery window was the sole incident report in Borteen that morning.

Ellie pushed down her feelings of shock and violation and set about the practicalities of clearing up and making the property secure. A window replacement company promised to come and measure the glass in a couple of hours and board up the window until they could replace it. She reasoned with herself that every shopkeeper was bound to get a smashed window every now and then, but the feeling that there was more to this wouldn't go away.

Putting on gloves to protect against splinters of glass, she began to sort the bigger pieces of glass and pottery and swept the rest of the mess into a bin bag. Only the evening before, she had arranged twelve of her orchard pots in what she hoped was a pleasing arrangement in the window. She'd added sparkly silk flowers in the top layer of the pots and had been so pleased with the result. "Pride comes before a fall" maybe? That was her mother's voice talking to her from the past.

She put the flowers in the bin bag too, not being able to face using them again. Was this a chance thing, or had she been targeted? Who could have taken objection to her work? Who had she upset? A cold worry about Rushton wriggled from the recesses of her mind.

Concentrating on a gap in the floorboards where several splinters had lodged themselves, prickles on the back of her neck alerted her to someone standing behind her. She looked back under her arm and fell sprawling on the floorboards, flailing to get away.

Her instincts had been right all along; Rushton Jacob leaned nonchalantly against the wall. He had a horrible smirk on his face as he ran a finger down the edge of one of Ellie's paintings, making it tilt alarmingly.

She sat up against the wall, dustpan and brush raised as a lame protection. He looked just the same as when she had last seen him and, of course, matched Nick's description of tall, rugby player shoulders and black hair, although his hair was tinged with new grey and he was unshaven. Unhappy memories flooded her mind and body, making the tension more acute.

'Hello, Ellie. Nice gallery. Doing well for yourself by the looks of things.'

Even now, the deep gravelly tones of his voice drove daggers of fear through her.

'Rushton! What do you want?'

'That's not a very nice way to greet your long lost husband.'

'Ex … Ex-husband,' she stuttered. She'd divorced him while he was in prison. He'd signed the papers for goodness' sake.

'Come on, Ellie. Divorce or no divorce, you'll always be mine. You know that deep down, don't you? You're mine.' He took a step forward and laughed when she scrabbled to get away.

She managed to get to her feet using the wall as support, trying to keep her wits about her and assess escape routes. Rushton was a big man. How could she once have thought his solidness meant safety? All she felt at the moment was an overwhelming fear that made her heart hammer in her rib cage. Nick had been right all along. The man who had been watching her was dangerous.

'How did you find me?'

How could she be safe, if a change of name and location didn't work?

'It wasn't difficult. I made lots of amazing contacts inside, you'd be surprised what strings they can pull, even from inside a cell. Just needed to put out a few feelers and you were found. Could have had you dealt with, but I wanted to do it myself. You and, of course, Tom.'

An icy chill travelled over her skin at the mention of her son. It was one thing threatening her, but quite another to threaten Tom. Every mother knew how far she would go to protect her child. Rushton was unaware that his words had flipped a switch inside her, a switch of determination to get out of this situation and get her son to safety.

He put his head on one side and looked her up and down. It felt like he was mentally undressing her. 'The medics made a good job of your face. Better than the original, I reckon. You should be thanking me.'

Ellie's legs began to shake. She had to move quickly or she would be incapable of getting away. She didn't like to think what Rushton had in mind for her.

'You broke my window?' The comment seemed irrelevant, but came out of her mouth anyway. She had to find some fight from somewhere.

'Have you proof?'

'You broke my window! How dare you.' She tried to summon anger, because she knew that the adrenaline would help her. He was blocking her escape route and was much too big and solid to push out of the way. She'd have to outwit him.

'You stole my money! How dare you.'

His eyes were bulging and he had a look that Ellie knew from experience spelled danger.

'What money?'

'Oh come on Ellie. The money you found hidden around the house.'

'I don't know what you mean. I stopped renting the house we shared years ago.'

She'd never been very good at lying. She focused on the pulse at the base of his neck, where his blood beat time.

He looked uncertain for one second, before the leer returned to his face.

'You owe me, Ellie.'

'I don't owe you a penny, given what you put me through.'

What now?

What next?

Was he going to hit her again or maybe kill her this time?

Would he finish the job he started when he rearranged her face and sent himself to prison?

They faced each other in silence. He raised his fist and she saw he had a knife in the other hand. Her blood turned to ice. It wasn't a large knife, but the blade glinted in the gallery spotlights.

It was still early, Maeve at the gift shop didn't open until ten thirty and the lady who ran the wool shop didn't always open at weekends. Unless someone was browsing for art early, a rescue party was unlikely to arrive. It was all down to her.

She couldn't even scream and despite her earlier resolve, knew it was worthless to fight. A cold resignation settled over her and she raised her eyes to his, daring him to ignore any feelings he might once have had for her, if indeed he had ever really cared for her at all. She'd just been a cover, a veneer of respectability to fool the police that he'd turned a corner and stopped his criminal activities.

Rushton had hatred on his face, every pore proclaimed his anger and distaste. How had they come to this? Ellie remembered those dark eyes full of … what was it? Not love, but at least lust. She even recalled saying to him once, "I love it, when you look at me like that", as he enfolded her in his arms. The smell of his blue denim jacket. The solid strength of him. She had never really loved him. She'd known even at the beginning that he was dangerous, that he was involved with a bad crowd, but that was somehow fine when he offered to protect her and her unborn child. It had been okay until he'd turned against her.

He took a step forward and she jumped. She'd been free of him for nearly eight years. Did he want to be free of her forever? Was this where it ended?

'Mum, what's happened?'

Tom shouted to her from outside of the broken window. He must only have been able to see Ellie inside the gallery.

She turned horrified and Tom seemed to sense movement, saw Rushton and leaped back, his huge brown eyes wide.

'Thomas! Come in and join the party.' Rushton opened the gallery door and gestured for Tom to come inside. He held the knife behind his back so that Tom couldn't see it. Ellie's heart was in her mouth.

A range of emotions passed over Tom's face.

'Run, Tom!' she yelled.

He turned and ran without saying a word. Her heart leapt in gratitude that he'd listened and not tried to protect her.

'Goodness, he's growing up, isn't he? Good at rugby too.'

'How long have you been watching us?'

'Long enough.'

A yelp escaped from her throat and she jumped up onto the window sill. She cut her arm on a shard of glass and blood began to ooze out of the wound. Her only chance was to make an escape through the broken window, but Rushton was too fast, he grabbed her hair and yanked her back into the gallery.

'No! No! Let me go ...'

The blade glinted again in the spotlights. Ellie tried to twist away, but he had a big handful of her hair and it hurt as he pulled. She could smell garlic on his breath, see madness in his eyes, feel his strength.

I'm going to die. A high speed film of his previous attack ran on a loop in her head.

'Where's my money, you thieving bitch?'

Tears ran down her face. Tears of fear and pain as he yanked her hair again. The knife blade kept getting closer. She didn't have his money any more. She'd used the cash, after much soul searching, to pay for things they needed and the lease on the shop. Squeezing her eyes tightly shut she resigned herself to her fate. She prayed for the end to be quick.

Just when she'd given up, and the tension began to flow out of her, there was an almighty roar from nearby. Rushton let go and she fell to the floor. Opening her eyes, Ellie rolled away as Rushton smashed into the display table in the centre of the room, scattering and shattering yet more pots. Thankfully, she heard the knife skitter away across the floor.

A man was wrestling with Rushton.

Harry Dixon.

How could that be?

Ellie cowered against the wall. Her head hurt where her

hair had been pulled. Blood smeared her jeans from the cuts on her arm.

She was transfixed by the writhing men, grunting and struggling in front of her as they tried to get handholds on each other. It seemed surreal. How had she ever trusted Rushton enough to marry him? She couldn't even remember living with him now. And Harry ... her heart went out to him for his bravery in tackling Rushton. What could she do? How could she help?

She grabbed one of her pots and tried to get a clear view of Rushton's head to smash it down on him, but the men were writhing together and she was just as likely to knock Harry out as Rushton.

When the men rolled to one side, she could see a clear route to the door and ran outside screaming. She needed to get help. Tom stood there, white-faced. She flung herself into his arms, sobbing, the pot incongruously still in her hands between them. He clung onto her, trying to push her towards the alley entrance.

'Mum, come on, we have to get away.' He pulled at her clothing, imploring her to move, but she was frozen in fear and disbelief.

'We can't leave Harry on his own. Rushton has a knife. He'll kill Harry. Phone 999.'

She pulled away from Tom, pushed him towards the entrance of the alley and returned and tried to see what was happening inside the gallery. Harry and her ex-husband were still locked together, rolling around the floor.

Heavy breathing and smashing sounds filled the air. They grappled with each other, pulling at clothing, trying to get a space to land a punch. Ellie's gallery was being wrecked in front of her eyes, but none of it mattered as long as Harry was safe.

Rushton head-butted Harry and he fell back stunned, but then leaped up again and grabbed Rushton, who pulled him to one side, stretching out his hand. Ellie realised in an instant what he was trying to do. She threw her pot on the cobbles, where it smashed, took a deep breath and dashed into the gallery, hearing Tom behind her screeching for her to come back.

The knife lay against the skirting board, its blade glinting dangerously. Ellie made a lunge, picked it up and ran back outside. Her heart hammered. She stood against the wall, examining the weapon in horror. This was the blade Rushton had intended to use on her. She couldn't believe he would want to risk going back to prison. Not familiar with the mechanism to fold the knife, she stood there holding the blade in front of her, fascinated.

The sounds of the struggle intensified, punctuated by crashes, as yet more of her work fell to the floor to be trampled, smashed and ruined.

Ellie came to her senses. 'Tom, phone the police again. Quick, Rushton is going to kill Harry. Go out on the main street to guide them here and stay out of danger.'

Her own phone was in her handbag in the studio at the back of the gallery. She felt vulnerable standing on the cobbles on her own, but she couldn't bring herself to abandon Harry, her rescuer. She couldn't believe Tom had found him so quickly, but she was sure that if he hadn't, she could be lying with her throat cut in the broken shards of her own artwork right now. Tom would have found her dead when he came to look for her.

As she went to peer into the window again, Rushton dashed past her. Dishevelled and bloodied, he must have realised that she would have alerted the police by now. He gave her an almighty shove against the wall.

'Now I understand everything,' he yelled mysteriously and ran off.

Ellie banged her head on the bricks and it hurt. She slumped against the wall, wondering what Rushton had done to Harry and trying to gather her senses to go and find out.

The same policeman, PC Giles, who had visited the gallery earlier, ran into the alley. His eyes widened when he saw Ellie holding a knife.

'He ran away. You must have seen him. He would have run straight past you. He went that way.' She pointed back the way the policeman had come.

'Can you give me a description?'

'Tall, dark-haired, broad chest. He was bleeding and his clothes were a mess. I have to check on Harry, he's in there, and where's Tom?'

'One thing at a time. Let me have that knife.'

She handed the weapon over gratefully and the constable wrapped it in a plastic bag he drew out of his pocket. He passed her some tissues from his other pocket and she dabbed at the cuts on her arm.

As she went back through the gallery door, she heard him alert the control centre to the dangerous man on the run, giving Ellie's description and Rushton Jacob's name. He asked for back up.

'Harry?'

There was no reply. Fear spiralled up her body and she began to shake uncontrollably. Was Harry dead?

She could hear sirens approaching. Her head reeling, she ventured further into the gallery, her shoes crunching on bits of pottery and glass.

Harry lay curled up on the floor by the far wall. She went over and knelt down gingerly on the splinter covered tiles, almost frightened to touch him, but needing to know he was still breathing.

'Harry?'

She put her hand on his shoulder and to her relief, he turned and lay on his back. She launched herself at him, tears wetting his T-shirt as she clung to him.

'Ow, Ow … sorry, Ellie, I'm covered in bruises.'

'Sorry … of course … sorry. You came to save me. How did you know?'

He pushed her gently off his body and sat up cautiously. 'Of course I came. Tom said you were in danger.'

A couple of policemen ran into the shop, faces serious, batons raised.

'He's already gone. Find him,' Ellie yelled.

They raced back out of the door. She almost laughed, as it was so like a scene from an old silent film.

Paramedics arrived and began to assess Harry and Ellie for injuries. Mercifully, they had only suffered cuts and bruises.

Rushton had escaped. She couldn't believe it. He'd escaped and he was angry, vicious and quite likely a mortal danger to Tom and herself if he wasn't caught.

Where was Tom?

Panic rose up in her chest and threatened to engulf her. She hoped to goodness he hadn't followed Rushton. He could be in real trouble if he had. She turned to the nearest policeman. 'Where's my son?'

'He's safe. He's outside.'

She let out a long breath and allowed the paramedic to bandage her arm.

After what seemed like forever, Harry and Ellie hobbled out of the gallery. Ellie grabbed Tom and held him in a tight hug, before turning to look at Harry in the daylight.

His face was dirty, bloodied and bruised; Ellie's heart did a little skip. Gratitude that he didn't appear badly injured flooded through her. Harry, who she had not trusted, and at times had not been very nice to, had saved her life, she was convinced. He was looking straight at her, with concern on his face. Then, he leaned in and put his arms around both Ellie and Tom. They clung together as a little group amongst the policemen.

As he released them, he winced. 'I seem to have bruises on my bruises.'

Ellie started to dab at his face with the tissues PC Giles had given to her.

'Hey, hey.' He tried to fend her off.

'Do I gather that this wasn't the man who attacked you?' asked PC Giles.

'I told you. The man who attacked me was Rushton Jacob, my ex-husband. He's just been released from prison. I had a letter to tell me he was out, but I never dreamed he'd find me here.' She was aware she was babbling but didn't seem able to stop.

'Can I ask, Sir, how you came to be involved in all of this?'

'I'm the headmaster of Borteen High school, Harry Dixon. I'd arranged to meet one of my pupils, Tom Golden for a run on the beach. I was walking down the promenade, when he ran up and told me his mother was being assaulted, so I came to try and help her. The man attacked me too, we struggled and then he ran off.'

Harry looked a mess. Ellie knew she didn't look much better.

PC Giles held up the plastic bag containing the knife. 'Is this yours, Mr Dixon?'

Harry's eyes widened. 'No, it's not mine.' He turned to Ellie. 'He had a knife?'

'Yes, it's Rushton's. He threatened me with it before you arrived.'

'Mum, are you okay? I was so scared. I tried to follow Rushton, but he ran too fast.' Tom's face was pale and he looked more child-like than he had for a long time.

'Which way did he go? Tell PC Giles.'

Tom turned to the policeman. 'He ran towards the old church, past the library, but I lost sight of him in the churchyard.'

PC Giles related the information on his radio.

Tom hugged Ellie tightly and then turned to Harry and did the same to him. She watched them embrace and it felt surreal to see them so close together. Her heart filled with gratitude that her son was safe and unharmed.

'Thank you for helping Mum, Mr Dixon. I was scared Rushton would hurt her ... again.'

Ellie glanced across at Harry and shook her head slightly. The last thing Tom needed was confirmation that Rushton had indeed intended to more than hurt Ellie.

'You'll all need to come to the police station in Sowden to make statements,' said PC Giles. 'If you would follow me.'

'My gallery isn't secure,' Ellie said feebly, wondering at the same time if there was anything left of her stock to salvage after the ferocious fight inside.

'I'll leave an officer to look after it, while you make your statement.'

She nodded gratefully. 'I've already asked a window replacement company to come to board up the front window. They should be here soon.'

Harry came over to her, wiping dirt from his face with the tissues.

'Are you all right, Ellie?'

She leaned in closer so that Tom couldn't hear. 'I'm alive. I don't believe I would have been if you hadn't come to save me. I've had my hair pulled, a bang on the head and cut my arm, but I think the worst thing is the shock. Shock that he's found me here in Borteen.'

She asked one of the policemen to retrieve her handbag from the studio. She couldn't face seeing the state of the gallery right now.

The policeman ushered them along the alley, just as Maeve arrived to open her shop. She stared at Ellie in disbelief.

'Whatever happened here? Ellie, are you okay?'

Ellie told her briefly that she'd been attacked in the gallery, before she followed the others to the police car, which took them to the police station in Sowden. The journey over the moor seemed to take forever, when all Ellie really wanted to do was to sink into a warm bath and go to sleep.

She sat close to Harry in the back of the car, Tom on her other side. Harry slipped his hand into hers and squeezed gently.

Chapter Twenty

They still hadn't found Rushton. There had been a report of a bloodied man being picked up by a van, but so far the police hadn't found the van or her ex-husband.

By the time the taxi dropped them near the gallery later on, Harry's eye had swollen badly.

'You look terrible,' said Ellie, guilt once more flooding through her.

Harry gingerly explored the swelling with a finger. 'Thanks. I'm going to look a sight in assembly on Monday morning. I can already predict all the gossip that's going to be doing the rounds. Tom, we're going to have to discuss what you can and can't say before Monday. Guess the eye is too bad to pretend I walked into a door?'

'Erm, yes, I'm afraid so. Thanks for saving me, Harry. It could have been a very different story if you hadn't dived in.' He gripped her hand for a second. It was the firm grasp of someone wanting to reassure another human being.

'Are you going to feel safe at your house tonight? I mean, I could sleep on your sofa if it would help.'

She laughed. Would Harry on her sofa help her to sleep? Er, no, but it was lovely of him to offer.

'That's very kind, but I can't let Rushton intimidate me. I'm hopeful the police will find him.' Her words sounded much braver than she felt. 'But, I'm being selfish. Will you be all right on your own? I mean you've been in quite a fight.'

'I'll be fine. I was checked over again at the police station. It's only bruising.' Harry had been interviewed separately to Ellie and Tom, presumably so they couldn't discuss what had happened and their evidence wasn't contaminated by each other's opinions. 'At least let me walk you home.'

'Before that, I need to check on the gallery. Make sure the windows are boarded up and the door locked. Although, I can't face the carnage till tomorrow.'

The gallery was secured and a note was taped to the locked door. It told her that the key to the gallery had been left with the bakery owner on the corner of the entrance to the alley. The bakery was shut until Monday and her spare keys were at home, but Ellie knew it was probably a blessing she couldn't get inside right now. It would be too upsetting to see the extent of damaged and broken artwork and she couldn't face the questions of the bakery staff yet either.

Harry insisted that he see them safely home. It was late afternoon already, as everything seemed to have taken so long.

'Why don't we collect a take-away on the way up the hill?' suggested Ellie. 'I'll pay, by way of a thank you for today. Hopefully, we can all calm down and decide what we want to tell others about what happened this morning.'

Despite her brave words, her heart was in her mouth as they walked down her road, white plastic bags swinging in their hands. She saw Rushton in every bush and felt her whole body tense when she unlocked the front door, in case he was lurking inside. From Harry's tense body, as she pushed open the door, she guessed he was thinking along the same lines.

They fell on the Chinese take-away like a pack of hungry wolves. Ellie hadn't been able to face the sandwich lunch they'd been offered in Sowden and she hadn't realised how ravenous she was until the hot food was in front of her.

There was something intimate about watching how Harry ate his food. She hoped he didn't see her observing him so closely. Tom and Harry talked about football teams. It was almost as if there was a common understanding not to discuss the events of the day until they'd eaten.

As soon as the meal was finished, however, Tom fell silent. He followed Ellie around the house like a slouching spectre, even if she only went into the kitchen. His replies to any questions were monosyllabic and Ellie knew she would have to tackle the attack and its aftermath, as it hung between them unspoken in the air. He was more than likely suffering from shock.

Harry looked very tired and battered. Guilt surfaced again because she was the cause of his disfigurement, even though she hadn't launched the blows. There were, thankfully, no injuries to his face deep enough to scar, but he would carry the signs of the fight for a good few weeks to come.

The doorbell sounded. All three of them jumped. Ellie, flanked by both Harry and Tom walked down the hall and Ellie put the security chain across the door before opening it a mere crack.

'PC Saunders. We've found no sign of your assailant, Ms Golden, so we wanted to reassure you that there will be extra patrols in Borteen and on your road tonight. If you have any worries, please phone the number the sergeant gave you earlier.'

Ellie thanked him and shut the door. The whole thing felt unreal now.

'I'm exhausted, Mum. I think I'm going to chill by playing some computer games in my room and then I'll get an early night.' Tom stood up.

Harry put a hand on his sleeve. 'It's probably best if you say as little as possible about what happened to your mates at school.'

'No worries,' said Tom.

'What if we say I was being threatened by an intruder at the gallery and you came to my rescue?' said Ellie. 'It's more or less the truth anyway. We don't need to elaborate about who it was or why they were there.'

143

She glanced up at her son. He had that "whatever" teenage look.

For once, Ellie didn't have to wince at the thundering of his feet on the staircase, as he trod so softly on his way up to his room that she couldn't hear him at all.

Harry and Ellie cleared away the take-away cartons together. She moved to the door to take the carrier bags of rubbish to the wheelie bin.

'Let me go outside.'

'You can't be here all of the time. I have to do this, or I'll become a virtual prisoner of my fear, scared of my own shadow.'

He stood aside. 'You're right. It's just …'

'Just what?'

'It was so horrible seeing that man with his hand on your throat. I … I've come to care about you, Ellie.'

'It's mutual.'

She smiled, squared her shoulders, went out of the back door and threw the rubbish in the bin. It made a loud bang that reverberated around the small garden. She paused, deliberately, to take a gulp of cool night air before returning to the kitchen. Even the bushes in the garden appeared to have eyes. Her heart thudded against her ribcage, but she wasn't going to admit as much to Harry. She locked and bolted the door behind her.

Harry's swollen eye was almost completely closed up. She wondered if he might try to continue the conversation about caring for her, so she spoke first to give herself time to think.

'I'll get a pack of frozen peas for that eye.'

'I've no doubt I'll be covered in bruises tomorrow, but thankfully nothing serious.'

'Where else do you hurt?'

He laughed and then grimaced in pain. 'Head, elbows, ribs, knees, stomach and eye. Your ex put up quite a fight.

144

I've not been in a scrap like that since my college days and I was a lot younger then.'

He walked over to the driftwood he had helped Tom to finish for Ellie's birthday. He caressed the wood and it reminded Ellie of the time he had played with her shoes on the beach. The movement of his fingers produced sensations in her body, just as if he was touching her.

'Thank you for helping Tom sand and varnish my lovely driftwood sculpture.'

'It's a nice piece. I'm glad you like it.'

The moment grew in intensity as their eyes met across the room.

'I'll get those peas,' stuttered Ellie, moving away to the freezer.

She handed him the frozen packet wrapped in a tea towel and he applied the cooling compress to his eye.

'Ow.'

There was something endearing about his expression. Ellie felt herself wanting to smooth the hair back from his forehead and kiss his bruises. *Why don't you?* She asked herself, but, inevitably, the old confusions and suspicions concerning Harry rose up to stop her.

'I can't stress enough how grateful I am for what you did today, but if we are going to "care" for each other, can we finally drop the pretence?'

He took the peas away from his eye. 'Pretence?'

'Stop it, Harry. Will you finally admit I was right?' Why was she determined to sabotage this relationship? Didn't she feel she deserved another chance of happiness?

'In what way?'

Ellie's frustration with both herself and Harry gathered pace. 'You were called Ben Rivers in Cornwall, weren't you?'

'Ellie, can't we draw a line under this and deal with the here and now, please?'

'I need to know. I just need to hear you say it.'

'I can't, Ellie. I can't tell you something that isn't true. Harry Dixon has never been to Cornwall apart from one holiday when he was ten.'

It was as if he was reciting a practised script and she guessed that was exactly what he was doing.

He sighed and reapplied the peas to his eye. The eye socket was starting to go purple. He was right about school assembly on Monday. Everyone in Borteen would be talking about his black eye, speculating how he came by it and in what way that was connected to Ellie Golden. A wave of guilt passed through her, but her dogged determination to get to the bottom of the mystery wouldn't go away.

'You are Ben, aren't you?'

'Ellie, you said yourself, this man you call Ben Rivers died in a surfing accident on a beach in Cornwall.'

'No. Unless you have an identical twin brother, you are Ben Rivers. I was there, remember?'

He shook his head.

She clenched her hands. She'd seen enough violence for one day, but she was so tempted to pummel his chest and keep going until he admitted the truth she wanted to hear.

'Rushton knew you back then. I wonder if he recognised who he was fighting? He made a comment as he left the gallery, something about *understanding everything now*.'

'Ellie, please, drop it. We were fighting at too close quarters to notice anything about each other.'

'You don't remember me at all, do you?'

He shook his head. 'As far as I am aware, we've never met before I came to Borteen. I'm sorry if it seems cruel and it's obviously not what you want me to say, but I have no recollection of our paths ever crossing before.'

Ellie went to the cabinet in the corner and rummaged around in a drawer. She pulled out a packet of photographs. Searching though the pile, she held one in front of Harry.

'A picture of me in Cornwall.'

It was a faded photograph of a girl in a bikini top and shorts. She was on a beach, with windbreaks and surf boards in the background. Her hair was tied up, but was unmistakably her mop of hair. Ellie felt strangely detached from her younger self. She handed the snapshot to Harry. She could tell he didn't want to take it, almost as if he feared he would recognise her after all.

She could see him comparing her face with the image in the photograph.

'Ellie, what did Ben do to you back then? It must have been really bad. I like you a lot, and I think that, given half a chance, we could be good together, if only you'd let go of Ben.'

Chapter Twenty-One

Harry had a good look at the photograph and then put it onto the table in front of him. The girl in the photograph was recognizable as Ellie from her hair, but her nose and the set of her cheekbones was definitely different. One thing he did recognise from the picture was his surfboard. It was one of the ones in the background and had three unmistakable green stripes. He knew he couldn't comment. This was dangerous ground.

He had no memory of the girl in the snapshot, but wondered again if Ellie's hair was the cause of his preference for wild locks. The fight seemed to have gone out of Ellie and she just looked sad.

His head was beginning to ache, in fact, he felt rather exhausted. Ellie still wanted confirmation that he knew who she was, that he'd known her in the past, but he couldn't give her what she wanted. He genuinely didn't remember her. It was weird, as he definitely remembered Rushton Jacob and he had a horrid feeling that Rushton had recognised him today. It was when Harry was lying winded against the wall and Rushton had looked at him closely.

His future as head of Borteen High was once more in doubt. As soon as his contact discovered what had happened in the gallery and found out that he knew the man he'd been fighting, it was likely he would be spirited away and have to start again somewhere else. The thought filled him with dread, as he'd started to enjoy the possibilities of his life here.

He was suddenly overwhelmed with tiredness and wished he hadn't eaten the Chinese.

'Ellie, I might have to ask to sleep on your sofa after all. I'm not feeling too good. Or, you could just call me a taxi.'

'Don't be silly. After what you did for me today, you must stay so that I can keep an eye on you.'

Ellie was still suspicious of him and it seemed a terrible imposition to ask to stay the night in her house, but he didn't think he could walk home, even if he wanted to. His body was beginning to protest at the punishment it had received in the fight.

He was surprised that Ellie didn't raise any objections. She dutifully fetched a pillow and a fleece blanket and offered him painkillers, before making her excuses and going upstairs to bed.

He lay in the unfamiliar room on the sofa, which was too short for his long legs. He was grateful not to have to talk any more, not to justify his existence, his name, his job, his self-worth. The room was tidy and neat. The whole house had a pleasant floral scent, subtle, but not overpowering. Surprisingly, the walls didn't have any of Ellie's art on them; instead, framed prints of the work of famous painters hung from the old-fashioned picture hooks. The furniture was too large for the space. Ellie favoured heavy oak old furniture. It was a revelation to him. He hadn't imagined an artist who painted such abstract, modern art would be a traditionalist, but then maybe this house was rented and didn't reflect Ellie's taste at all.

He wondered vaguely where the light switch was located, but couldn't be bothered to get up and find it. His body ached all over and he was sure it wasn't going to be helped by lying cramped on Ellie's small settee. He closed his eyes. It felt right to be here tonight, despite the throbbing sensations in his body, rather than lying in his own bed wondering if Ellie and Tom were safe. Ellie under attack had brought out protective instincts he wasn't aware he had. She must be getting under his skin more than he had admitted to himself. She was a very attractive woman, must be to make her way through the steel shutters he had erected over his heart. Yet could they have any sort of future unless he tackled her lingering doubts? He genuinely didn't know the woman in the photograph, but back then, he'd been so focused on his job and had lived on a knife edge of danger.

He contemplated for a moment what it would be like to be allowed upstairs to sleep in Ellie's bed and then he fell asleep.

Ellie crept down the stairs. She was hot in the pyjamas she had chosen simply because Harry was in the house, instead of her usual skimpy nightie. She always took a glass of water upstairs for her bedside, but in the haste to get away from the recumbent man on her sofa and the disconcerting emotions he caused, she had forgotten. At the bottom of the stairs, she peeped round the edge of the wall, telling herself it was ridiculous to be creeping around in her own home.

The light in the kitchen-diner was still on. Harry was breathing heavily, not quite snoring, but almost. His swollen eye was turning a deep purple with yellow highlights.

Ellie quietly scooped up the peas he had been using as a compress from where they had fallen on the floor. They were completely defrosted. Every movement she made seemed too loud, especially opening the freezer door to return the peas and turning on the tap to fill her glass that seemed determined to ding on every object. She came back through the room as silently as possible.

The blanket had slipped from Harry's shoulders. She put down her glass and pulled it over him, tucking it carefully around his body. She was holding her breath, hoping he didn't wake and find her performing such an intimate, nurturing gesture. When he didn't stir, she couldn't resist studying his relaxed face. He appeared younger, despite his poor swollen eye. His lips were bruised too and she had fleeting fantasies about kissing his mouth gently enough not to hurt them. Butterfly kisses around his neck would come next and then she'd reach her hand under his T-shirt. *Stop it, Ellie*. How could her thoughts see-saw so wildly between suspicion and attraction? She picked up her glass and moved away. After a last glance at Harry's sleeping form, she switched off the light and bolted up the stairs. She was breathless and flushed as she got into bed.

She couldn't sleep of course. Her mind kept replaying the events of the day, a blow by blow account of her encounter with Rushton, the sound track of the fight between Rushton and Harry and the conversations she'd had with Harry during the evening. In the small hours, a vivid video played behind her eyelids of her time in Cornwall and Ben Rivers.

Ellie had been eighteen when she first spotted him. Ben was oblivious to her; despite the fact they had many mutual friends and went to some of the same events that summer. Ellie wondered why her girlfriends had no difficulty in attracting and dating guys. What was wrong with her and why didn't Ben notice her at all?

He had a VW campervan, which was always parked on the beach road. Like so many others in a line at the side of the road, it had surf boards on the roof and his wetsuit hanging from the roof rack. The van was bright orange and a previous owner had adorned the paintwork with stickers. CND emblems vied with smiley faces and flowers.

It didn't matter how many times Ellie walked past, how she wore her hair, how short her skirt or how skimpy her bikini, Ben appeared to look straight through her. She began to wonder if he preferred the male members of the group.

Ellie's frustration morphed into annoyance. Why didn't he notice her? Her only consolation was that he didn't date or attempt to flirt with any of the other girls. She should know, as she watched him all of the time. Ellie began to fantasise about other ways to grab Ben's attention and capture his affections.

He was a master on the surfboard. She'd watched him riding huge waves, dipping and somersaulting, often to the applause of the other surfers. Would he rescue her if she got into difficulties in the surf? Would he dive in and drag her to safety?

If she pretended to hurt her leg on the beach, would he help her to the beach café and buy her a drink? Or, would someone else beat Ben to it? Annoying Colin had started to show an interest in Ellie. She'd have to be careful that these imagined plans didn't backfire.

What if she went to see a witch and asked for a love potion? Ellie had laughed to herself, these ideas were getting out of control. Her imagination supplied moving images of her administering the procured love potion and Ben suddenly finding her irresistible. But, where would she find a witch, if they even existed at all? She was more likely to be taken for a ride by a fake.

Her ideas might be getting more outrageous and desperate, but she had to have Ben hold her and kiss her. He was the one she wanted to give her virginity to. She had made her decision and it became an obsession.

Her fascination with Ben had even kept her in the group, largely consisting of people she knew from school, when some of them had started taking drugs. Now they were eighteen, they could go into bars. The one nearest the beach was most popular, run by a guy called Norrie. Ellie recognised him as a sleaze. He took every opportunity to touch the girls on their bottoms and breasts. It was he who had introduced Louisa and Fran to Ecstasy tablets. Ellie managed to avoid taking any, her parents' warnings ringing in her ears, but the others quickly became hooked. How they acted when they had taken the stuff frightened Ellie and despite the peer pressure she had resisted.

If Ben hadn't died, she liked to fantasise that maybe they would have stood a chance at making a go of a relationship after their brief encounter on the sand or else it would have all been over completely after that night.

Just a one-night stand.

Not even that really, more a fumble on the beach.

Then, he was dead.

Or, so she had believed.

She had spent nearly fifteen years wondering what happened after they had made love and she had left the beach. If Harry refused to admit his previous identity as Ben, refused to discuss what had happened in the past, she would never know. Equally, however much she fancied Harry, she wasn't sure she could pursue a relationship with him on anything more than a superficial level.

They could never be lovers or real friends, could they?

She turned over in bed, trying to find a comfortable position and eventually cried herself to sleep with confusion and frustration.

Chapter Twenty-Two

'Where's Mr Dixon?' asked Tom, when he came downstairs the next day.

'He went home as soon as I got up.' Ellie didn't add that Harry had been walking very stiffly and his face was badly bruised. He'd refused breakfast, drank a large glass of water, asked her to be careful and observant, then left.

Since he'd gone, she'd been sitting at the dining room table sketching designs. Throughout her life, she had taken refuge in drawing and painting. Whatever difficulty beset her life, she could escape for a while by putting pencil or paint on paper. She had wondered at one time about becoming an art therapist, as it had helped her so much with her own problems.

She would have to make, glaze and fire a completely new batch of pots, it seemed a little early to put out the Christmas ones, and she had decided to make the new pots very different to the first lot. She had been pleased with the original design, but it would forever remind her of Rushton and his actions, so she didn't want to make and sell any more of that type or even use the same colours. The new design centred around stylised gold and silver pine cones.

'Mum, shall I come and help you clear up at the gallery?' Tom was watching her sketch.

'Thank you. That would be great. I'm not looking forward to the job at all.' Her pencil pushed a little harder into the paper at the thought.

Tom went to get a bowl of cereal, returning to sit at the table with Ellie. 'Do you think Rushton might still be around?' His voice betrayed his wariness.

'I'm hoping not. The police have promised to keep a more open presence in Borteen for a while. Having said that, make sure you carry your mobile phone everywhere, in case you spot him, but promise me you won't challenge him on your own. He's dangerous, remember?'

'Was he trying to kill you?'

'Who knows what he was thinking.' Ellie averted her eyes, so that Tom wouldn't see the depths of her fear.

'It somehow all seems like a dream this morning, or a nightmare.'

'I know what you mean, but I'm sure it doesn't to Harry Dixon; he came off worst from the fight.'

'I did do the right thing though, didn't I, Mum? I was on my way to meet Mr Dixon for a run when I popped into the gallery, so I bumped straight into him when I went for help. He was looking in a shop window around the corner from the gallery.'

'Of course you did right, darling. Harry was marvellous. He saved me from serious injury or worse. I just feel terribly guilty he got hurt.' Ellie gave Tom a brief hug.

'He didn't hesitate, when I told him you were in trouble he just ran towards the gallery. I think he's got a soft spot for you.' There was a twinkle in Tom's eye and a cheeky smirk on his face, when Ellie looked up.

'Don't be silly, Tom. He was doing what he would have done for anyone.' She rubbed the plaster on her arm, her cuts were beginning to itch.

'Yeah, right.' He stopped smiling, his face becoming serious. 'But why would Rushton be so angry with you after all this time? Why would he risk being sent back to prison by attacking you again?'

'He wanted money. Maybe he didn't mean to hurt me, but lost his temper, or perhaps he imagined he could get away before anyone discovered what he had done. I've also heard a lot of people get addicted to a life inside prison, so maybe he wanted to get sent back.' Ellie didn't want to explain to Tom the background of the money Rushton had been after.

'He was involved with drugs before, wasn't he?'

Ellie nodded.

'If he was involved in drugs, do you think it could have been him selling them outside school a couple of weeks ago?'

'Possibly, although it does seem a long time for him to be watching me without confronting me. Patience was never his strong point.'

Her hair stood on end at Tom's next comment. 'You know if you wanted to date Mr Dixon, I wouldn't mind. It would be kinda cool to have him as my step-dad.'

'Thomas Golden!' Ellie was aware her face was the colour of beetroot.

They walked down to the gallery and, on the way, Ellie was heartened to see a policeman walking down the promenade. She used her spare keys to open the gallery door. She would have to retrieve the other set from the bakery on Monday morning. The gallery felt very dark with a large piece of chip board covering the broken window.

Ellie feared Rushton would have broken into the shop in the night and would be lurking in the shadows waiting to get her. She took a deep breath and tried to cover her trepidation from her son. Nonetheless, she opened all of the internal doors and put on the lights to illuminate the spaces, even though she caught her breath at the extent of the devastation.

She re-examined her conscience about the money she had found in the house she had once shared with Rushton. It had been hidden in several places in plastic bags, at the back of cupboards, wardrobes and drawers, never more than a thousand pounds' worth of notes in each packet. Ellie was all too aware that it must be the ill-gotten gains from some scam or other, but she was packing up the house to move away with Tom. What was she supposed to do, leave the money where it was for the next tenant to find? Invest it for her attacker? She knew that she should have handed it into the police, but Rushton had injured her badly and traumatised Tom. Didn't she deserve compensation for what she had been through? She'd never had a moment's guilt about using his money, or rather, the guilt she had felt was for the poor souls who must have been cheated out of it in the first place.

Rushton wanted his money back, but how could she possibly find such an amount? Would he ever let it go, or would he keep turning up in her life? She was just about making enough to live on from the gallery and even that meant she had to live frugally with Tom. Unless she became an overnight art sensation, she would never be able to repay the money, even if she wanted to. So, they were likely to be always in danger whilst Rushton was at large.

Tom had obviously had the same thought as she had about the possibility of Rushton lurking in the gallery. He did his own search, which included the cupboards, before returning to where she was standing and giving her the second long hug in two days. Ellie decided not to comment, just to be grateful and proud of her son.

'He's not here.'

'You wondered if he was too though, didn't you?'

'Yes, of course I did. Given what happened yesterday, it was highly possible he was hiding here. He'd think it was the last place the police would look for him. He always was devious.'

'Why did you ever marry him, Mum?'

'I've asked myself that question many times over the years. At the time he seemed to offer me protection and a sanctuary.'

'Because my dad wasn't around?'

'It's difficult to explain. I felt stunned when your father died and lost for a while. Rushton seemed to be the answer to my prayers. He was being kind to me, offered me a home. My parents weren't nice when they found out I was pregnant, but they soon came round when you were born. I guess I went for the safety and survival Rushton seemed to offer … but then you know how that one ended.'

Tom hugged her again. 'I'm sure you were just trying to do the best you could.'

Tears blinded her as she took out the two pairs of protective gloves and large black sacks for the debris she had brought with her. She couldn't decide whether to say more to Tom or not. Things had become so much more complicated with the appearance of Harry Dixon, but how did she begin to explain that to her son? His father had come back from the dead, or at least that was how it felt.

Thankfully, he went through to the storeroom to collect the dustpan and brush.

In all her practical preparations, Ellie hadn't reckoned on her emotional reaction to being back in the shop after the attack. Not only was a large proportion of her stock of pots and paintings damaged, but the memories of her tussle with Rushton, his fight with Harry and the overwhelming emotional fear rose up to choke her. She fought against the tears and couldn't stop shaking. Tom seemed to sense what was happening to her.

'Mum, let me clear up. You go next door and paint. Clear your mind and relax. It always makes your mood better when you work. I'll sort out the mess and then we'll need to re-stock so you have something to sell. The news about the broken window and the fight will get around town in no time. You need to use this as a marketing opportunity to sell things.'

'Tom Golden! That's mercenary thinking to take advantage of the pity of locals and sightseers.' The smile was back on her face.

'Yup! But, we need to eat, Mum. You should cash in if you can.'

They both laughed.

His caring attitude and mature thinking brought on a fresh batch of tears. For once, she didn't argue with him. She went into the studio, but turned away from the easel. Instead, she set the potter's wheel turning.

By the time Tom had dumped several black bags in the wheelie bin and swept and cleaned, she was well on the way to replacing the broken pots. In fact, the new batch was much better than the originals.

'Wow, that was quick work,' said Tom, looking up and down the row of pots on the rack, drying before being loaded into the kiln.

'A product of my bit of forward planning at the table this morning. I reckon these new ones will sell more easily than the ones that were broken. I've got to look on the bright side anyway.'

'I've finished cleaning. The worst bit was collecting up all those marbles. Oh and throwing away your lovely art. Do you want to take a look at what I've done?'

She hugged him, keeping her hands away from his back because they were covered in clay.

'Thank you, Tom. You can't know how much this means to me.'

'It means a lot to me that you are still here to tell me that.'

His words came out awkwardly. He smiled weakly, but Ellie could tell he had been badly shaken by the whole incident.

'Haven't you got a rugby match after lunch?'

'Yes. I'd better get a move on. Do you want help hanging new pictures?'

'I'll wash my hands and tell you which ones I want to put up. It's always easier to get them level with two people.'

'Will you come and watch me play, Mum?'

Ellie had avoided the rugby matches up until now, because Harry was on the side lines, but confronted by her son, she had little choice but to say yes.

Chapter Twenty-Three

Ellie stood on the edge of the rugby pitch, hair standing on end, both because of the wind and the fact she was scared. She knew that rugby was a contact sport, but she hadn't counted on her reaction to seeing huge towering members of the opposing team pushing and shoving her son, despite the protection of his rugby padding and scrum cap.

At one point, Tom had the ball and three players launched themselves on top of him. Ellie let out a yelp, fearing he would be badly injured. It was all she could do not to run onto the pitch and pull them off.

Why did people enjoy this game? Ellie couldn't understand what was going on, despite having asked the man standing next to her to give her a potted version of the rules. It was cold, windy and the field was incredibly muddy. Most of the mud looked as if it was plastered all over Tom and his kit, and the rest was stuck to the bottom of Ellie's boots.

Harry stood on the opposite side of the pitch, but he was too busy coaching the members of his team, or rather yelling unintelligible things at the players, to notice her. Or if he had, he hadn't acknowledged her.

Tom's team were eventually declared the winners. Team members and spectators retired to the hut at the end of the field, which doubled as the cricket pavilion in summertime.

To Ellie, the best part of the entire match was the cup of tea afterwards. It didn't taste very nice, but at least it was hot and doubled as a hand warmer as she drank it.

Tom showed her his match wounds, various stud marks on his legs and arms. She winced at the sight of the circular black bruises and scrapes, some of which she could tell would be purple the next day.

Harry came over to speak to her, a tentative grin on his face. His eye was black, yellow and purple this afternoon, giving the impression of elaborately applied make-up. The swelling gave him a piratical air. Ellie felt a surge of attraction and hoped that Harry couldn't read her reaction to him in her face.

'How are you, Ellie?'

'I should be asking you that question.'

'I'm fine, just a bit battered and bruised. I could have come off worse on the rugby field if I'd played today.'

'We've cleared up at the gallery, or rather Tom did it for me.'

'He's a great lad. Did you see his three tries? He was definitely man of the match.'

Ellie must have looked puzzled, because Harry repeated what he had said. 'He scored three tries, sort of goals if that makes more sense. He played brilliantly. And we won.' He did a jig on the spot, as if he'd regressed to being a schoolboy himself. Ellie liked his childlike reaction to the win.

'You've done well getting the team up to such a high standard in a short time. I won't come to see him play every time though, as his mum I found it very difficult watching my son being pummelled by boys twice his height and width. I nearly joined the field myself at one point!'

Harry pulled a face. 'I'd like to have seen that, but sad you won't be joining us more often. We could do with more spectators.'

'You'd have to give me rugby lessons, so that I could understand what was going on.'

'Gladly. How are you in a scrum?' He winked his undamaged eye. She fought a rising blush.

'I led myself into that one didn't I?' She grinned at the infuriating man, aware her face was now bright red. Something unwound within her. Harry was flesh and blood and right here, Ben Rivers was dead. It was time to let him rest peacefully in his grave. She made a solemn vow to herself never to mention Ben out loud again, just to remember him in the deep recesses of her heart. But, could she keep to that promise?

Mandy had been very concerned about the events at the gallery. She hugged Ellie hungrily the first time she saw her after the attack and asked for a full description of Rushton so that she could be on the look-out for him.

There had, thankfully, been no sign of him since the incident at the gallery. She hoped he was far away by now, but Ellie was still extremely wary, especially when she left or arrived back at home, the school or the gallery. She wondered if she would ever relax again. It was tiring being on high alert all of the time.

Harry had somehow forgiven her for badgering him, yet again, about Cornwall; she still couldn't understand why. He always made a point of visiting her after art class to ask how she was and to admire the artwork of the students. They were almost like moths and flames, as if they couldn't keep away from each other.

Ellie recognised how much Nick Crossten came alive during the headmaster's visits to the art class, as it gave him the opportunity to talk to the revered Mr Dixon and show off his pictures. Many of the children, including her own son, idolised the headmaster. Harry was good for Borteen High.

Mandy had now sold several of Nick's canvases. He had proudly shown Ellie his new school shoes today, bought with his own money.

The mentoring scheme had been declared a success after only half a term. The students who had been chosen for the scheme had shown marked improvement in their attitude and level of commitment to school work. The scheme was set to continue and grow.

Even Tom told Ellie that his weekly chats with John Williams were giving him the opportunity to share his views, voice any problems and have a sounding board for difficult homework. She was overjoyed that Tom had taken to the meetings, despite his initial negative reaction. It allowed him to have a male viewpoint in his life, rather than the female-only influences, mostly from herself and Mandy, he'd had before.

Did she imagine that her own mentee, Zack, had calmed down a lot? He'd taken to tying his tie in the normal way. It could be just that he was growing in maturity, but Ellie hoped that having her full attention in the mentoring meetings had meant that Zack didn't feel he had to win attention from troublesome behaviour at school.

The only real cloud on the horizon of an otherwise settled life, as half term came and went, was not knowing if Rushton would reappear, or what his next move might be.

Chapter Twenty-Four

The weather on November the fifth was changeable. One minute the skies were blue with fluffy white clouds and the next, those clouds were tinged with grey and it drizzled. Ellie couldn't believe the date, Christmas was just around the corner and she hadn't even started making preparations, apart from at the gallery, where she had to think ahead. She had been busy producing more Christmas-themed pots and increasing her stock of smaller paintings she hoped people would buy for Christmas presents. Where had the time gone since the start of term?

Borteen High school had an annual fireworks display on the school field. Ellie had volunteered to butter rolls for the hot dog stall. Wrapped up to keep warm, wearing jeans and a jumper and her hair tied tightly back, she had butter on her sleeves already. Her buttering companion was one of the chattiest women in Borteen, Mrs Edgar. Ellie was almost regretting taking on the job.

They were part of the chain of a production line for hotdogs. The school secretary used a bread knife to cut the rolls in two, Ellie and Mrs Edgar buttered them and put them on trays, two sixth-formers took them over to the barbecue to be loaded with sausages and the sales team on another table sold them with a squirt of either red, brown or mustard sauce. Sales were brisk.

A big queue began to develop at the sales table. Ellie was being urged to speed up. It had become almost a game to see whether she or Mrs Edgar, who never shut up for one moment, could butter a tray of rolls faster.

Ellie was beginning to enjoy her task and was laughing and buttering faster and faster, until she heard Louise, Tom's girlfriend calling her name. Glancing at the girl's face, she knew there was something wrong. Tears glistened on her long eyelashes.

Ellie stopped buttering and abandoned her post, passing the butter knife to one of the sixth-formers and grabbing her bag from underneath the table.

'Whatever's the matter, Louise?'

'Do you know where Tom's gone?' The anguish in the girl's voice made Ellie's stomach turn to ice.

'What do you mean, where Tom's gone?'

Ellie put her hands on the girl's arms to force her to look into her face.

Louise took a big shuddering breath. Ellie held her own.

'Tom got into a van by the school gate. He didn't answer me when I called his name, didn't even turn round. It seemed really weird, not right at all. I thought for a moment he was ignoring me, but now I think he was trying not to draw any attention to me.'

Ellie fought to stay calm, but a maelstrom began churning in her stomach. 'Did you recognise the van ... the driver?' An image of the blue van she had thought was following her the previous month came to mind.

'No. I've never seen the van before and it had dark windows, so I couldn't see the driver,' Louise sobbed.

'Did you get the registration number?' Ellie rummaged in her bag for her mobile phone and tissues for Louise.

The girl continued to cry. 'No, I'm so stupid. I didn't think quickly enough.'

'Hey, hey.' Ellie pulled the girl into her arms for a hug. 'I wouldn't have thought either.' She let go of Louise and put her hand on her chest where her heart was beating fast. She had to think, couldn't let herself dissolve into a useless puddle with fear. 'You probably weren't close enough to see anyway. I'll try Tom's mobile.' She took a deep shuddering breath. 'There could be an innocent explanation.' Deep down she knew it was a vain hope. Rushton!

'Tom looked so straight and stiff, as if he didn't want to get into the van. I tried to ring him after it had driven off, but he didn't answer.'

The cold feeling had spread all over Ellie's body and she began to shiver. She tried Tom's mobile number anyway. *No answer*. Eventually it cut through to her son's beloved tones on his bright voicemail greeting. She didn't leave a message. What now? She really needed to stay calm and think clearly.

'Have you seen Mr Dixon this evening?'

'He's on the doughnut stall.'

Ellie made her decision. Positive action was needed. She dialled the police.

She reported Tom missing and gave details of the incident with Rushton at the gallery to add weight to the fear that her son had been abducted by her ex-husband. The officer asked her to make her way to the main school gate, together with Louise, to meet the police car that would be sent to them.

She stared at the screen of her mobile for a few seconds, took another shuddering breath, grabbed Louise's hand and marched over to the doughnut stall, explaining to her on the way what the policeman had said.

Ellie could see Harry as she approached. He was busy bagging up doughnuts. Tonight, he was dressed in faded denim jeans and a light-coloured denim shirt with a padded body-warmer on top. He looked twice at the pair as they walked into the halo cast by the temporary lights near the stall. Immediately, he put down the bag he was holding.

Ellie stopped walking, momentarily stuck dumb.

Harry said something to the teenager working on the stall with him and came out from behind the tables wiping sugar off his fingers.

'What's wrong, Ellie? Louise?'

'Tom's been taken.'

'Taken?'

'Abducted, kidnapped.'

'What?'

'Louise saw Tom getting into a van. I can't get hold of him on his mobile. I thought a van was following me the other day. I've reported it to the police. We've got to meet them by the gate.' A huge sob shook her body.

'Your ex?'

'What better way to get at me?'

Ellie put her hands over her face as another violent shudder hit her. She had to pull herself together. Now was not the time for a meltdown.

'Sorry, Harry, I didn't know who else to ask for help.'

Ellie began to have difficulty catching her breath.

'Hey, calm down. Deep breaths. He might be with a friend. All this is probably nothing. Recent events have made you nervous, that's all. We'll find him.' Harry reached out and put his hand on her arm. 'Deep breaths.'

Louise stood back, turning to tell one of her friends what had happened.

Ellie launched herself into Harry's arms. It felt such a relief to slump against his strength and warmth. As soon as she realised what she had done and in public too, she pulled away, but he kept hold of her arms.

'But, what if Rushton *has* got him? I'm scared.'

'Hey, calm down. We don't know anything for sure yet. Stop imagining the worst. You go to the gate with Louise and meet with the police. I'll ask around quickly and see if anyone else saw anything, then join you.'

Harry was still holding onto her.

She realised he was trying to calm her down, get her to think rationally, but all his words were doing was making her more worked up. Panic rose up inside, fuelling sudden anger. She pulled away.

'I don't want to calm down … I want my son … Help me.'

'I will, Ellie, but for that I need you rational and clear-headed.' He was smoothing his hands across the air between them, as if he could soothe her with the gesture.

'Harry stop it. This isn't about me, it's about Tom.'

'Hey, hey. We're wasting time. I'm going to go and ask around. See if anyone else saw anything. I'll meet you by the gate.'

'But as you said … we're wasting time.'

She didn't feel he was taking her fears seriously and he wasn't doing anything.

Fear and frustration overwhelmed her and before she knew it she grabbed his arm and whispered fiercely in his ear.

'For goodness' sake, do something Harry. He's your son too.'

Chapter Twenty-Five

Harry was stunned. He must have misheard.

Ellie gripped his arm with such force that he had to bite his lip. She leaned forward again to speak closer to him.

'He's your son too,' she repeated, her voice a little calmer.

The whole world closed down to the words coming out of Ellie's mouth.

'What? What did you say?'

'He's your son too.'

Even the third repeat didn't compute in his brain.

'Ellie, how on earth can he be my son?'

Harry was conscious of the possibility of those nearby overhearing and lowered his voice to a whisper.

'You asked me why I can't forget Ben Rivers. It's because he fathered Tom on the beach in Cornwall on the night before he was found dead on the sand.'

'You're talking nonsense. We've had the discussion about my similarity to this Ben person so many times.'

He was saying the words. Looking at Ellie's anguished face. His rational mind told him she was delusional, but somewhere in the deep recesses of his brain, it all made sense.

His feeling that he must have known Tom's dad. The way he felt that Thomas Golden was an equal match for him. The rapport that had built up between them. The way looking into Tom's face was like looking into a mirror. However impossible it seemed, however he couldn't imagine how it had happened, it felt right.

There was no need for genetic tests. He knew, with the full force of recognition that what Ellie was saying was the truth. No wonder she had been badgering him for an admission about his past with so much at stake.

He had a son and that son was missing.

Although his mind was in turmoil, he had to maintain a calm exterior, had to act as if nothing unusual was happening. He was the headmaster of this school. It was a search for a missing child and he would search for any student of the school who went missing.

His son! He felt a surge of emotion gathering, panic almost. Tom could be in the hands of Rushton Jacob and that was not a happy thought.

He had to do his best to shield Ellie from his worries. Sure, Rushton had it in for Ellie and could have taken Tom to exact revenge, but there were other possibilities. It could be an innocent misunderstanding. But, if someone else had worked out his relationship to Tom, if Rushton had recognised him that day, there could be real danger. But how was that even possible, if he himself had not guessed? It was more likely the link to Ellie that had put the boy in danger.

Ellie had wondered many times if and how to tell Harry the truth about Tom. None of those imaginings had included a terrified admission in the darkness of a field, surrounded by people she would rather not know all of her personal business. Neither could she have foretold leaping into Harry's arms in front of so many witnesses. The gossipmongers would have enough to keep them going all winter long.

To his credit, Harry hadn't publicly proclaimed her insane. He'd kept his voice to a whisper and taken everything seemingly impassively in his stride. He hadn't sought to denounce her accusation about him fathering Tom, instead he'd chosen to keep a cool head and to focus on the search for a missing child from his school. She guessed his opinions and questions about the truth of her claims would come later.

They met the police by the gate and related what little information they knew. Harry had rounded up some of Tom's classmates and asked them to recall any sightings of Tom Golden that evening. Another lad had also seen Tom getting into the big, dark blue van, but hadn't thought there was anything sinister in it.

They promised to begin searching, putting out several patrols and the police helicopter.

Harry and Ellie saw Louise safely home, explained to her parents what had happened and then drove around the streets of Borteen in Harry's little sports car. They walked every inch of the beach. There was no sign of Tom or the van.

The beach in darkness could be a magical place, but tonight the atmosphere was sinister, especially as it began to rain. Ellie added a few more tears to the moisture in the air, as they searched mostly in silence.

They went to the gallery, in case a note had been pushed through the door, but there was nothing. The newly replaced glass shone in the street light's glow. They paused to watch the Borteen High firework display from a distance.

Her house was the next stop, but it was in darkness and there was no note or answering machine message, no sign that Tom had returned.

Ellie checked with Louise, but she had still heard nothing from Tom. Ellie promised to update her when she knew anything.

She phoned the police again and they drove to the station in Sowden to make a formal report about what had happened. It all felt surreal. She had to relate the details of the earlier attack and her worries about Rushton Jacob. The officer was reassuring and promised they had put extra patrols on the streets and would view CCTV footage to see if they could identify the direction the van had travelled, although there weren't many cameras in the town. Nothing had been found as yet, but the search had begun and there didn't seem any more they could do. Ellie was offered a support officer, but she refused and Harry assured the man that she would not be alone as he would stay with her.

They returned to Borteen to wait for news. Ellie had left a light on in the lounge, so her house was lit up as Harry drew up at the kerbside. She looked up at the windows and offered up a prayer. Her hair was frizzy after the drizzle and the sleeves of Harry's denim shirt were wet through. She had resigned herself to the fact Tom wouldn't be there, but it didn't stop her yelling his name brightly as she opened the door. There was no note and no Tom.

Ellie fetched two towels and offered one to Harry. She slumped on the sofa and checked her mobile phone for the umpteenth time. A few more tears escaped and ran down her cheeks.

'Probably a stupid question, but you don't happen to have a contact number for Rushton?' asked Harry.

'No, nothing. His last known address as far as I'm concerned was the prison in Bristol.'

Harry sank down on the chair. 'Ellie, we're going to have to have a serious talk about what you said earlier, but the priority right now is finding Tom.'

'Let's have a drink and then go out searching again.'

Harry agreed, but the second search didn't find anything more than the first. They spotted a heavy police presence out searching too. Ellie felt tired and distraught. When they got to her house, she made two mugs of hot chocolate and they sat warming their hands on the mugs.

'I don't see what more we can do ourselves tonight. We have to hope the police come up with something. Unfortunately, it's most likely Rushton who has him and I know what he wants from me. He'll be enjoying stringing this out and terrifying me.'

'What does he want?'

'Money I found after he'd been arrested.' She glanced at Harry. 'No doubt you're thinking I should have given it to the police, but I had a child to support.'

'I won't judge you, Ellie. How much money, exactly?'

'About fifty thousand pounds.'

'Blimey! No wonder he wants it back.' Harry ran his hands through his wet hair.

'I just can't stand the thought that Rushton might hurt my baby.'

'Imaginings aren't going to help us. We have no reason to suspect Tom has been harmed, or will be harmed, and we're still making assumptions that he's in any danger at all.'

She knew he was only attempting to keep her calm, but the expression on his face suggested he didn't believe his words any more than she did.

He glanced at his watch. 'Midnight. I hate to say it, but I don't think we'll hear anything till morning, unless, of course, Tom appears in the next few hours excited about some club or other he's visited with his mates.'

'I think the chances of that are slim, but I'll try to cling onto that thought and imagine being angry with him for not telling me where he was going.' She undid the laces on her boots. 'Poor Louise thought Tom had broken up with her when he didn't respond to her calls.'

'She does seem besotted with him.'

'I assure you it's totally mutual. That's why the behaviour Louise described seems so odd. He wouldn't have ignored her if everything was all right.'

Having taken off her boots, Ellie played with the edge of the pages of a magazine on the table by the settee.

She had no way of knowing why Tom had got into that van. It could belong to one of his friends' parents or anything, but however many scenarios she imagined which made this situation harmless, her gut instinct was telling her things were not right. Tom would surely have told her if he had intended to go somewhere other than the school bonfire party.

'Ellie, we should try to get some rest. I know you won't want to, but we need to have our wits about us for whatever tomorrow holds. Can I borrow your pillow and blanket again, please?'

She knew what Harry was saying made sense. She didn't even question that he was going to stay over. She fetched the bedding he'd used before and left him to settle down on the sofa. Not undressing, apart from taking off her fleece, she slid underneath her duvet. She got too hot and threw off the covers and then she got cold and pulled them back on. Sleep was the last thing on her mind and the novel that had been so gripping to read the night before held no appeal, the words merging and blurring in front of her tired eyes.

Harry lay looking at Ellie's ceiling, wondering how he could possibly have conceived a child without being aware of it.

Even though she seemed pretty certain about his identity, he hadn't yet confessed to Ellie that he had indeed once been known by the name of Ben Rivers. Although, even that wasn't his real name. The fateful night in Cornwall, when he suspected he had fathered Tom, was a complete blur. The night he'd been yanked out of Ben's existence.

He'd somehow been drugged, beaten and left for dead. He'd been told that he'd been found with a surfboard on the beach, but he hadn't been surfing. He'd been beaten so badly that he hadn't regained consciousness for days, not until Ben Rivers was well and truly buried.

They'd shown him a picture of the grave marker, so he knew his existence in Cornwall was finished. He could never return to that identity. Never be Ben Rivers, surfer dude, ever again.

So he'd become Harry Dixon and he had to admit to being attached to the name. *Harry Dixon, headmaster.* It had been touch and go whether he would be able to remain in Borteen given the events of the last few weeks and he guessed, or rather, he knew, that this latest development would be the last straw. Harry Dixon would have to die too, or at least go away or disappear. The thought of letting down the people at the school and in the community weighed heavily on his shoulders.

What about Ellie? What about Tom? If he told his contact about the complication of a son, would they want him to disappear without explaining things even to Ellie? Without having that important conversation? He knew they would. There was no room for compassion. They would take him away without a moment's thought for the mayhem and upset he left behind. Therefore, Harry decided, against his better judgement, he would keep quiet a little longer, even though it could be potentially dangerous to his personal safety.

Chapter Twenty-Six

Ellie had imagined a lot of possible developments for the morning. The mobile phone call before dawn from an unknown number had, of course, been one of them.

She jerked out of the fitful sleep she had finally slipped into and scrabbled for the phone. It was an accident that she knocked the books off the bedside table. At least the noise alerted Harry and by the time the call had connected, he was rushing through her bedroom door. He stood next to her, white-faced and bleary-eyed, as he strained to hear the conversation on the phone too.

'Tom, where are you? Are you okay?'

'Morning, Mum. Yes, I'm ... okay. I'm sorry I went off without telling you yesterday.'

Anger rose in her chest. Had Tom left her worrying for a whole night unnecessarily? But then, he wasn't using his own mobile and even though the words were delivered in a bright voice, the tone was unlike Tom's normal way of speaking.

'Where are you?'

'I'm ... with ... Rushton, Mum.'

'Right. I see. And what are you doing with him?'

'He said I had to go with him or ... you'd get hurt ... badly. I was scared not to do as he ...'

Ellie could hear a man clearing his throat and muttering in the background. Tom returned to what he was obviously meant to be saying.

'Mum, we're on loud speaker now, Rushton can hear you. He says if you want to see me again, he wants his money back. Mum, I'm getting really scared.'

Ellie closed her eyes. 'It's okay, Tom.' She offered up a fervent silent prayer that it was. 'I've already told you,

Rushton, that I can't pay you back. The money has long gone. How did you expect us to survive after you went to prison? You need to view the money as my divorce settlement. I want my son back.' Ellie felt desperate. How could she hope to get Tom back safely?

There was silence at the other end of the line and then she could hear a commotion.

'Take the lad away.'

'Mum!'

Ellie could hardly breathe.

'If you want to see Tom again, there's something else I'd like. If you can deliver this, I'll write off your debt and call it even.'

Her heart lurched with hope. 'And what exactly would that something else be?'

'Ben Rivers.'

Ellie paused as her heart rate increased beyond where it had speeded up to already. She looked up into Harry's eyes. His face was white.

'Rushton, you know as well as I do that Ben Rivers died in Cornwall. We were both at the funeral for goodness' sake.'

Rushton laughed and then his voice barked so loudly from the phone that the sound made her cower. Pulling the phone away from her head to take deep calming breaths, she had to put it to her ear again to hear what he was saying. She would have put the call on loud speaker, but in her panic she couldn't remember how.

'Do you think I was born yesterday, Ellie? The man I fought in your shop was our old acquaintance Ben Rivers.'

Ellie hesitated. 'The man you came to blows with is called Harry Dixon.' Ellie met Harry's eyes again. She couldn't read his expression.

'Whatever he's calling himself these days, I know him. I have scores to settle with him, as do some of my friends.

I'll swap him for Tom and as much money as you can get together. Knowing you, Ellie, the man is probably standing next to you right now.'

She watched Harry rubbing his damaged ear.

'Ha, ha, good joke.' It took all of her resolve to keep a tremor out of her voice. 'So, assuming I can get Harry Dixon to agree to this, how do we do the swap? Where and when?'

'Car park, end of the beach. Nine-thirty. No funny business. No police. I hope you haven't contacted them, Ellie, or you'll never see Tom again.'

The line went dead, leaving Ellie staring at the handset in disbelief. She began pacing the bedroom. She felt drained and anxious. Rushton wouldn't harm Tom, would he?

'He must know I can't pay him back. His money has long gone. How did he expect us to live after he was taken to prison?'

Harry pulled her into a big bear hug. The air disappeared from Ellie's lungs. She lay against him, her mind a turmoil of emotions.

'It's going to be okay. Tom's going to be fine.'

'I wish I could believe that.'

She pushed her head closer into his body.

'He said if I involve the police, I'll never see Tom again … What have we done? … He wants me to bring money and Ben to the car park at the far end of the beach at nine-thirty this morning.' A sob escaped her and she battled to regain control. 'Harry this is hopeless. You can't go near Rushton and I haven't got much money.'

'I've some cash I keep for emergencies. We'll get that from my flat.'

'But is it enough? And how can I take your money?'

'We need to get Tom out of Rushton's clutches safely. We have a little while until the meet. Let's go and get some breakfast and talk. I think it's time for both of us to lay our ghosts to rest, don't you?'

She nodded against his chest and then pulled away. 'Oh, Harry ...'

'I'm going to give you a telephone number, just in case. As soon as you and Tom are safely away, you need to ring it and tell the person on the end of the line exactly what has happened. I should be making that call right now, but it's safer for Tom if I don't. They'll sort out the local police too.'

'I can't believe you are considering going along with this.'

'I don't see we have much choice. Besides, I have a few tricks up my sleeve too.'

'Do I phone the police again as well?'

'This number is enough, trust me.'

'Now you're scaring me.'

'If I'm honest, I'm scaring myself.'

They clung together again, united in uncertainty. The warmth of Harry's body seeped into her as he held her closer.

She pulled away slightly so that she could look into his eyes.

'I'm sorry. I've not always been nice to you.'

'Now I know there was a reason for that and I can see it wasn't simple for you to tell me about Tom.'

'I've never regretted having him. He's the joy of my life.'

'It can't have been easy though. I need to know everything and we haven't much time before the swap.'

She nodded. 'I have lots of questions too.'

Chapter Twenty-Seven

Was this how the loved ones of condemned criminals felt before they were sent to the gallows or firing squad? Huge waves of guilt kept passing through her. She wanted her son back, but giving Harry to Rushton instead seemed dreadful.

Harry briefly returned to his flat, to shower, change and fetch his emergency stash of cash. Ellie got ready while he was away. She had to pretend this wasn't happening to avoid breaking down in tears. It was important to stay as calm and clear-headed as possible for what was to come.

They were the first customers at the local greasy-spoon café. They sat at the most isolated table in an alcove and Harry ordered a huge full English breakfast. Ellie settled for toast, but wasn't sure she'd be able to eat even that.

'My last supper,' joked Harry, as the plateful of eggs, sausage, bacon, beans, fried bread and mushrooms was placed in front of him.

'Don't say that, please.'

Ellie gripped her toast so tightly, she made a hole in it.

'I've managed to escape some pretty hairy situations in my time. All will be well. You'll have to trust me.'

A tear ran down her cheek. She gave up on the toast and threw the piece onto her plate.

'It still feels too dangerous to consider, even if I did think you were dead for fourteen years. I gather you're not pretending any more. You are Ben Rivers.'

'There's no point denying it now. I was Ben Rivers once upon a time, in a galaxy far, far away.'

A huge belt of tension departed from her body. She hadn't realised she was carrying it. He was right, ghosts needed to be laid to rest, as long as it didn't mean Harry would become one.

'Police?'

He nodded. 'Ex-police. Undercover.'

'You'd better give me that telephone number.'

'I don't want to write it down, you'll have to put it straight into your mobile and delete it and the record of the call as soon as you've used it.'

He recited a number from memory and Ellie copied it carefully into her phone.

'What will happen when I make that call? Will helicopters fill the skies and commandos parachute down to save us?'

Harry's expression was very strange as he replied. 'Something like that. I don't want you to be around whatever happens. If Rushton has found you once, he can find you again. You must go, Ellie. Take Tom and get completely away.'

'You mean leave Borteen?' A coldness settled between her shoulder blades.

'Will you ever feel completely safe here again?'

Ellie toyed with a piece of toast again, folding it over and over, trying to take in the enormity of what he was suggesting.

'I wouldn't have a clue where to go. We've only just begun to settle here. I have the gallery and friends.'

Ellie remembered Rushton's words in the gallery. *I could have had you dealt with, but decided I wanted to do it myself.*

Harry handed her a fat, brown envelope.

'I know, but you have to go. This is for you.'

She looked quizzically at him. 'What's this?'

'It's a packet of money I always keep around in case I have to make a quick getaway. I want you to have it. Don't ask any questions. Just accept it. There's money for a fresh start in the envelope. You can give Rushton a small part of it … if you have to.'

Ellie's mind was reeling. 'But how?'

'Don't ask, Ellie. Go to Australia, America, New Zealand. I don't want to know exactly where you're going, so I can't tell anyone. I want you as far away as possible, where they can never find you both again.'

'But is he really that dangerous? He'll hopefully be caught and put in prison again.'

'Don't be naïve. Do you really think he'll ever leave you alone? He'll sit in his cell and plan revenge. You have to take this seriously and go, for Tom's sake if not your own.'

Her eyes were as wide as saucers. She was vulnerable and upset. He worried she wouldn't be able to carry out her role in what was to come without falling apart. She needed to be strong, at least until this was over. He was taking a big gamble handling things his own way.

'Stay calm. You can fall apart later if you need to, but not until Tom is safe.'

He gulped his tea to swallow the big lump that had developed in his throat. Would he even be considering this if he wasn't convinced that Tom was his own flesh and blood? 'Time's marching on. You'll need time to go home and pack some bags, but before that, I need to understand your part in Cornwall and, of course, about Tom.'

'I'll never see you again?'

'Never is a long time.' He stretched his hand across the table to clasp her fingers. 'I can't predict what will happen later, but I hope we can all get away safely and then leave the police to find Rushton.'

'Harry, you'll hate me when I tell you the story of Cornwall.'

'I doubt that, but it doesn't matter in any case now, just tell me. You'll feel better if it's all in the open.'

She gulped coffee and batted tears from her cheeks. He watched the emotions playing over her face.

'Okay, here goes. My confession. A potted version of

what happened in Cornwall. I was eighteen and besotted with you, but you never noticed or even spoke to me. How old were you then?'

Harry thought about it, 'I was twenty-seven.'

'One evening, Rushton's friend Norrie spoke to me about being lovesick. He gave me a bottle of beer and said if I gave it to you and stayed close, you'd find me irresistible and you did. I've thought about it so many times over the years, but when you said about your career being ruined by a drug-laced drink, suddenly everything became clear. I guess the beer I gave to you was drugged.'

Up until now, Ellie had been talking to the table top, now she turned those beautiful blue eyes on him. He kept his face calm and impassive, so as not to distract her.

'I was involved in some pretty deep shit in Cornwall. I was walking a tightrope, trying to keep people such as Norrie and Rushton on side. I was an undercover cop, working to expose a huge drugs ring.' He squeezed her hand. 'All I remember about that night is packing the camper van, but not being able to face leaving my surf board behind. I can see myself walking down to the beach to get it …'

'Norrie told me to give you a message. He said to say that "He was sorry you were leaving, but he knew your job was done." I said that to you and you just grabbed the beer and drank it in one. I thought you were going to leave, but then you turned back and kissed me. I linked my arm in yours and led you down the beach into the shadows by the sand dunes and you made passionate love to me on the sand. At the time I thought I was in heaven, it was the perfect first time, the best any girl could wish for, but of course, now I can see you weren't aware it was me, probably weren't conscious of what you were doing. It was the drug driving you to have sex with me.'

She was talking to the table top again and Harry pulled her hand slightly to encourage her to look up.

'I was your first time? Really?'

She nodded. 'I took advantage of you.'

'Oh, Ellie, Norrie used you. You have nothing to be guilty about. If you hadn't given me that beer, they'd have found another way to get me, they'd have been waiting for me when I got back to my campervan. They'd more than likely been called about the raids at the drug warehouse, realised I was the link and what I'd been doing. I was living on borrowed time.'

'Even before I put two and two together about the drugged beer, I have … have felt guilty all these years. It was as if I took the life force out of you, because I left you on the beach and by the next morning you were dead, as far as I knew anyway.'

Harry realised as Ellie spoke, he could remember more. He could recall walking into the sea and feeling strange and woozy, then being surrounded, but not being able to defend himself.

'The tests I had in hospital showed I'd taken a drug, probably in the bottle you gave to me. They used you to get me drugged up. They were on to me and wanted to know who I'd told about the drug chain and if there were any more undercover cops in their midst. They beat me up and when I didn't tell them anything, they beat me some more. I was told I'd been left for dead with a surfboard so it would look like a surfing accident.'

'But whose body was buried in your grave?'

'I was told later that it was an unidentified tramp found in a river.'

'You mean I used to visit and cry over a stranger's grave?'

'You used to visit my grave?' He was touched anyone would do such a thing for him, whatever the circumstances.

'Yes. I put flowers on the memorial stone too, right up until we left Cornwall.'

'Thank you, Ellie.' He captured her other hand and squeezed them both. Her fingers were surprisingly cool.

'Another thing that felt strange was that you died on the same night as Tom's life began, as if you'd passed the spark of your life force to him. I still can't quite believe you're alive after all.'

Harry held his breath before he spoke. 'Don't take this the wrong way, but are you one hundred per cent sure Tom is mine?'

She looked at him sideways. 'Come on. You only have to look in the mirror. I'm surprised no one has ever commented on the similarities between the new headmaster of Borteen High and Thomas Golden. There's hardly a need for DNA tests.'

'I must admit, he does look like me, or rather, he looks like I did when I was surfer dude, Ben Rivers.' Harry's smile lit up his face.

'The similarity is heart-breaking some days. If I'm not careful, I can fall in to what ifs and maybes.'

'I can't believe I fathered a son with a gorgeous girl and I don't remember doing it. I mean how unfair is that, not remembering the pleasurable bits on the beach?'

She blushed. 'You were pretty amazing that night. I can honestly say I've never had a time since that's matched it.'

'Pander to my ego, why don't you. A man likes to hear he's the best time a girl ever had. It's pretty infuriating I don't remember any of it. Is Golden your real name, by the way?'

'No. Two can play at that game. Changing our surname to Golden was a vain attempt at evading Rushton. As you're aware, it didn't work.'

'Why on earth did you end up marrying someone like Rushton Jacob? You must have known he was a bad lot.'

'He can be very charming and persuasive if he wants to be.'

'But what did he say when he knew you were pregnant with another man's child? I take it he did know the baby wasn't his?'

Ellie traced the edge of her discarded toast with a finger. 'He knew. He lived his life on a knife edge, but always seemed to avoid being held responsible for things. I think he'd got himself in hot water again and wanted the appearance of a settled family home life. A wife and a baby must have seemed like a good idea at the time.' She lifted her eyes to look at Harry. 'I gave him an alibi whenever he needed it.'

A stab of unknown emotion overwhelmed him. Could it possibly be jealousy?

'I believed you were dead. I was eighteen and pregnant. My parents took a while to get used to my news, so they weren't speaking to me. Rushton wanted me. I was scared and lonely, so I gave him what he wanted and for a while, it worked. He acted as Tom's dad. It sounds really callous said like that, doesn't it?'

'You forget. I have a degree in survival. You were trying to survive in the best way you could and you seem to have done a pretty good job up until now.'

'Our marriage worked while Tom was little. I pretended not to see the things Rushton was up to, even if sometimes it did make my hair stand on end. My parents, when they calmed down, were thrilled with a grandson. They weren't very keen on Rushton though. They looked after Tom while I finished college, but when they died, mum not long after dad, Rushton became a lot more controlling. He wouldn't let me do anything without his permission. I guess he knew I'd lost my escape route.'

'I'm sad you had to go through that. Did he try to get you involved in his activities?'

'No, thankfully. I think I was more value as an honest alibi.'

Phew! At least that was one thing off his mind, Ellie

wasn't complicit in Rushton's dodgy activities, apart from by association.

'When Tom was five, Rushton got angry when someone commented that he didn't look anything like him. He stopped pretending to be his dad that day. Poor Tom didn't understand why, of course. It was horrible to see him in pain and bewildered. Rushton started to use more serious drugs and soon after he went off me too.'

'Is that when he started to hit you?'

'Yes. He wasn't in his right mind most of the time. You speak about survival – I was walking that tightrope you talked about every day.'

Harry squeezed her hand.

'Water under the bridge. You can't do anything about the past, the future might not arrive, all we have to work on is right now, right here.'

'That's Mandy's favourite saying.'

'Well it's very true.'

'Why does Rushton want you? How did he ever recognise you?'

'I guess he's angry about me supplying evidence that led to some of his friends going to prison. I exposed a major drug ring in the South-West, complete with warehouse and cannabis growing facility. Made his supply routes dry up for a while. Norrie died in prison in a fight with another inmate. Rushton knows those friends might be interested in knowing I'm still alive. I'm still surprised that he recognised me too, but then you did.'

'True. Are you still an undercover cop?'

'No. It took me a good while to recover from the attack. I still have little memory of the events of that night, but interestingly I remembered more as you were speaking about it. I bowed out of the police force soon afterwards and retrained as a teacher. Went to work abroad for a few years after qualifying, South Africa, Singapore ... I enjoy teaching. It's just a pity I've never been able to relax completely or feel settled.'

Ellie stroked the brown envelope.

'My lifeline?'

'Ellie, you do understand how dangerous Rushton is, don't you? I mean he was dangerous before, but after being in prison, he will have made contacts and learned new skills. He'll also know how to find you if you don't disappear quickly and completely.'

'I understand that and I'm grateful for your help. I feel bewildered and I'm not sure how Tom is going to react when I tell him we're leaving. He's madly in love with Louise for one thing. How will I get him to leave her behind?'

'It will be tough, but he has to go and that means no contact with Louise on social media either.'

'How on earth am I going to stop that?'

'I think if you explain to Tom about the danger to you, he'll understand. Besides, I'm sure his experiences over the last twenty-four hours will have had an impact. Social media is probably a no no for both of you. Connections can be made so quickly these days.'

Ellie put her hands over her face and shook her head. 'I just hope he's okay.'

Harry stood up.

'Come on, let's do this before I have time to consider the consequences.'

'Hang on a minute. Why don't we just give Rushton this money?' She held up the packet.

He pulled a face. 'Do you honestly think that would work? Would that ever be enough for him? Even if it was for now, he'd be back for more in time.'

She knew deep down that Harry was right, this was about more than money.

They left the café and bumped straight into Mandy on her way to open the gallery. Ellie hugged her friend tightly.

'Hey, Ellie. What was that for?'

'Just because,' said Ellie, praying she didn't cry or give anything away with her expression.

'Have you two finally realised that you are perfect for each other?' Mandy moved back and looked at the two of them. 'That's it, isn't it? I've guessed. You're dating Harry at last. Whoo hoo.' Mandy hugged them both in turn and neither said anything to confirm or deny what she had said.

Ellie was relieved that the news of Tom's disappearance hadn't reached her friend. She felt guilty not telling her, but there wasn't time and Mandy was sure to want some involvement in his rescue.

Despite the situation, she laughed aloud as they parted, because Harry deliberately linked his arm through hers. Mandy whooped in the background.

'Tease.' She shoved Harry playfully, then immediately remembered the nightmare they were living in and her delight departed.

He reminded her of the time and they hurried up the hill to the house she had imagined she would call home for many years to come. There was just time to quickly pack before the exchange.

Chapter Twenty-Eight

Ellie packed a bag for herself and one for Tom. Harry had insisted they were only small holdalls or backpacks, so as not to attract any attention.

The whole process was gut-wrenching. What to take and what to leave. She wasn't overly attached to possessions, but she had a few sentimental mementoes of her early years with her parents, Tom's first pair of shoes, his tiny Babygro, photographs. She was being torn in two at the choices. The selection had to be made quickly. It made the decisions seem more acute, but didn't allow her time to procrastinate. Two sets of clothes apart from what you stand in, Harry had said, with a few extra items of underwear.

'Do we really have to leave this quickly?'

'It depends how everything goes this morning, but I'd suggest the sooner you leave the better. You have to be ready in any case.'

Harry helped her to write a note to Mandy, leaving her friend the keys to the gallery and house, and giving her permission to dispose of the rest of Ellie's art and possessions as she saw fit. She asked Mandy to explain to Louise that Tom had no choice but to go away.

She could foresee that keeping Tom from contacting Louise would be one of the biggest challenges facing her.

Harry kept having to repeat things twice, as Ellie veered from one wave of panic or worry to another. He told her to leave her car keys with Mandy's note.

'When you make the phone call to my contact, he'll help you with travel documents. He'll know what to do when you ring and explain the situation. They owe me. When you leave the country, you need to leave from an airport as far away from here as possible and try to change your appearance, even if only with a scarf; your hair is very distinctive.'

Ellie ran to find a scarf.

It felt like a scenario from a novel or a film. How could this be happening to her? Was she dreaming? Harry was trying to give her advice and she was trying desperately to remember what he was saying, despite the emotional turmoil.

'I can't believe they want you after all of these years.'

'Ellie, in my short time as an undercover policeman, I helped put away enough drug dealers to be hot property even now. Rushton has probably already started negotiations to sell me on to another party. The potential threat to my safety increases as the years go by and yet another batch of criminals is released after serving their sentences. There is plenty of time in prison to plot revenge. I made the wrong career choices early in my life. At least the chance to start again with yet another new identity enabled me to lead a sort of normal life. It meant I could teach. It's what I should have done in the first place. Only perhaps I did it too well, or got overly ambitious for someone in my situation and ended up with promotions. I'm a good headmaster, dammit.'

Ellie didn't quite know what to say to him.

They left the bags at the gallery. Ellie took a wistful look around. She had a feeling that she would never see the pots she had firing in the kiln as finished products on the gallery shelves. Having said that, she hadn't felt the same about the gallery since the window had been smashed. Rushton had invaded her world and spread his own particular brand of poison even here.

Harry picked up on her thoughts.

'Your business and your way of life can be recreated elsewhere. As soon as we've got Tom away from Rushton, don't look at me, don't look back, go, make your escape.'

'But will you be okay? I can't stand this. What is your real name anyway?'

'I haven't really got one any more. Right now, I'm just Harry.' He pulled a funny face and looked so endearing her heart felt like breaking. It was so unfair that they'd made peace with each other and obviously felt a connection and not just through Tom, but there was to be no happy ending, no falling into each other's arms, no passionate embrace.

'What did it say on your original birth certificate?'

'You won't laugh?'

'Why would I?'

'Percy Pretty.'

Ellie found it hard to suppress a smirk. 'No wonder you wanted a different name.'

'I know. My mother named me after my grandfather, but you can imagine how I was teased at school with that first name. Pretty isn't an easy surname for a bloke either.'

They both laughed and although Ellie was taking part in the amusement and the joke, it seemed strange to find something funny given the circumstances. Dread was creeping up her body.

'Right, come on. It's time. Lamb to the slaughter and all that.'

'Don't say that! Harry, I don't think I can do this. It's unfair to swap you for Tom. Maybe we'd better ring the police again after all.' Ellie's eyes brimmed with tears, just as her mobile phone rang.

'Change of plan.' Rushton's voice announced.

'What?'

'You've had time to plot, so I'm swapping the venue. Be at the school cricket pavilion in five minutes.'

The line went dead. Ellie repeated what Rushton had said.

'Flow with it. This is normal behaviour in this sort of situation. And as for swapping me for Tom, he's my son too.'

She pulled Harry against her, a fold of his shirt bunched in her fist. She kissed him, fiercely.

Then, as if the kiss hadn't happened, they broke away from each other and walked out of the door.

It wasn't far from the gallery to the school. Ellie marched up the hill again next to Harry. Like in a dream, or a nightmare, she felt strangely detached. She clutched the smaller envelope of cash Harry had prepared.

They reached almost the exact spot where she'd been told Tom was missing at the bonfire party the night before. Things appeared to have gone full circle.

The weather was fine, crisp and dry, but the rain over the last few weeks had left the school field squelchy underfoot. As they approached the pavilion, Ellie was relieved to see Tom standing next to Rushton. Tom, the most precious thing in her universe.

There were two other men lurking behind them. Nameless thugs. Ellie couldn't begin to catalogue where Rushton stood in her world – deceiver, tormentor, bully, aggressor. How had he appeared to be a lifeline when she was eighteen and newly pregnant? She must have been mad. She'd discovered his volatile moods and very bad temper too late to escape; they were already married and she was caught in his web of deceit and fear.

A lot of his behaviour was no doubt due to the cocktail of drugs and alcohol he'd been taking. She'd lost count of the times she'd had to clear up broken glass and pottery, because he'd thrown things in temper, sometimes at the wall and sometimes at her. Seeing him now bought back all of those memories, made it difficult not to slip into a defensive, submissive role.

The tension escalated inside her as she fought her thoughts.

'Remember what to do,' Harry whispered, dragging her

193

mind back to the present. 'Take care of yourself and my son.' He accentuated the word "my".

He gripped her arm for a second, leaving behind a ghost of a touch, and then he walked forward. She stuffed her hand against her mouth to stop from crying out.

No one said a word. He stopped with three metres to go and Rushton nodded his head. He gave Tom a shove and her son began to walk towards her. Harry continued towards Rushton, and Ellie wanted to run and pull him back. She hadn't said good luck or anything. All of the tension had meant that she hadn't thought of it. The omission left a hollow space within her.

Rushton spoke. 'Well, well, well, Harry Dixon I understand? Where's my money?'

'No money. Just me.'

Rushton moved so fast that Ellie didn't realise what was happening for a moment. He shoved Harry behind him to be caught by his two associates, then he sprinted and yanked Tom back.

Ellie screamed. Tom looked so shocked.

'Money first.'

She started to walk towards the group on automatic pilot, holding out the envelope, but Harry yelled.

'No, Ellie. Get away now.' He doubled over as one of the thugs punched him in the stomach.

Ellie continued to hold out the packet.

'I can tell by the size of the envelope it's not enough. You can get me more. You will get me more.'

Rushton started to move towards the silver van parked at the side of the pavilion. Her mind registered that they had changed their vehicle. The police were looking for a blue van. Tom looked back at his mother, his expression grim, his eyes heart-wrenchingly desperate.

'Bye, Ellie. Get my money. I'll be in touch. No police or else. See you soon.' The threat in Rushton's words was obvious.

She watched numbly, as the van drove off, then cursed herself for not memorising the number plate. She reasoned that knowing Rushton he would probably have several plates for the same vehicle to avoid detection in any case.

Shock kicked in and she fell to her knees. Racking sobs shook her body as she ranted at the injustice of Rushton getting the upper hand yet again.

What now? She felt very alone and unsure.

Walking in circles on the field, she tried to think. She had absolutely no idea where they would take Tom and Harry.

No idea what to do.

Chapter Twenty-Nine

Her heart was beating so fast, she thought that she might pass out. Tears threatened her eyes again, but she needed to stay focused, in control and decisive. She had to talk this through with someone.

She dialled Mandy's number.

'Mand, can you meet me at the gallery as soon as you can? It's Tom. It's urgent. I need your help.'

Mandy didn't argue or ask questions, but Ellie could hear the worry and uncertainty in her voice as they made their arrangements to meet.

Ellie walked fast back down the hill towards the seafront and the gallery. For once, she didn't even notice the clouds, the colours or the quality of the light over the ocean.

When she rounded the corner of the alley, she was dismayed to find Nick Crossten leaning against the gallery window. He had his cap on backwards and resembled one of his own paintings come to life.

'Miss Golden. I've been waiting for you.' He straightened up and put his cap on the normal way round.

'Hi, Nick. Is everything all right?' Ellie put her key in the lock. Her hands were trembling so much it took her several attempts. She hoped that Nick didn't notice.

'Yes, I wanted to tell you I'd spotted that man again. The one who was hanging around outside school and your gallery before. The one who was watching you. And being as your Tom went missing last night, I thought it might be linked.'

'Where did you see him, Nick?' She turned to face him.

'He was going into one of the holiday cottages on The Point.'

Ellie felt a strange sensation beginning to build inside of

her. The Point was an area at the far end of the beach with sheer cliffs.

'What was he doing, Nick? And come to think of it, what were you doing over there?'

'Me? I get everywhere round here. Prefer being out than at home, so I mooch around all over the place. Know Borteen inside out. You'd be surprised what I see when I'm wandering around.' Nick looked proud of himself.

'What was the man doing?' Ellie tried to mask her impatience, Mandy should be here any minute. As Nick spoke, a rebellious, excited, almost hopeful feeling was beginning to build up inside of her, however much she wanted it to go away. A chink of light seemed to open up in the general blackness of her mood.

'Another man arrived at the cottage. He got out, shook hands with the man who followed you and gave him a packet. Then, he drove off.'

Drugs no doubt, thought Ellie. Rushton was up to his old tricks again.

'Did you see anyone else there? Was there a van?'

'I only saw the dark-haired man and, yes, there was a big van.'

'Colour?'

'Silver. Would you like the reg?' Nick held up his arm and showed her letters and numbers scrawled on his skin in biro.

'Well done, Nick.' As she noted down the number, Ellie's mind began to work on different scenarios. Rushton might take Harry and Tom back to that cottage and maybe ...

'Can you remember what the cottage is called?'

Nick drew himself up proudly. 'Of course I can, Miss. It's Quarry Cottage. Really hidden away, it is. Can't see it from the road. In a quarry, but I guess that's why it's called that.'

Quarry Cottage, she was sure she'd seen a sign saying that on the road out of the town.

Ellie unlocked the gallery door at last, pleased that she had put their bags in the studio not in the gallery, so Nick wouldn't see them.

'I could show you where it is, Miss.' His eyes were excited.

'No, thank you, Nick, although it's very kind of you to offer. You must promise me that you'll not go near the cottage for a few weeks at least.'

'But …'

'Nick, I need your solemn, cross your heart and hope to die, promise.'

She thanked the boy, whilst making a quick assessment of how long it would take her to get to The Point. She showed Nick out and offered up a prayer that he would indeed keep away from the cottage and wouldn't trail after her.

Mandy greeted Nick as they met at the entrance to the alley. They high-fived. Since Mandy had been selling his art, the two had become friends.

Ellie lurked inside the gallery door. Her friend's face was flushed with rushing and her eyes wide.

'What's happened?'

'Rushton, my ex, kidnapped Tom last night. He agreed to swap Harry for Tom, but everything went wrong. Rushton took both of them away. He wants money.'

'I'm very confused. You didn't say anything earlier. You let me think everything was romance between you and Harry …'

'I'm sorry. It was just too complicated to explain right then.'

'Why on earth would Rushton want Harry?'

'It's a long story.'

'Have you told the police?'

The enormity of everything hit Ellie full force and she slumped against the central display table. Mandy caught a vase just as it began to teeter.

'They know Tom is missing, but Rushton made threats

about their safety if I involve the police, so I haven't told them the latest developments.'

'He would make those threats though, wouldn't he?'

'There are things you don't know about Harry. He used to be an undercover policeman.'

Mandy cocked her head on one side. 'Don't tell me, in Cornwall?'

'Yes.' Ellie's mind was working in the background.

'So you were right. You did know him before.'

'Yes.'

'So, what do you want to do? What do you want me to do?'

'I'm confused, which is why I needed to talk it through with you. Harry gave me a police contact, at least I think it's a police contact. It's the number for the man responsible for keeping an eye on his safety now he's no longer a cop. The local force know Tom is missing, but Rushton's changed the van they were looking for. Nick's just given me the registration number of the new van.'

'Hey, hey, slow down. Say that again. What has Nick got to do with it? I need to get up to speed with all of this.'

Ellie repeated what she'd just said.

Mandy shook her head in disbelief.

'Nick's just told me where Rushton might be hiding out. So, I don't know whether to check the address out before I involve anyone else, to see if Rushton is there or just to ring the local police, or ring Harry's contact, or even to set up a meet and give Rushton his money.'

'Have you got the sort of amount of money he'd want?'

'Harry gave me an envelope full of cash to make a new start somewhere new.'

'Why on earth would he do that?' Mandy's face was full of confusion. When Ellie didn't answer the question, Mandy shrugged. 'Ellie, if I'm honest, this sounds far too big and dangerous to go it alone.'

'I know, but do I have a choice?'

Mandy ran her hands through the marbles in the vase by the door. They clinked and jangled against each other. Her expression changed.

'We need to ensure Tom's safety as a priority, and Harry's. I think the only way you are going to feel safe in the future is for Rushton to be caught and put back behind bars, so giving him money is not an option.'

'I know you're right, but what do we do?'

'Ring Harry's contact, ask for advice.'

Before she had any more time to ponder her misgivings, Ellie located the number Harry had insisted that she put carefully into her phone contact list.

Nagging at her mind was the fact she was only supposed to dial this number when they were safely away from the area, but if she left it any longer, anything could happen to Tom and Harry. For a second, she could feel the warmth of Harry's hug, see the way Tom's hair flopped on his forehead. There was no option but to try to rescue them both.

She dialled the number, her heart drumming a military beat, surprised by her own forcefulness when the call was answered. The man on the other end of the line sounded very wary and suspicious.

When she told him her name, he appeared to already know about her and her connection to both Harry and Rushton. It was a relief not to have to explain everything. She related what had happened to Tom and Harry, followed by what Harry had told her to do before her son had been snatched back. She let him know Nick's information about Quarry Cottage as a possible location for Rushton and his hostages and recited the silver van's registration plate. 'What about the local police?'

'I'll liaise with them. Ellie, Rushton Jacob is dangerous. You must not, repeat not, go after him.'

'I know very well that he's dangerous, but he's got my son. Do you really think I can just sit here and wait?'

'Yes. You must.'

Ellie looked at Mandy.

'But I'm not going to do that!'

'What?' The man protested loudly, but Ellie was adamant. She looked across at Mandy. Her friend had a grim smile playing on her lips.

'You do what you can from your end, but we, that's my friend, Mandy and I, are going to the vicinity of Quarry Cottage to see if Tom and Harry are still there. If we can, we'll rescue them, or at the very least delay any plans Rushton has to move on. It should give a rescue party time to arrive.'

'We're a distance away, but will be there as soon as we can. Do you realise how risky this course of action could be? Well done for finding where they are, but, Ellie, keep away from there. Promise me. You have done enough. We can handle things from here.'

'We are going anyway. I'll go mad if I sit and wait. We'll do what we can. Do what you have to do and do it quickly please. It's Quarry Cottage, The Point, at the end of the beach in Borteen. Rushton wants money. I'm going to pretend to give him what he wants. So if you want to stop us,' she paused, 'or save us, you'll have to be quick.'

Harry had told her to delete the number from her phone once she had spoken to the contact, but the man on the other end of the line, who said his name was Sam, told her to keep it for now in case she had further information to share with him.

'Ellie, be careful and put your phone on silent. I can't tell you how many people have been given away by their mobile phone ringing at the wrong moment.'

There was silence in the gallery for a few moments after the call ended. Ellie and Mandy just looked at each other.

'How much money does Rushton want in exchange for Tom?'

'I found a load of cash hidden in our old house. No doubt the proceeds of drug deals. A lot of money. That's what he's after.'

'I still don't understand how you could have married a man like that.'

'Goodness knows. I was young. We all make decisions we regret later, don't we? It's just some are bigger mistakes than others.'

Ellie grabbed the larger envelope of money to take with her, tucking the smaller one into her rucksack instead. She turned to find Mandy filling her pockets with marbles.

'What are you doing, Mand?'

'Think I've watched too many *Home Alone* movies. They always use marbles to trip up the baddies.' Mandy ran a hand through her hair and tied it back in a ponytail with a scrunchy she had on her wrist. 'Humour me. I need something to make myself feel better about going into the lion's den. We must be mad.'

'You don't have to come with me.' Ellie grabbed a handful of marbles too, just in case they could ever be remotely useful.

'Just try stopping me. You know how much Tom means to me.'

Ellie covered her hair with her scarf and the two friends left the gallery.

'Car or no car?' asked Mandy.

'Would you drive? We may need to follow them if they make a getaway.'

'Sure.'

They jogged round the corner to where Mandy's four-by-four was parked in the craft centre car park. Ellie put the envelope of money in the glove box and took deep breaths to fight down her nerves as Mandy started the engine.

The rescue party was on its way.

Chapter Thirty

How stupid had he been? Harry wriggled ineffectually against the bindings on his wrists and ankles. The blindfold forced him to rely on his other senses for information.

He could smell fabric softener on the surface he was lying on, probably a bed. Waves sounded on a beach somewhere nearby and seagulls called overhead.

Despite his earlier words to Ellie, he'd mistakenly believed he could outwit Rushton and get himself and Tom to safety. He had been wrong. So wrong. He'd been about to dart away when Rushton grabbed him. The man was fit and strong.

He didn't know for sure, but from the little he'd seen before he was bundled into the van, he thought Rushton had taken Tom back too. Poor Ellie. She would be distraught, helpless and alone. He willed her to ring his contact number before she called the local police. Sam would know what to do and mobilise a search and rescue party.

In the meantime, his side ached horribly where the burly minder had taken great delight in thumping him several times.

Where was Tom? The boy must be terrified. Oh, why had he been so stupid as to underestimate Rushton?

There was a bang. It must be the door opening. Harry braced himself. Something landed on the bed next to him and the bang came again as the door closed.

'Mr Dixon?'

'Tom. Are you okay?'

'I've been better.'

'Can you take off this blindfold?'

'My hands and feet are tied too, but I'll try.' There was much grunting and creaking of the bed, as Tom tried to get into the right position to pull at the blindfold with his fingertips. He was almost sitting on Harry. Eventually, he succeeded in pulling it down and it fell around Harry's neck.

Harry blinked in the strong sunlight coming through the big window. He tried to move and waves of pain and nausea swept over him. When he opened his eyes again, a white-faced Tom was staring at him, fear and concern written all over his features.

'Are you all right?'

'I'm fine.' Harry chuckled at the ridiculousness of the statement. 'Or rather, I'm as fine as someone whose been abducted, tied up and thumped can be. How about you?'

'Physically I'm good, but a bit scared and worried about Mum.'

'Your mum will be okay. At least we know there is someone out in the world on our side.'

'Rushton warned her about involving the police though.'

'I know. We have no control over what happens out there. All we can concentrate on is the here and now. Like, can we get these ties off, where are we and can we escape?'

Harry looked at the boy. He was pale and a deep furrow had appeared on his forehead.

'Was Rushton okay with you last night?'

'Yes. It was kind of weird. He came over all step-dad-like, as if mum had asked him to mind me while she went out with Mandy. We had a take-away and he made sure I had an extra blanket for the bed so I didn't get cold. He's different today though. He's angry.'

'Did he tell you why?'

'No, I guess he's not going to confide in me.'

Harry tried to sit up and gasped at the pain in his side.

'You're hurt.' Tom tried to help him sit up, but everything was clumsy with both of them tied at the ankles and wrists. All he could do was nudge Harry with his body.

'Just the thump one of those Neanderthals gave me. Do you know who they are? Did Rushton introduce them?'

'They're Gus and Frido. I almost burst out laughing when Rushton said that. They seem almost like characters from a comedy film.'

'Hmmm. Don't underestimate them. They are baddies all right. I can recognise one a mile off.'

Tom's smile died on his lips. 'Shall we try to untie each other?'

'I don't think there's any point until we make a plan. They'll only tie us up again if they come back.'

Harry thought, but didn't say that he wanted to avoid another thumping if possible. He rested his back against the headboard of the bed and looked around. The bed was piled with cushions that co-ordinated with the wallpaper and curtains. It seemed an unlikely place to keep hostages. He tried to get his feet to the edge of the bed and then thought better of it. Pain radiated through his abdomen and he felt sick.

'What can you see out of the window?'

Tom rolled to the edge of the bed and jumped over to the window.

'It's a sheer drop down to the beach. It's like this house is built into the side of the cliff.'

Maybe not such an odd place to keep captives.

'Can you tell where we are in relation to the town?'

'I know exactly where we are. I've ridden past here on my bike lots of times. Far end of the beach, down a side road. It's a house that looks like a bungalow from the front, but it's actually two, if not three storeys at the back. I know, because it intrigued me at the time, so I made a point of looking the next time I was on the beach. Built into the cliff. It's a holiday cottage.'

'Strange choice for a hideout.'

'Maybe not. You can't see it from the road. Views from all sides so no one could creep up on you and two ways to get away onto the main road.'

'Pity we can't phone your mum and tell her to pick us up.'

'Rushton took my phone off me.'

'Mine too.'

'Why are you here, Mr Dixon? Why did Rushton nearly swap you for me?'

'I knew him years ago, Tom. He recognised me when we fought in the gallery and I guess he fancied settling some old scores, especially if your mum couldn't give him any money.'

Harry wondered if the boy would recognise the name Ben Rivers, if anyone called him that. Surely Ellie would have told Tom his father's name? It was a difficult situation and he didn't think it was his place to tell Tom about his parentage, that should be Ellie's job. He decided to remain quiet unless the need to confess arose. He felt uneasy, but this situation was already complicated enough.

Tom jumped back to the bed and sat on the edge, nearly falling off again as he was off balance with his hands and feet tied.

'What will they do with us?'

Harry saw Tom's lip tremble and realised he would need to try to lighten the atmosphere, so the boy didn't get overwhelmed by their situation.

'Let's just focus on escape plans. Come on, let's brainstorm. Throw any ideas out and see what we can come up with.'

'Sheet ladder.'

'How far is it to the beach?'

'A very long way.'

On one hand, it seemed like madness, on the other, it felt like the right thing to do. If there was a chance to find Tom and Harry, surely she should take it. Wouldn't she always wonder if she didn't act? Ellie had spent the last fourteen years wondering if things could have turned out differently if she'd stayed on the beach with Ben that night. Okay, maybe she'd be dead, but even that might have been better than years of turmoil and wondering. This time she was going to act on her instincts and be brave.

Would Rushton be armed? She'd not reckoned on the possibility of weapons. Rushton had only ever used his fists when she'd been living with him, but who knew what he'd learned in prison. He'd had a knife in the gallery, but it was little more than a large penknife. All she and Mandy had were pockets full of marbles.

The same thoughts must just have occurred to Mandy. 'Did Rushton have weapons?'

'He came to the gallery with a knife, but the police have got that. I'd guess he'll have another by now. He's also got two other men with him, big guys.'

'Thugs to protect him, I suppose.'

'Can you think of anything else we should take with us?'

'Nothing we can carry easily without attracting attention. Let's go.'

Ellie started to feel sick with apprehension. She hadn't thought this through, but if she started to now, she knew she wouldn't do it at all and she definitely wouldn't let Mandy be involved. A vision of Tom's frightened face came into her mind and a surge of protective instinct strengthened her resolve.

Just act, Ellie. Don't think too much.

Mandy revved the engine. The situation started to feel even more unreal.

They drove out of Borteen along the coast road and for once Ellie didn't even notice the spectacular views on each side. The quarry road was easy to spot; the sign saying "Quarry Cottage" was a bit of a giveaway.

Mandy stopped a little further along the beach road in a layby and faced Ellie as the engine fell silent. 'Do you think we're doing the right thing? Should we just leave it to the police?'

Ellie noted the pallor of her friend's face. 'Do you want to go back and wait for me? You don't have to come.'

'No way. If you are going, I'm coming with you.'

Mandy was more like an auntie to Tom. Ellie felt guilty for a moment that her friend wasn't aware of the relationship between Tom and Harry, but now was not the time to begin to explain.

'I guess I'm starting to lose my nerve a bit. I've never done anything like this before and I couldn't bear anything bad happening to you. I'm not normally brave. I'm afraid of my own shadow for goodness' sake.' Ellie chewed her finger, aware she was voicing her thoughts out loud.

'I suppose we don't have to actually confront Rushton. Let's just go for a walk and gauge the situation. At least then, we'll be able to give useful information to the police when they arrive.'

'True. We'll just go for a walk. When we find the cottage, we'll decide whether to go in, all marbles blazing, or run back to the car. We haven't actually committed to anything yet. We don't even know if they are still there. Hopefully, the rescue bid will happen soon. If we're lucky, we'll only need to watch, at most distract the baddies, or maybe the rescue party will get there before we do. Sorry, I'm nervous. Hence the babbling.'

'Let's find Quarry Cottage and take it from there.'

'Okay. I'm going to leave the money in your car for now.'

They walked back along the road at double speed. Ellie dragged Mandy into the hedgerow every time she heard a car coming.

'Just in case it's Rushton.' She apologised, as her friend brushed twigs out of her hair yet again.

The pair fell silent.

Ellie hadn't the breath for walking fast and talking at

the same time. She was wearing the scarf over her hair that Harry had suggested for disguise at the airport. She wondered if she looked glamorous or like a sit-com cleaning lady. It was not a fool-proof disguise, but it might confuse Rushton for a few vital moments.

Reaching the sign to the cottage, they walked cautiously down the track.

Ellie grasped Mandy's hand and squeezed.

Mandy squeezed back. 'It might have been better if we'd been able to wait until dark.'

'I know, but I have the feeling that there isn't a moment to lose. Harry said something about the possibility of Rushton selling him on to another group.'

'I wish I understood what all of this is about, Ellie, but I guess you can explain later.'

They crept around the bend in the road and the track levelled out and straightened. The cottage was set to the side of the track right in front of them. Ellie pulled Mandy against the hedge.

After watching patiently for five minutes, she could detect no sound or movement around the cottage. The silver van was parked to the side of the door, exactly as Nick had reported. If they walked further down the track, they would be totally exposed to anyone looking out of the cottage windows.

They both jumped as Ellie's phone rang out. Her hands were shaking as she silenced it by answering the call, Sam's warning about keeping it on silent echoing in her head.

Rushton's chilling tone came from the handset.

'Now you've had time to think, I guess you're more willing to empty your bank account for me.'

Ellie instinctively began to walk back up the track away from the cottage as she spoke.

'You know I am. How do I get the money to you?'

His horrible laugh came from the mobile. 'As much

money as you have remember. The last breakwater on the beach furthest from Borteen.'

'And Tom?'

'He'll be released as soon as the money is in my hand. I'll ring my friends.'

'How can I trust you?'

'Okay, I'll bring Tom with me.'

'And Harry?'

'He's not part of the deal.'

Ellie toyed with arguing, but decided against it.

'When?'

'Eleven, on the dot.'

Ellie stared at the handset for a long while after Rushton's voice died away and then she switched her phone to silent.

Mandy was waiting tucked into the hedge. Ellie wondered how Nick had been able to watch the house without detection. She told Mandy what Rushton had just said.

'Can you trust him?'

'Not at all, but what choice do I have?'

'It will be quite exposed on the beach, the police patrols might see us and there could be dog walkers and tourists. I wonder if he's thought of that?'

Mandy turned her attention back to the cottage. 'If we could get to the other side of this hedge we might be able to get closer.'

'There must be a vantage point. Nick said he watched the cottage for quite a while.'

She pushed her way through the hedge and Mandy followed.

The pain in Harry's side was intensifying. He was having to fight very hard not to pass out. Tom was trying hard to keep the conversation going, probably because he could see the look on Harry's face.

'Did you know your dad, Mr Dixon?'

Harry jolted back to full awareness, his ears alert and the hairs at the back of his neck standing to attention. 'I didn't. He was out of my mother's life well before I was born.'

'Same as me. Only my dad died in a surfing accident.'

'I'm sorry. My mum married when I was very young, so I had a great step-dad and step brother.' Harry didn't know what else to say.

Tom shuffled up the bed to sit next to Harry with his back against the headboard. The mirror on the wardrobe opposite showed them side by side.

'You know, you and I look so alike. You could easily be my dad.'

Harry didn't trust himself to say anything. His stomach did a strange somersault. They sat for a while examining their reflections. Harry couldn't blame Tom for saying what he had, they truly did look alike.

He felt a renewed drive to get out of this situation, so maybe Ellie could tell Tom the truth. Was there a remote chance he could be part of his son's life?

It was starting to drizzle. Ellie pulled her scarf closer round her face and looked at Mandy. 'What now? Any ideas?' Her adrenaline had been keeping her going, but as it began to seep away, despair and uncertainty reared up to engulf her.

'There's no sign of the rescue party.'

'No, I'm starting to get anxious and annoyed. If we meet Rushton on the beach, we might not see Tom or Harry again.'

'We could go and knock on the door.'

'What! Then what? It would be madness.' Ellie silenced her outcry and ended her sentence on a whisper.

'Well we have to do something. Time is slipping past.'

Ellie nodded. 'You're right … If we have to run, split up and meet behind the hedge near the car.'

Chapter Thirty-One

The women were just about to move. Mandy grabbed Ellie's arm and pulled her down.

'They're getting ready to leave.'

Ellie looked at her watch. 'But it's nowhere near five.'

'I hope Rushton hasn't changed his mind.'

Ellie's head was full of images she didn't want to see. There were only a couple of scenarios which would cause Rushton to leave without his money. Maybe they were panicking. Maybe someone had told them the police were on the way. She peered through the leaves again.

Rushton's two henchmen were loading backpacks into the van.

'They could just be getting ready for later.'

'Phone your contact quick.'

Ellie ran doubled over along the hedge line, until she judged she was far enough away not to be heard.

Sam answered the call on the first ring.

'They're packing up. How far away are you?'

'Five minutes.'

'Hurry up! We're going in.' Ellie felt her resolve returning.

'Do not under any circumstances make your presence known. It's not safe, Ellie.'

'Maybe not, but he's my son. Get here as fast as you can. Mandy and I are going to do what we can to delay them.'

'Ellie, this is crazy. What are you going to do if Rushton attacks you?'

'It's happened before. I'll be cautious and if the worst happens, I'll just have to make it up as I go along.'

'Please. Just stay where you are. We'll be there in moments.'

Ellie drew in a deep breath. 'I know he's dangerous and

nothing about him would surprise me. I lived with him after all, but that still doesn't mean I can just abandon Tom and Harry.'

She heard Sam's exasperated sigh. 'I can see I'm not going to be able to dissuade you, but please be doubly wary and, hopefully, my team will get there first.'

'We'll be careful,' said Ellie, with a bright tone she didn't really feel.

She cut off the call before Sam could argue with her and returned to Mandy.

'They are definitely getting ready to go. I've been watching those two big men carrying stuff to the van.' Mandy was scrabbling through her handbag and Ellie didn't have to ask if she was going to help, when her hand emerged from the depths of the bag with a metal nail file. 'I'm on tyres. You see if you can trip up Rushton, or even better, punch him in the face.'

'Don't put yourself in danger though, Mandy. Stay outside and run if anyone comes out.'

They hugged, waited until the two men went back into the house, then squeezed back through the hedge and darted across the road. Ellie knew she had to move before she thought too much about what she was doing.

Mandy stabbed at a tyre and Ellie rushed past her and rang the doorbell.

Chapter Thirty-Two

'*Ow, Ow.*'

Harry was in pain. Either he had a bruised kidney or something more serious was going on inside him. He tried not to dwell on the possibilities, clinging instead to the feeling of the tightness of the bindings on his wrists and the bruising on his face to remind him he was still alive. He was trying not to make too much fuss about how he was feeling, as he didn't want to frighten Tom.

He'd deduced that Rushton's helpers hadn't known him before. They were much less vocal than Rushton, but no doubt also ex-cons. Perhaps Rushton had met them in prison.

Before Tom had been brought to join him, he'd heard Rushton outside the door, ranting about Ellie and his money, including a threat that chilled him – "I'll get that bitch if it's the last thing I do. I'll enjoy finishing her off. I bet she's been laughing while I've been inside. Well I'll show her."

There had been telephone conversation after telephone conversation with Rushton spreading the word about his captive and starting to auction him to the highest bidder. Harry knew that Rushton had wanted him to hear those calls.

He mentally listed the criminals he'd been responsible for putting in prison and wondered which reprobate he'd end up being owned by, no doubt someone with a grudge, who would delight in settling it. Things were likely to get much worse. That was if he lasted that long. He really didn't feel at all well.

He worried that Rushton still intended to go after Ellie and that meant both she and Tom were always going to be in danger while her ex was at large.

Tom was staring out of the window. Tom, his son. Would

he ever get over the strangeness of saying that? Yet, if he could have chosen a son, he would have chosen someone exactly like Tom. He hoped that Sam would help them to get away, that Ellie would choose wisely for their next location to live and prayed that Rushton would be dealt with in such a way that he could never threaten them again.

Harry's future involvement in their lives was secondary to them being safe, after all he'd not known of his link to either of them until he had arrived in Borteen. But now he knew, he could never forget, or cease to wonder what life would have been like if he'd known before.

He strained to hear if his captors were close by and when he couldn't hear them, he tried to loosen the ties on his wrists, only succeeding in setting off another wave of pain in his side. Harry lay still, hoping he wasn't going to pass out.

'Tom, let's see if we can untie each other.'

They lay wriggling on the bed and fumbled with the bindings. Harry told Tom to try untying his wrists. They could tackle their ankles later. He gritted his teeth against increasing discomfort.

Harry didn't know what his future would hold, if indeed, he had any future at all, but one thing was clear, he had to get Tom to safety.

Ellie pulled the scarf further forward on her head as she banged on the front door of Quarry Cottage.

Rushton peered through a tiny gap, when he opened the door. Ellie didn't hesitate, she pushed her weight against it and took him by surprise.

Recognition dawned across his face, as he lurched backwards. 'You!'

He stumbled, but didn't lose his footing. Ellie stepped into the room, her heart thundering. *Show no fear. Show no fear.* She repeated the words like a mantra.

She'd forgotten Rushton was so tall. He towered over her. Had she really been married to this man? She recognised that menacing look. What had her self-defence instructor said? Strike first, they'll expect you to cower.

There was a vase of artificial flowers on the sideboard next to her. Ellie realised with a strange slow-motion moment of clarity that it was one of her own pottery vases. How appropriate. She grabbed it and smashed it into Rushton's face, plastic flowers showering around them. He howled and leaped back, blood rushing from his nose. Ellie tipped the rest of the flowers onto the floor and struck again. A part of her brain was thinking how strong the pottery was, as it didn't shatter. She was horrified and exhilarated all at the same time that she had hit him.

'You've broken my nose.' Rushton howled.

'If I have, then we're part way even at last. You broke my nose, both cheek bones and one eye socket ... and my wrist.'

He recovered himself and lunged towards her. She ducked under his arm and ran to the far side of the room only to be caught by Rushton's two thugs as they came from the staircase in the corner. She squealed as they grabbed her arms. The pottery vase fell to the floor and smashed to pieces. In another seemingly slow-motion freeze frame she noticed there was blood, Rushton's blood, on some of the bits.

She heard a sound and saw Mandy standing at the door rolling handfuls of marbles across the wooden floor. If it hadn't been such a serious situation, Ellie would have laughed.

Rushton growled and turned round, marbles flew everywhere under his feet. Ellie looked from side to side at the men who held her and knew she and Mandy had taken on more than they could deal with. What had they been thinking? Sam was right.

'Run, Mand!'

Mandy ran, but Ellie heard her scream before she'd gone very far.

Rushton pulled Ellie from the two men who held her as if she was a rag doll. He pushed her and she fell against the table. He grabbed her by the arm and hauled her upright. 'Meet my wife.' He shoved her back towards the two burly men, just as four uniformed men came bursting through the open front door. It was Ellie's turn to scream. The policemen had guns and, in seconds, Rushton and his friends had their hands in the air.

'Are there more of them?' asked a thin man with glasses who had followed them in.

'I don't think so.'

Rushton was cuffed and manhandled out of the door with the other two. Mandy darted back in and pulled Ellie into a big hug. As they stood against the wall, Ellie recognised several of her own paintings on the wall. It seemed somehow ironic that the owner of this cottage had bought her artwork to decorate this property.

'Where are Tom and Harry?' Ellie asked. Fear once more surfaced to engulf her, as she shrugged off Mandy's embrace.

'Search the rest of the house,' commanded the thin man. The men disappeared down the staircase. He remained behind.

Nausea rose in Ellie's throat at the sight of the blood on the bits of vase and the floor. How had she managed to hit Rushton? The thought made her feel ill now the adrenaline was seeping away.

'Which one of you is Ellie?' the thin man asked, but he was looking at her, so he'd already guessed.

'I'm Ellie and this is my friend Mandy.'

'I'm Sam. We need to get you out of here.' He put his hand on her arm.

Ellie shrugged him off. 'Not until I've seen my son and Harry.'

She began to cry, as the tension overwhelmed her. It was as if all of this effort had been useless. What had she been thinking? Thank goodness the cavalry had arrived in time, but were Tom and Harry safe? The pressure inside of her felt unbearable.

She recognised Tom's thundering footsteps on the stairs before he appeared. He flew into her arms. After a fierce hug, she held him at arm's length to assess him for injuries. 'Are you hurt?'

'I'm fine, Mum. Just sore wrists and ankles from being tied up.'

'Thank heavens!'

Mandy grabbed him next and held him very close.

Ellie's elation only began to dissipate because there was no sign of Harry; she'd hoped he'd follow Tom into the room.

She turned to Sam, who had been talking to one of the armed policemen, and lifted her eyebrows in question.

'We've called for a medical team.'

She felt the colour drain out of her face. 'Can I see him?'

'Not now, he needs a doctor. We'll take you away to make statements.'

'Can't that wait?'

Tom took her arm. 'Come on, Mum. We need to go. Harry needs help, he's been trying not to show it for my sake, but he's badly hurt.'

Reluctantly, Ellie allowed herself to be led outside, her mind in turmoil. She pointed at Rushton's van with its flat tyres and smiled at Mandy.

There were several big vans parked beyond the drive. Ellie, Mandy and Tom were led to the back of one of them and as soon as their seatbelts were fastened, the vehicle took off at an alarming rate. Ellie judged they had gone east away from Borteen.

'What now, Mum?'

'I guess we get asked lots of questions. I just hope Harry's okay.'

'He was in terrible pain, he said one of the big men punched him hard.'

Mandy had been quiet, listening to the other two. 'We did well though, Ellie. You were ace. You definitely got your own back on Rushton, although I must admit to being scared that he would hurt you again.'

'It was very close for a minute there. If the cavalry hadn't turned up right then it might have been a different story. But on balance, we were both amazing and I'm glad that we acted, rather than just waiting for news. Thank you for your support, Mand. At least we tried and I, hopefully, have nothing to beat myself up about later.'

'Unlike last time,' she said under her breath. An image of Ben Rivers' coffin being lowered into his grave floated into her mind and she offered up a silent prayer for Harry's safe recovery.

The next few hours passed in a blur. Ellie, Tom and Mandy were taken far away from Borteen and Sowden. All Ellie could see was the looming shape of an industrial looking building in the darkness. They were led down endless corridors into a room with no soft furnishings or colour.

Ellie swallowed down a thought that it felt like a prison, like the sort of place that once you entered, you never left. She kept reminding herself that she'd done nothing wrong.

Sam came and sat at the desk in the corner.

'I'm afraid we'll have to question you all separately and it might take some time. Mandy, my colleague will take you to another room. Tom, I'll start with you and your mum can stay with you as you're a minor.'

Sam went through the events of the past hours since

Tom's abduction in meticulous detail, whilst Ellie tried not to interrupt when he said things that surprised or shocked her. Poor Tom's face was ashen and he was having difficulty staying awake by the end of the interview.

Sam took her to another room for her own interview, so that Tom could get some rest. He could hardly keep his eyes open and snuggled up on the uncomfortable looking bed in the corner of the room.

Ellie's interview was as detailed as Tom's and, at the end, Sam broached the future.

'Ellie, we have grave concerns about your safety. Rushton Jacob is a dangerous man, if you didn't know that already. I think Harry has spoken to you about the possibility of you moving far away. I don't honestly think it would be wise for you to return to Borteen.'

'But, is it really necessary to go away now that Rushton is in custody?'

'I'm afraid so. Harry overheard Rushton making threats about you and speaking to some of his associates about "getting you".' He paused to let his words sink in. 'Now, we can move you elsewhere in this country and give you some police protection, or how do you feel about a different country altogether?'

A cold feeling enveloped her, as if ice had been pumped into her veins. This felt unreal, like the subject of a film at the cinema. 'Harry made me pack bags in case we needed to get away. They're at the gallery.'

'Give me the keys and the address and I'll have them brought here for you. The photos I took of you both earlier are being used to make new documents in any case. Have you thought about where you would like to go?'

'... Australia?' The word came out as a strangled whisper. 'I've looked before at emigrating as a specialist teacher of art. It was one of their required occupations when I researched it, but getting a visa takes ages.'

'I'm sure I can speed things up and we can get you out there on temporary visas to begin with.'

It all sounded too easy, but she didn't doubt Sam could sort everything out for them. The logistics were one thing though, the feelings and emotions of leaving behind her gallery and friends quite another.

'Will we need to return for a trial?'

A strange expression passed across his face. 'I think I can assure you that it won't be necessary. Your ex went on quite a revenge spree when he was released from prison. There will be no shortage of evidence against him. If the court does need to speak to you and Tom, I'm sure it can be done by video link.'

He left the room briefly to send a driver to retrieve their bags.

'Can I see Harry?' Ellie asked, when he returned.

'I'm afraid that won't be possible.' Sam's brow furrowed into a frown.

'At least tell me if he's alive, if he's going to be okay ...' she pleaded.

Sam studied her for a few moments, as if he was considering how much information he could give to her.

'He's alive, but not very well at the moment.'

Alarm jarred her body. 'Is he badly injured? He'll pull through though, won't he?'

'Our medical staff will give him the best possible attention.'

'Am I allowed to send him a note?'

Sam shook his head.

'A message?'

'Best not to.'

Ellie felt a mixture of upset and anger rising.

'Look, Sam, or whatever your real name is, Harry risked his life to save my son, to help me. I know you lot, whoever you are, think we have to disappear, be spirited away in the night, I accept that, Harry prepared me for it, but how do you expect me to ever settle into a new life, ever to find peace and contentment, unless I know what's happened to Harry? I need the chance to say goodbye. I need, what would you call it … closure.'

She felt out of breath after her outburst. Her stomach churned uncomfortably.

Sam sighed, he took off his glasses and rubbed his hands over his lined face. He looked as tired as Ellie felt.

'Look, Ellie, this is a difficult situation. Let me go and speak to someone.'

He took her back to Tom. He was deep in conversation with Mandy, who had returned to the room after her own interview.

'Would you three like anything to eat or drink?'

Ellie was the first to reply. 'A cup of tea would be nice, but I'm not sure I could eat anything after the day we've had.'

'Yes please to a cup of tea,' said Mandy, who was obviously recovering her composure as Ellie was sure she fluttered her eyelashes at Sam.

Ellie felt so churned up inside, she didn't believe she'd ever want to eat again. She lifted her eyebrows at Tom.

'Tea please and maybe some toast?' he replied. As if in answer, his tummy rumbled. 'Lots of toast,' he added.

Sam left and refreshments appeared in a short while like magic. Ellie found she was hungry after all and the toast was gone in seconds.

'Mandy, Tom, there's something I have to tell you.' Tears coursed down her face as she told them that Sam was making preparations for them to relocate. She didn't give any details.

Tom was silent for a few moments as he digested what she had said. 'What about Louise?' His face was full of pain.

She didn't know what to say. How did she tell her lovely

son that he had to give up his first love? She knew what that pain felt like. 'Tom, you know what we've been through these last few days ... we were lucky to get out of this unhurt. I know it's hard and how difficult we are going to find it, but for our safety and actually for the safety of our friends too ... I'm afraid this means we won't be able to contact Louise or Mandy again.'

'No!' howled Tom, throwing himself on the bed and thumping the hard pillow.

It was Mandy who provided the voice of reason. 'Tom, look at me, Tom.' She pulled him to a sitting position and put her hands on either side of his face, so that he was forced to listen to her. 'You are one of the most precious people in my world, one of the others is your mum, but even I can see the sense in this. Rushton Jacob is a horrid, horrid man. Now that he's found her again, he will never leave your mum alone, not as long as there is breath in his body. So, much as I can't bear to see you both go away, I'd rather that than any harm come to you. Louise will be upset, sure, but you are both young, you will both find other relationships in time. I will take time to explain things to her. I promise to be there for her. Besides, I'll need someone to give me a hug too when I get lonely.'

Ellie could tell Tom was calming. Mandy had always been able to get through to her son.

Mandy took a deep breath and released his face. 'How exciting for you both, starting again somewhere new. I wish you both the happiest of lives. Pity I can't come with you.' A tear ran down her cheek. She wiped it away and Ellie could tell she was trying to be strong, to put a brave face on things for their sakes. The thought sent pain shooting through her and a big lump lodged in her throat.

'You have a spare key to our house, Mandy. I've left you a note asking you to deal with the rest of our things. Have what you want, sell the rest. I'd like to think you could maybe help Nick pursue his art dreams with some of it. Sam said he'll act as go between to get money from the sale of the bigger things to me.' She hugged her friend. 'Sorry to land you with this.'

'Anything for you guys, you know that.'

The three of them clung together and finally allowed their tears to flow.

Shortly afterwards, a man came to take Mandy back to her car, which was still parked near to Quarry Cottage. It was one of the hardest partings Ellie could ever remember.

'I'll send the packet you left in my car back to you with this gentleman.' Mandy was referring to Harry's packet of money. She smiled at her driver, but her bottom lip was wobbling, as she hugged them both. 'Take care of each other.'

Ellie sobbed out loud as the door closed behind her friend. She worried about the effect all of this was having on Tom. He looked washed out, grey with tiredness, as she took his hands in her own.

'Go and lie down, Tom. Have a sleep. We're safe here.' She glanced at the obvious surveillance camera in the corner of the ceiling. 'Try not to think about things too much. I'm a little scared too, but it will all work out in time. I promise.'

He nodded and looked younger than his fourteen years. This time, he didn't argue about having a rest. He went back to the bed in the corner and Ellie pulled the rough blanket up around her son's ears and tucked the cover down either side of his body. She hadn't done this for a few years, but it had been a ritual when Tom had been young, tucking him in with a teddy bear on each side of him. He mumbled in acknowledgement and fell straight to sleep.

Ellie sat watching the covers rise and fall. Her heart ached with emotion. Her beloved son, safe for now, but if Harry and Sam were to be believed, they needed to start over again somewhere else to be sure of that safety. It was a daunting thought, but she knew she could be strong for Tom's sake, if not her own. They would be fine. The thought didn't stop that little nervous jiggle inside of her though.

Tom was snoring gently by the time Sam returned. He tiptoed over to Ellie, the gesture somehow making him human instead of an interrogation machine, as he tried not to wake the sleeping boy.

He looked down at Tom. 'I've got two boys, they take your heart, don't they? He's been through a lot the last few days.'

'At least he wasn't hurt, but, yes, they turn you inside out.'

'It's highly irregular, but Harry wants to see you too. I warn you, it will be strictly for five minutes.'

Panic clouded Ellie's mind. Five minutes and so much to say. Still, it was better than nothing.

She'd thought he must have been taken to hospital, but Sam led her from the room and into a different part of the building.

The corridors were grey and bleak. The floors were the same colour as the walls, giving the appearance of some sort of puzzle game. She couldn't help imagining placing a few of her more colourful canvases on those walls to brighten them up. They passed no one, but Ellie reminded herself it was, by now, the middle of the night.

The room they arrived at was small and stark. Harry lay on the bed covered by a thin sheet and hooked up to drips and monitors. He twisted his head as the door opened and she was reassured by the warmth of his smile. She breathed out.

'Five minutes, Harry. Ellie, you know I'm putting my neck on the line here. I'll be waiting outside the door. The medical team will be back soon.'

Ellie walked to the bed, struck dumb by the relief of seeing Harry alive. She went to hold his hand, but settled for gripping a couple of fingers to avoid touching the lines, which came from the back of it.

They stared at each other for precious long moments.

'You're a bad girl,' said Harry, smiling. 'You disobeyed my orders.'

'I know and I'm glad I did. I wouldn't have had this chance to see you otherwise.'

'It was the general opinion of the team that your information saved my life; by the time the team arrived my condition was deteriorating rapidly. Thank you, Ellie. Where's Tom?'

'He's fast asleep in the room they brought us to. He was exhausted.'

'But, he's okay?'

'Yes, he's fine.'

'He asked me lots of questions about my father and told me about his own dying in a surfing accident when we were together. From the way he was talking, and I might be reading too much into his words, he's noticed how alike we look and I think … I think he might suspect that I'm his dad. Does that seem possible?'

'It's probably wishful thinking. He idolises you, probably even more so after the past few days. He can't know for sure, even if he does suspect and as we are unlikely to see you again … if he asked me, I'd have to tell him the story I've always told … which was the truth I believed, his dad died on a beach in Cornwall.'

They both fell silent and Harry wiped away a tear at the same time as Ellie brushed at her own.

'And, how are you?'

'I'm surviving,' Her choice of words jarred her, was Harry going to survive? 'But there's a lot to think through and come to terms with when I have the head space. I'd never have thought myself brave enough to wallop Rushton, but I did.'

'Sam told me the basics. You did well, Ellie, very brave,

if a little reckless. I hope the inner strength you found will help you in the weeks to come. You know you can't return to live in Borteen?'

She nodded her head, wishing she'd combed her hair. 'Neither can you.'

'It's a pity. I was enjoying being Harry Dixon, the headmaster of Borteen High. We haven't long, Ellie. Live a happy life and paint lots of pictures of me running across the beach.'

She grinned, despite the tears that came flooding to her eyes. She wiped them away with the back of her hand, she wanted to see Harry clearly. 'You guessed it was you in the picture? That image will be forever etched on my mind.'

'Mine too. You can't tell me exactly where you are heading, but which continent please? So I can think of you fondly in the right direction.'

'Australia. Sam thinks he can accelerate a visa for us, with me as a specialist art teacher. I almost applied a few years back, when I found that was on the list of wanted occupations.' It actually sounded a logical move when she talked about it. 'Tom will like the surfing there if he's anything like his father.'

'Take care of each other. I won't tell you to look after him, as he's rapidly becoming a man. He's more likely to look after you.'

The door opened. Ellie gripped Harry's fingers more tightly.

'Are you going to be okay?'

'Internal bruising, thanks to Rushton. I'm sure I'll be fine.' He tried to smile, but it became a grimace as pain registered in his face. Ellie knew he was glossing over his injuries, but there wasn't time to ask him more.

Ellie ignored Sam clearing his throat by the door. 'I don't want to leave you, Harry.'

'But, you must. Be safe.' The corners of his mouth lifted,

but it was like the first time she met him as Harry Dixon, the smile didn't quite make it to his eyes.

'I'd like you to know that I like Harry Dixon even more than I did Ben Rivers.'

He swallowed. 'Hold that thought. I'm very honoured, to be liked twice by you.' He put a stress on the word "like".

'More than *like*. Come with us.'

He smiled. It was a weaker smile than before. He was getting tired. He didn't need to reply. He wasn't fit to go anywhere.

She brushed her lips over his, then kissed his forehead, trying to capture the warmth and scent of him before she turned reluctantly for the door. She didn't dare look back or she wouldn't have made it out of the room. The lump in her throat threatened to overwhelm her and she could hardly put one foot in front of the other.

Ellie followed Sam down the long corridors again. He glanced around him almost nervously, as if he expected them to be caught by someone at any moment. She tried not to break down in tears, as she knew Sam was desperate to get her back to their room.

Tom was still sleeping soundly.

'Thank you, Sam. That meant a lot to me.' The tears had begun to escape, flowing freely down her face.

'I'm sure it meant a lot to Harry too. I'll leave you to rest. Try to get some sleep. You have a long journey ahead.'

When Sam had gone, Ellie curled up on the other side of the bed to Tom and cried silent tears into the musty-smelling pillow. How was she going to find the strength for a new life after this? But then, she'd carried Ben in her heart for all of these years, so why not Harry?

Was she destined to be plagued by might-have-beens?

Chapter Thirty-Three

One Year Later ...

He watched from a distance.

Having pulled all the strings and favours he could to discover their location, he didn't just want to go blundering into their lives, not after this long. He had to be sure he'd be welcome. If necessary, he could just disappear again and they would be none the wiser that he'd been here. He didn't have to take up the job he'd secured at the high school. He could always return to England and start again, however unappealing that option might be.

He'd spent a year trying to recover, to move on, trying to forget, but he hadn't been able to stop thinking about them on the other side of the world.

His son looked relaxed here, tanned, his hair longer and bleached by the sun, even more the spitting image of himself when he was younger. Judging by the steady flow of young adults to the door of the gallery with the house above, Tom, or rather Lucas, as he was now known, was popular and had plenty of friends.

Lucas left early each morning on his bike, a book bag slung across his shoulders. He always yelled bye to his mum and whistled on his way to school. He had never seemed this happy in Borteen. He'd had his fifteenth birthday in Australia. *Fifteen already*. He was almost a grown man.

Ellie, or rather Freya Wheal, as she was now called, was tanned too, her wayward hair long and uncontrolled. The sight of it still made his heart lurch, as it had that first day at Borteen High.

He had to be sure she hadn't set up home with a new man or had a steady boyfriend, before he revealed himself, but so far things were looking good. He felt hopeful.

The Wheal Gallery was full of the distinctive paintings and pottery he had come to associate with her. Freya, he tested the name on his tongue. It suited her. Her trademark "man running on the beach" pictures featured regularly in the window display of the gallery. *I've been immortalised.*

Rushton Jacob had been sent back to prison with a reasonably long sentence for abduction, grievous bodily harm and various drug-related offences.

It worried him that he had found Freya and Lucas on the other side of the world relatively easily. If he could, couldn't someone else? Someone paid by Rushton. But then, if all went to plan, he intended to be close by to protect them.

How would Ell ... Freya react if he did make himself known? He'd rehearsed so many versions of the expression on her face and the words she would say, that he was driving himself mad. How would he convince her that he'd come to Australia for both of them, not just to be close to his son?

Freya counted her blessings every day, but especially today, the first anniversary of their arrival in Australia. When they'd found themselves on a plane to Sydney with new identities, she couldn't have imagined anything better than the lives they were now living.

She and Lucas had discussed their name changes before boarding the flight, in whispers while they were sitting at the boarding gate. They had decided that the only way they would ever be convincing was if they ceased to use the names Ellie and Tom straight away and used their new names all of the time, even when they were alone together. So, Ellie and Tom Golden had become Freya and Lucas Wheal.

The organisation that had rescued Harry, which she never did discover the name of, had supplied the flight tickets, arranged a short stay rental in a suburb of Sydney and sorted out any red tape so that she could start teaching at a school part time and begin a gallery business in Australia.

They'd explored the city, enjoying a couple of weeks acting like tourists; visiting the beaches, the Opera House, Taronga Zoo, walking over the famous Sydney harbour bridge and taking ferry rides around the harbour. The heat was difficult to get used to and they had to sip water all of the time to remain hydrated. The scenery and views were amazing. She felt as if her eyes were standing out on stalks every day with the sensory overload and inspiration for her artwork.

To begin with, she hadn't been able to stop herself scanning the crowds for Rushton or his cronies. Even though she'd tried not to unsettle her son, she still didn't feel completely safe and, at first, her new identity felt odd, as if she was wearing an outfit that didn't fit.

There was, however, a freedom associated with her new name. It had been truly like being born again. She'd had the opportunity to choose a new character and way of living. *I am Freya Wheal*, she kept repeating to herself, dreading the time someone called her name, in case she didn't recognise it and didn't respond, or she called her son Tom by mistake. Her fears had been unfounded and that had never happened, or rather she'd managed to stop herself up to now. A year on, she didn't have to even think. They were totally Freya and Lucas even in her dreams.

She wanted to scan British newspaper websites for any news of a trial or conviction for Rushton Jacob, but had convinced herself that focusing on his name could bring him back into their lives, so she resisted. Somehow, although she never advocated violence, making his nose bleed had put to bed a lot of the demons that had tormented her for years. She felt free from the shadow that had dogged her, free to make a new start and live life to the full.

It was, on one hand, very exciting to go to a new country and start a new life; on the other, there was still the ache and flatness associated with what they had left behind and the knowledge that she would never see her friend Mandy or, more importantly, Harry again. She would never know if they could have made a go of a relationship born of their fledgling friendship.

Would she ever dare tell Lucas about his connection to Harry? She believed that it would be too cruel to do so, when he would never see his father again. Better to let him continue to believe that his father died in a surfing accident on a Cornish beach on the other side of the world. Even if she told her son the truth, he would be unlikely to be able to trace Harry, as undoubtedly, he too would be living in a new place with a new name, identity and maybe, a sick feeling rose to her throat, romancing a new woman. She shook her head to dislodge that thought.

Freya had been stunned about how much money had been in the envelope Harry had given to her. Where had it come from? Why had he given her so much? Then again, it gave her freedoms she might otherwise not have enjoyed.

She discovered the shop with living accommodation above it, close to a beach, in the newspaper and everything had gone so smoothly with the move that she was convinced they were meant to be there. The shop had nearly the same layout as the one in Borteen and was perfect for her gallery and studio. There was even an outhouse in the yard to house a pottery kiln.

When they returned for a second viewing, Freya had turned to Lucas with shining eyes, believing this to be the right place for their new start, but she needed him to be convinced too.

'What do you think?' She'd asked.

'I think it's perfect.' Lucas became serious for a moment and hugged her tightly. 'We're going to be all right here in Australia, aren't we, Mum?'

'I do believe we are.'

'Can I get a bike? I can keep it in the yard.'

'I might even buy one for myself.'

Lucas pulled a face. He'd never seen her ride a bike.

The area was criss-crossed by safe cycling paths. There were parks, shops and cafés nearby. The estate agent had described it as an up-and-coming area, with new families and businesses moving there because it was affordable.

Their house was comfortable and it was lovely having the gallery underneath, rather than a journey away. The rooms had been sparse to begin with as they had arrived with hardly any belongings from England. She was gradually adding to their possessions, but she didn't want to overcrowd the space.

The balcony upstairs had intricate wrought iron work, like many of the buildings in the area. Freya enjoyed tending her balcony pots and experimenting with new Australian plants and seeds.

The only possessions she truly missed from her old life were her rocking chair and the gorgeous piece of driftwood Harry had scavenged from the beach and helped her son to sand and varnish for her birthday. She hadn't found the right replacement rocking chair yet, but she would. She had a photo of the wooden birthday sculpture on her phone and had to be content with that, but it wasn't the same as running her hand along the smooth wood and feeling connected to Harry.

One thing she firmly believed in was the adaptability of the human race. On that first day in Australia, she had made promises to herself that a year on she had largely fulfilled. She'd vowed that they would adapt to their new names, that they would live in their new country wholeheartedly and learn its customs and ways, that they would make new friends, try new activities, laugh, sing and that she would have an art gallery again to sell her paintings and pottery.

It had made things easier that her son had settled here

in a way he never did in Borteen. His new school was on a modern campus a short cycle ride away from the house and after only the second day, a blond-haired lad in shorts came to call, asking if he wanted to play volleyball on the beach.

Lucas had asked if he could grow his hair longer and was tanned and tall in his Aussie school uniform. He laughed more than she remembered in England and his laughter gladdened her heart. He'd stopped talking about Louise, his first love, but Ellie knew he would never forget her. They'd both avoided social media, beyond what was necessary to promote the business.

He'd also taken to playing electric guitar and they would spend many happy hours with Lucas strumming and Freya singing along to his tunes. They hardly watched any television.

Lucas was thriving and Freya knew in her heart that he would grow up, finish his education, get a job and have his own family in Australia.

The shop had done well from day one. She had to paint as often as she could to keep up with demand. The most popular paintings were, of course, her paintings of a man running on the beach. The only problem with painting these images was that Harry was never far from her mind.

She ran specialist art classes at two schools in the area and had several mentees already, who she was coaching for art college entrance exams.

The beach near to the house was amazing. She felt as if she had been transported to paradise. If she was honest, there was one thing missing and that was a special man in her life. Several tanned Aussies of their acquaintance had shown an interest in her and one flirted outrageously, but Freya couldn't yet let go and relax into a romance. She would be ready one day, but not just yet.

Eventually, she might find a man to share her new world. However, she was certain that part of her heart would always belong to the man who had once been Ben Rivers and also Harry Dixon. She'd been besotted by Ben, but truly believed she could have loved Harry. Freya Wheal had much to be thankful for and hope for the future, but deep in her heart, she would never forget her past.

Too much pondering and reminiscing had lowered her mood. She had a sudden urge to be out in the elements, away from other people, away from the gallery. She locked the door of the shop and walked the short way to the beach. As always, she looked for inspiration everywhere and stopped to take a few photographs on her phone of things that caught her eye – a pattern on the concrete paving, an aboriginal styled graffiti painting on a wall.

Reaching the beach, she took deep gulps of sea air and stood watching the seabirds circling the sand. The beach was deserted apart from an elderly man with a dog far away by the rocks. The tide was a long way out. The wind whipped her hair in her face, but she didn't care.

She had a sudden desire to shout to the sky, but twirled around instead, spreading her arms wide.

Happy one year in Australia birthday, Freya Wheal. I love Australia. I love my new life.

Giggling to herself, she wiggled her toes in the sand and watched a man running along by the distant shoreline. He wore blue shorts and an orange T-shirt. The similarities to another man on that far away beach in Borteen tore at her heart. He raised his hand in greeting and she waved back.

Harry was never far from her mind. Before she'd realised she'd done it, she'd written his name in the sand with her toe.

As always when she left the beach, she offered up a silent prayer for the well-being of her friends in Borteen, especially Mandy.

Returning to the studio, she set to work on a new series of paintings inspired by the beach and her impressions of

Australia so far. These pictures had an Aboriginal influence, using animal shapes and coloured dots. She still signed her name with the stylised signature she had always used, but then no one had ever been able to tell what it said in any case, so they wouldn't guess it stood for Ellie.

The day sped by and before she knew it, Lucas was back from school. Freya made him stand back to back with her by the mirror in the studio to confirm he had indeed grown again and was taller than her by at least five centimetres.

He told her about his day, excitement in his voice, what he had learned in lessons and what he was expected to do for homework. She carried on painting as they talked. He looked relaxed and tanned and the sight warmed her heart.

They had a ritual of sharing the worst and best things that had happened to them each day.

'Worst thing?'

He looked thoughtful. 'Perry told Veronica Lewis that I fancied her.'

'And do you?'

'Mum please, she's not my type at all.'

'Best thing?'

'I've been chosen for the football A-team.'

'Well done, love.' She ruffled his hair. 'Presumably that's Aussie football?'

He nodded.

'You realise we've been in Sydney exactly one year today?'

'I knew it was about that, but couldn't remember the exact date.'

She noted the way his sentences finished with a high note now in true Aussie style, but then she often caught herself doing the same.

'I've planned a special tea to celebrate.'

She loved these times of closeness, as Lucas wanted to be independent more often than not these days.

'Right, I'd better get my homework finished and our special tea eaten, some of the lads want me to go fishing tonight.'

'It won't be too late will it? You've school tomorrow.'

'Mum, I'm not eleven, I'm fifteen.'

'I forget, but you'll always be my baby.'

He pulled a face. 'Mum!'

Fifteen, how had that happened?

She looked proudly at her tall, long-haired son. He was handsome; there was no doubt about that. The cleft in his chin becoming more pronounced as he got older. He was heart-breakingly like his father. How could she ever forget Harry when she had his spitting image with her every day to remind her of what she had lost? She resumed painting to cover up the emotion passing over her heart. She felt particularly sentimental today after her reflections on the beach.

Lucas turned back, 'By the way, Mum, some funny news. There's a new sports teacher starting at the school next week. His name made us laugh so much. I don't know how we're going to keep a straight face when we meet him or during lessons.'

'What's his name then?'

'Mr Pretty. Have you ever heard such a bizarre name?'

Freya dropped her brush, a great splodge of orange spattered on the wooden boards of the floor. Her heart had taken up a lurching beat of premonition. Harry's birth name had been Percy Pretty. She would never ever forget that. Was the new teacher's name too much of a coincidence? It couldn't be, could it?

'What's the matter? Are you okay, Mum?'

'Yes, sorry. It just gave me a shock, as I knew someone with that name in the past, but it couldn't possibly be him.'

Chapter Thirty-Four

Alex knew his appointment at the high school had been announced to the students. *Alex, Alex, Alex.* He had to keep repeating the name to get it into his head. Would news have got back to Freya about the new sports teacher, Alex Pretty? Would she have put two and two together?

He didn't normally think twice about what to wear, but today, he hesitated in front of his wardrobe. He settled on a crisp short-sleeved shirt and his newest shorts.

The worst thing was not knowing how she was going to react to his reappearance.

Casting an eye around the small rented flat, he knew exactly where he would hang the picture he was about to buy. He could visualise exactly what it would look like hanging there. A piece of Elli ... no, Freya on his wall.

Deep breath, Alex. Let's go. You know what you have to do.

Walking the short distance to the Wheal Gallery, he tried to imagine how he would handle this, but his mind was blank. He'd have to make it up as he went along.

He thought his heart might stop as he pushed open the gallery door and the bell above it rang to announce his entrance.

Lucas sat at a desk reading a magazine. His head snapped up as the bell sounded and his eyes opened wide, very wide, then his mouth dropped open.

'Har ...' he began.

'Good afternoon,' Alex strode over to the desk and extended his hand. 'Alex Pretty.'

Lucas looked at his hand with his eyes still abnormally wide and confusion on his face. He appeared to be struck dumb.

Alex looked around the gallery to confirm they were alone and smiled broadly.

'We're not in danger again, are we?' gabbled the teenager.

'No, no, not at all. I've just moved to the area and came to buy a picture for the bare walls of my rented flat.' He grinned again.

Lucas grinned back.

'You're my new sports teacher, aren't you?'

'Sure am.'

Lucas punched the air and laughed. 'Wicked!'

At least his son was pleased to see him. One down, tick, but he had yet to see Ell ... Freya.

Freya paused on the stairs, listening to the conversation in the gallery. Had she heard right? It was like being transported back in time. Harry had said similar words before in her shop in Borteen. Her heart began to thump and her mouth went dry. She paused to hear enough to be sure, to hear his voice. She'd been painting and scrubbed ineffectually at a paint blob on her shirt. She realised she had paint on her hair too. Oh well, no time to change.

Coming down the last step and around the corner into the gallery, she was greeted by the sight of Lucas and Harry embracing. Both had tears on their cheeks.

Lucas spotted her over Alex's shoulder. 'Mum, look who's here. Meet my new sports teacher, Alex Pretty.'

Alex disengaged himself from Lucas and turned to Freya. 'Hello.'

'Hello ... Alex.' She tested the name on her tongue, as she looked him up and down. She didn't trust herself to say anything else and felt frozen to the spot.

'I came to buy a picture of a man running on the beach ... if you have one.'

'It was you, wasn't it, running on the beach the other day?'

239

'Yes.' He smiled, but a wariness had crept into his face, as if he feared she wasn't pleased to see him. 'Was that you at the top of the beach?'

She nodded.

'What a coincidence. Fate even. Seeing a woman watching me, I was reminded of another time at Borteen and couldn't help but wave.'

'I wanted to believe it was you, but didn't allow myself to hope.' The tension overwhelmed her and she began to cry.

Then, his arms were around her, pulling her close. He felt warm and strong as he supported her body, wiping her tears away with his fingers, stroking her hair.

Lucas had retreated to lean against the desk.

When she'd calmed down a little, she turned to her son. 'Lucas, would you go and get us some coffees?'

'It's okay, Mum. I get that you want some time alone. Lattes all round?'

Alex and Freya nodded in unison. Lucas turned the gallery sign to closed as he darted off to the coffee shop down the road.

She turned back to Alex. 'I can't believe you're here.'

'I can hardly believe it myself.'

'Are you okay? I mean after the beating you took?'

'I'm fine. I was quite poorly due to internal bleeding and bruising. It took a while to recover fully.' His hand moved to his abdomen, as if he was remembering the pain.

She grimaced. 'I've thought of you so many times.'

'And I've been sending thoughts back to you too – always in the direction of Australia.'

She traced a finger around his face, drinking in his features and revelling in the warmth of his skin. When she'd finished, he echoed her movements by moving his finger around her face, stopping to rub gently at a patch of paint. Her body tingled at his touch. They moved closer, but neither seemed to be able to make the final move that would lock their lips together. Freya could feel sparks of electricity passing between them. She moved forward at the same time as he did.

There was silence for a while as they made up for lost time. Freya kissed Alex, the only man she had ever truly loved, as if she would never get another chance. They seemed to fit together perfectly, his kiss made her breathless and her body longed to get closer.

She clung to him. 'I don't care what your name is, you're the only man I have ever wanted.'

He was whispering softly into her ear and making her senses go into overdrive. 'It's so lovely to be able to hold you and kiss you properly without restraint or suspicion getting in the way. Everything finally open between us.'

The gallery door bell sounded as Lucas came back with the coffee. They reluctantly disentwined, but kept hold of each other's hands as if they couldn't bear to break contact after finding each other again.

Lucas gave out the coffees, raising his eyes heavenwards. 'You two!' But, his broad smile belied his words.

'I was just telling Alex about how we came here on a visa based on my art teaching.'

'Yeah right!' nodded Lucas.

Freya felt her face blush red. 'I teach at two after-school clubs and do specialist teaching when required, especially for pottery. I still run school art competitions and am mentoring again because I found it so rewarding.'

'Sounds a busy life. Have you got room for a new friend?'

She couldn't answer, as the lump in her throat was so large.

Lucas appeared to ignore what Freya was saying. 'Fetching the coffees, I was thinking back to a conversation we had in Borteen when things looked bad for us both. I commented how alike we look and that you could pass for my dad. You had such a strange expression on your face. You are, aren't you?'

Freya and Alex leaped apart and turned as one towards him.

She spoke first. She knew she needed to tell her son the truth, no matter how she worried what he would think. 'Yes, Lucas, this man, by whatever name we call him, is your dad. I thought he was dead for many years, which is why it was such a shock when I met him again in Borteen.'

'And I truly didn't know you were mine, didn't even know I had fathered a child, until you went missing on the night of the firework display.'

They all stood looking at each other for long moments.

Alex broke the silence. 'How do you feel about all this?'

'I feel as if I should be angry or something with both of you, but if I'm totally honest, I think it's great having a cool guy, even if his surname is weird, for my dad. In fact, it's great having a dad. I've never had one before.'

Freya looked from one to the other and laughed. 'You are very alike, especially since Lucas has grown. How did you find us?'

'I pulled every string and favour imaginable.'

'You couldn't bear not to be with your son?' She glanced across at Lucas. His face was full of joy. She knew that his reaction could have been so very different. She was pleased, but then a little disappointed that Alex hadn't come to Australia for her.

Alex tugged her toward him and put his hands either side of her face, so she had no choice but to look into his eyes, his big brown eyes, the ones she had fallen in love with all of those years before.

'I must admit I couldn't stop thinking about my son, but I couldn't stop thinking about his mother either.'

His face softened and her tears began to flow again.

'Do you think we might make it third time lucky for us?'

'Oh Har … I mean Alex, I hope so.'

Thank You

Dear Reader,

Thank you for reading my debut novel, *The Girl on the Beach*. I hope that you enjoyed meeting my characters and sharing their story. I'm a little in love with Harry Dixon (Shhh don't tell my husband) and I hope that you are too.

It is both exciting and scary to be able to put my work out into the world. Writing is quite a solitary occupation, as you wrestle the plot, characters and words into order and sense. Ideas come from many sources and join together in a writer's imagination to make a book that you hope your readers will care about.

If you enjoyed this book, a review is always welcome on the retail site where you made your purchase. Reviews help to improve a book's profile and sales, so are always appreciated.

Details of how to contact me are given at the end of my author profile.

Love
Morton x

About the Author

Morton S. Gray lives with her husband, sons and Lily, the tiny dog, in Worcestershire, UK.

She has been reading and writing fiction for as long as she can remember, penning her first attempt at a novel aged fourteen, the plot of which closely resembled an Errol Flynn film.

Life got in the way of writing for many years, until she won a short story competition and the spark for writing was well and truly reignited. She carries a notebook everywhere as inspiration strikes in the most unlikely places.

She studied creative writing with the Open College of the Arts and joined the Romantic Novelists' Association New Writers' Scheme in 2012.

Previous 'incarnations' were in committee services, staff development and training. Morton has a Business Studies degree and is a fully qualified Clinical Hypnotherapist and Reiki Master. She has diplomas in Tuina Acupressure Massage and Energy Field Therapy.

She enjoys history, loves tracing family trees and discovering new crafts. Having a hunger for learning is a bonus for the research required for her books.

The Girl on the Beach is her debut novel and winner of the 2016 Search for a Star competition.

For more information on Morton:
www.mortonsgray.com
www.twitter.com/MSGray53
www.facebook.com/Morton-S-Gray-253028955038417/

More from Choc Lit

If you enjoyed Morton's story, you'll enjoy the
rest of our selection. Here's a sample:

You Think You Know Me

Clare Chase

Book 1 – London &
Cambridge Mysteries

**Sometimes, it's not easy to tell
the good guys from the bad …**

Freelance journalist, Anna
Morris, is struggling to make
a name for herself, so she's
delighted to attend a launch
event for a hip, young artist at
her friend Seb's gallery.

But an exclusive interview isn't all Anna comes away with.
After an encounter with the enigmatic Darrick Farron, she is
flung into the shady underground of the art scene – a world
of underhand dealings, missing paintings and mysterious
deaths …

Seb is intent on convincing Anna that Darrick is up to no
good but, try as she might, she can't seem to keep away from
him. And as she becomes further embroiled, Anna begins
to wonder – can Seb's behaviour be explained away as the
well-intentioned concern of an old friend, or does he have
something to hide?

Available in paperback from all good
bookshops and online stores. Visit
www.choc-lit.com for details.

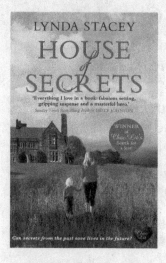

House of Secrets
Lynda Stacey

A woman on the run, a broken man and a house with a shocking secret …

Madeleine Frost has to get away. Her partner Liam has become increasingly controlling to the point that Maddie fears for her safety, and that of her young daughter Poppy.

Desperation leads Maddie to the hotel owned by her estranged father – the extraordinarily beautiful Wrea Head Hall in Yorkshire. There, she meets Christopher 'Bandit' Lawless, an ex-marine and the gamekeeper of the hall, whose brusque manner conceals a painful past.

After discovering a diary belonging to a previous owner, Maddie and Bandit find themselves immersed in the history of the old house, uncovering its secrets, scandals, tragedies – and, all the while, becoming closer.

But Liam still won't let go, he wants Maddie back, and when Liam wants something he gets it, no matter who he hurts …

Winner of Choc Lit & Whole Story Audiobooks 2015 Search for a Star competition.

Available in paperback from all good bookshops and online stores. Visit www.choc-lit.com for details.

Never Coming Home
Evonne Wareham

*Winner of the Joan Hessayon
New Writers' Award*

All she has left is hope.

When Kaz Elmore is told her
five-year-old daughter Jamie
has died in a car crash, she
struggles to accept that she'll
never see her little girl again.
Then a stranger comes into her
life offering the most dangerous
substance in the world: hope.

Devlin, a security consultant and witness to the terrible
accident scene, inadvertently reveals that Kaz's daughter
might not have been the girl in the car after all.

What if Jamie is still alive? With no evidence, the police
aren't interested, so Devlin and Kaz have little choice but to
investigate themselves.

Devlin never gets involved with a client. Never. But the more
time he spends with Kaz, the more he desires her – and the
more his carefully constructed ice-man persona starts to unravel.

The desperate search for Jamie leads down dangerous paths
– to a murderous acquaintance from Devlin's dark past, and
all across Europe, to Italy, where deadly secrets await. But as
long as Kaz has hope, she can't stop looking …

Available in paperback from all good
bookshops and online stores. Visit
www.choc-lit.com for details.

Introducing Choc Lit

We're an independent publisher creating
a delicious selection of fiction.
Where heroes are like chocolate – irresistible!
Quality stories with a romance at the heart.

See our selection here:
www.choc-lit.com

We'd love to hear how you enjoyed *The Girl on the Beach*.
Please leave a review where you purchased the novel
or visit: **www.choc-lit.com** and give your feedback.

Choc Lit novels are selected by genuine readers like yourself.
We only publish stories our Choc Lit Tasting Panel want to
see in print. Our reviews and awards speak for themselves.

Could you be a Star Selector
and join our Tasting Panel?

Would you like to play a role in choosing which novels we
decide to publish? Do you enjoy reading women's fiction?
Then you could be perfect for our Choc Lit Tasting Panel.

Visit here for more details…
www.choc-lit.com/join-the-choc-lit-tasting-panel

Keep in touch:

Sign up for our monthly newsletter Choc Lit Spread for
all the latest news and offers: www.spread.choc-lit.com.
Follow us on Twitter: @ChocLituk and Facebook: Choc Lit.

Where heroes are like chocolate – irresistible!